TRACE EVIDENCE

TRACE EVIDENCE

ELIZABETH BECKA

HYPERION NEW YORK

ISBN 1-4013-0174-6

Printed in the USA

To my mother, Florence,
who always believed in me
and my father, Stanley,
who taught me to believe in myself

TRACE EVIDENCE

CHAPTER

1

EVELYN JAMES PARKED THE county's battered station wagon behind a knot of cars on the side of the road. She pulled her crime scene kit from the passenger seat and stepped out into a puddle of slush, slamming a door with the words *Medical Examiner's Office* stenciled on the side. Flakes of snow fell at a deliberate pace, the day's mood darkening by the hour.

A maze of construction signs and sawhorses was spread over the bridge. Workers in bright orange safety jumpsuits watched the action as a jackhammer echoed from work at a new plaza on the next block—a forlorn attempt at urban renewal barely visible through the trees. Over their branches, the downtown skyline stretched toward gray clouds. Two marked Cleveland Police Department cars and two unmarked ones—worn Ford Crown Victorias that screamed cop— were pulled onto the softened grass. Except for two unlucky rookies directing traffic, the uniformed guys had long since taken to the warmth of their patrol cars, leaving the detective work to the ones who got paid for it. Each person present turned a wary eye to the riverbank, where the supine form lay as white and still as marble.

The Cleveland Metropark system covered over twenty thousand lush acres, enjoyed by forty-two million visitors per year, but today the trees were stripped bare, and Evelyn was not there to have fun. She uncapped her camera and recorded the scene—bridge, river, body, the downtown skyline looming beyond the forest—as her socks grew icy wet. Another day in the glamorous life of a forensic scientist. Her lens caught Bruce Riley as he stood on the bank, watching four men in scuba suits pack up their equipment. She moved carefully over the sloping grass to join him. "Afternoon, Detective."

Riley grunted in greeting, still the only man in the world who could wrinkle polyester slacks. "The divers got her out—two construction divers and two of ours, but it wasn't easy. You've got to see this. Ten years in Homicide and this is a first. It makes our nail-gun murder last year look positively normal. But hey, what's up with you? Planning a big Thanksgiving?"

She shook her head with a rueful smile. "I can't decide whether to cook dinner for Angel, or be magnanimous about it and tell her to spend the day with her father, or just screw the stupid turkey and go out—though any restaurant that makes its employees work on Thanksgiving doesn't deserve my patronage."

"Hear, hear."

"Tell me, Riley—you've got two ex-wives and four kids. What do you do on holidays?"

He lit a cigarette, a questionable practice in light of his pallor. "I go to Flanagan's Pub in Ohio City, buy a round for the house, and pop in a tape of the last World Series."

"Very traditional."

"Hey, they have chicken wings. They're like turkey."

Evelyn sighed, flexed her toes, and felt every minute of her thirty-eight years. "My entire family gathering will be my mom and a daughter who thinks it's entirely my fault that her father left me."

Riley frowned. "Why does she—"

"Because I've never enlightened her. So the three of us might meet you at Flanagan's." She grinned at him, getting a half smile in return. The Homicide detectives were older guys, white and black, married and divorced, who did a sometimes hellish job for always lousy pay, because somebody had to and it happened to be them. "But no chicken. Angel's gone vegetarian, unbeknownst to her steak-loving father."

No doubt Little Miss Perfect Stepmom would be *so* understanding.

Riley nodded toward the body. Beside it, the river formed a small valley through the wooded area. It had been deepened by a rainy fall and melting snow. Although driving a block in either direction would reveal a tightly fit neighborhood of dilapidated wood houses and pockmarked streets, the patch of earth by the river was quiet, isolated. "I don't think they lost any parts. Maybe the cold water kept her from decomposing. I can't say I envy our divers—they've got to be freezing even in wet suits. Ever pee in a wet suit?"

"I've heard that's how you stay warm," she said absently, moving closer. The body lay uncovered on the sparse weeds and mud. The lack of a covering sheet meant that they had not called EMS, and no wonder. The woman was very, very dead.

Though she was a Caucasian, the dark marbling of decomposition had spread through her limbs like a poison under her skin. In a short period of time she would turn completely black. Dark brown hair lay plastered against her face and neck. Everything seemed to be present—two arms, two legs, nose, eyebrows—and there were no signs of violence other than abrasions and skin slippage, made worse by her rescue from the depths. She wore what had been a pink long-sleeve shirt and denim shorts. Her feet were encased in a cement-filled five-gallon plastic bucket with a wire handle. Bright lettering on the side read *Stay-Clear Chlorine tabs, 1 inch.*

A tall man about her age stood beside the body. He had a shock of black hair and the cop look, indescribable but unmistakable. Riley waved his cigarette back and forth in a gesture of introduction. "Evelyn, our forensic scientist, is from the Medical Examiner's Trace Evidence Department. Evie, this is David Milaski. He's working with me until he gets me killed. He's known to be hard on partners."

Evelyn assumed this was a joke and smiled. Milaski didn't.

"David's new to Homicide. Real new—as in, today's his first day."

"Hell of a way to start." She gave him a sympathetic look, but he merely shrugged.

Riley clapped his new partner on the back, pushing him slightly off balance. "It could be worse, Milaski. On Evelyn's first day, the boiler at Hanna's in Playhouse Square blew. Took out the whole restaurant."

Evelyn groaned. "Don't say it."

"Three local actresses lost their parts."

"Didn't anyone ever tell you a pun is the lowest form of humor?"

"Yeah, but I don't believe it. Anyway, the construction divers were working on the base of that middle support, or whatever it is they call it—"

"Pylon," Milaski said.

"Whatever. One of them swam right into her. She was upright, like she was standing on the bottom. Scared the shit out of him."

Evelyn crouched next to the dead girl, nostrils pricked by the faint but persistent odor of disintegrating flesh, thinking, *She must have been pretty when alive.* High cheekbones set off wide-spaced eyes, now filmy and dull. Her slender frame seemed firm, almost the same height and weight as Angel, with the same delicate wrists. Thin chains bound those wrists and snaked around her waist and neck before plunging into the cement.

Uncharacteristically, Evelyn swore. Then she said, "Someone wanted to be sure this girl wasn't found."

"Yeah," Milaski breathed, stooping beside her, his coat hanging open over a stiffly new suit jacket. "But why?"

"You know what I want to know," Riley said. "Why is she wearing shorts in the middle of November, that's what I want to know."

The dead woman appeared to be about five-five and in her early twenties, but Evelyn couldn't be sure. The older she got, the younger everyone else looked—and the more any age at all seemed too young to die.

A shout of laughter echoed from slightly down the street, where members of the media had congregated behind police barricades. Milaski glanced in their direction and asked the older detective, "Can those cameras get a shot of her from there? I'd hate to have this girl's parents ID her from the six o'clock news."

"Nah, the bank's too steep. As long as they stay behind the tape we're okay."

Evelyn pulled on gloves and picked up the right hand, restrained by the chains and rigor mortis, the last touches of which still remained thanks to the cold water slowing the decomposition process to a crawl. A veneer of ice had solidified over the prunelike skin.

Milaski interrupted her thoughts. "Aren't you going to wait for the medical examiner?"

"You've been watching TV again, haven't you?" Her joking seemed to confuse him and she relented. "The doctors—the pathologists—never, but almost never, come to the scene. They stay at the office and do the autopsies. Though I'm not a doctor, out here at the crime scene I *am* the ME's office."

He nodded and she turned her attention back to the victim.

A piece of duct tape still clung to one cheek; it had obviously been over her mouth but the water's current had worked most of it off. Evelyn noticed a slight indentation from the middle of her nose to the end of her left cheekbone. Her nails were short and three were broken. The chains had left angry purple marks on her wrists and neck, but the ones around her neck would have been deeper if she had been strangled. She gave the woman's hair a cursory examination but didn't see any gashes or other damage. A pathologist would have to determine the exact cause of death, but because the woman had no obvious signs of fatal injury, it looked to Evelyn as if she had gone into the water alive.

Who could have done this? Who could have been so unspeakably cruel as to kill someone this way, to permit her to feel the frenzied pumping of her own lungs as they filled with water, to let her flesh be tortured by the icy water? Evelyn had worked through stabbings, beatings, the ubiquitous shootings, a deliberately scalded baby, and a teenager whose boyfriend had tossed her off a fourth-floor balcony. But she wanted nothing to do with this. It was horrific, wanton.

Bet it was cold, Evelyn thought, and straightened up, her foot sliding in wet mideastern clay. Milaski caught her arm.

"You okay?"

"Yes," she snapped.

"What do you think?" He released her elbow when she found firmer ground.

Evelyn sucked in a deep breath and summoned a friendlier tone. "She could have drowned. She could have already been dead, drug overdose or whatever, and someone just wanted to get rid of the body. She may be from a warmer state and just have been dumped here. That would explain the shorts. But it must have been a quick trip or she'd be more decomposed. Her epidermis is getting ready to peel off, so she was in there a couple days but not much more than that. If the water had been warm, it would have come off in a few hours."

"So how long do you think she's been dead?"

"As a general rule, two weeks in the water equals one week in the air, but you'll have to ask the doctors. And with the cold water slowing things down, it's going to be tough even for them." She glanced at the river. It moved along with a whispering sound, taunting her with its secrets.

"What about that bucket?" Riley asked of no one in particular. "Chlorine tablets?"

"Maybe the perp has a pool," Milaski suggested. "Can we trace the chains?"

Evelyn looked at him without seeing him, wondering about the woman's family, people who would need answers. "We can hit every Home Warehouse and Lowe's in the area, sure. If we find him, we might be able to match the chain, the composition, the manufacturing toolmarks."

"What about the cement?" Milaski asked.

She grinned without mirth. "As far as I know, cement is cement. But I'm sure there's an expert somewhere in the country who charges more an hour than I make in a week, and will be happy to take a look. It tends to be manufactured in large quantities, so it still wouldn't do you any good unless you have a suspect in mind—a suspect with a supply of cement to compare it to."

"Give me time," Milaski said. "I'll find him."

She raised her eyebrows, unsure if she found such optimism refreshing or foolish.

"I'll be honest with you, Miss James." He leaned forward. "I'm on my fifth life here, and this alley cat can't afford to screw up his first big case. So I'll get this guy."

If he thought sharing his vulnerability would warm her, he had miscalculated. "This woman isn't a big case. She was a person with a family and a job and a past, who's just been robbed of her future. And it's Mrs.," Evelyn added, unable to ignore a slight glow of satisfaction as his ears turned redder than the cold air would warrant. "*Mrs.* James. Now how about getting your guys off the bridge and out of camera range so I can finish photographing the scene before frostbite sets in, Detective?"

"Shit," Riley said suddenly, "what's *he* doing here?"

HE ISN'T GOING TO speak to me, she thought. *He hasn't spoken to me in seventeen years.*

Cleveland's mayor, Darryl Pierson, crossed the grass with a skeleton entourage and the county prosecutor in tow. The African-American mayor's face radiated concern. He stopped on the other side of the sagging yellow police tape and called to Evelyn as if he had last seen her around lunchtime. "Tell me where to stand, Evie. I don't want to mess up your scene."

Evelyn had hoped this reunion, if it had to occur, would have taken place on a balmy day while she wore a low-cut cocktail dress and fire-engine-red lipstick. Instead she stood in her worn blue parka with snow-dampened dull red curls, without a single word for her chapped lips to form. Best-laid plans. *I can't just ignore the man—we loved each other once, even if we were barely out of our teens at the time.* She forced her chilly feet to move.

Riley fell into step beside her, then Milaski. They met the mayor and county prosecutor Harold Rupert at the top of the bank, out of earshot of cops and reporters alike. The entourage maintained a discreet distance.

For a man of medium height, medium build, medium-dark black skin, wearing a perfectly fitting but conservative overcoat, Pierson somehow managed to tower over everyone present. He straightened his shoulders and took a moment to gaze at each of them. Only his eyes seemed tired, and in them Evelyn saw flecks of yellow like fragile spots, vulnerable areas; they were cat's eyes, cautious and a bit cold.

"How have you been?" he asked her soberly, as if a great deal rested on her answer.

"Good. Fine." Her voice cracked and she cleared her throat. Her nose started to run from the cold and she fumbled in her pocket for a tissue.

"I'm sorry to hear about your divorce."

"Last year's news. Really, I'm doing great."

Riley interrupted, to rescue her from a clearly awkward situation or simply out of impatience. "Have they told you the circumstances here?"

The mayor nodded. "I hate to say it, but cement shoes go with 'sleeping with the fishes,' don't they?"

"We'll be checking out the mob angle," Riley told him.

Evelyn applied a crumpled Wendy's napkin to her nose. "Do we even *have* a mob in Cleveland anymore?"

"You better believe it," Prosecutor Harold Rupert told her, supporting Pierson's theory with brownnosed enthusiasm. "They keep a low profile here, but that's why they've lasted. Remember Danny Green? Libertore? You might want to be careful whose toes you step on."

"Since when do I step on toes?" she protested. "And whose feet are we talking about?"

"Well," Rupert hedged, careful to keep his voice down and bending over the tape as if he were leaning on it, "I've had my eye on two different men, rival families. There's Armand Garcia, he works the near west side. Every time we get something on him, the witness develops amnesia or the evidence mysteriously disappears. Then, on the east side, we've got Mario Ashworth."

"Uh-huh," Riley said. The mayor nodded, still looking at Evelyn. Milaski remained silent.

She recognized the name—anyone in Cleveland would. Ashworth Property Management. The Ashworth Fund. Ashworth Construction: Current projects included the new Brook Park High School, the aquarium remodeling, and the South Fork Mall Annex. Lots of money, high profile. No wonder the prosecutor and the mayor had abandoned their warm offices for this. "He's in the *mob*?"

Rupert chuckled at her naïveté. "The Big M himself. Why do you think he gets the largest contracts? He's got a piece of every pie in northern Ohio." He turned to the senior detective. "Look, Riley, this has to be wrapped up, and quickly. If organized crime thinks they're going to take the city back, they're wrong. We have to present a united front and strike back hard." He spoke with the perfect amount of righteousness, and Evelyn knew he had a mental picture of the cover of *Cleveland Today* bearing his image with the caption *Mobbuster!*

The mayor grinned at her while responding to the prosecutor. "Don't criticize too loudly. He just might build the new medical examiner's office."

Evelyn raised an eyebrow. "So we can fight crime from a building built by a criminal?"

"The idea has a certain flair, doesn't it?"

"I don't know about flair, but to get out of the declared disaster area we're in now, I'd consider an inferno built by Satan."

"The council will support Jurgens Limited." Rupert carefully maintained his political correctness. Jurgens happened to be the largest minority-owned contractor.

"Their costs are out of control," Pierson said. "Reuters Limited has the best price but the worst reputation, and North Coast can't handle a project that size. That leaves Ashworth. Mobster or no, his buildings are energy efficient and free of problems."

Riley lit another cigarette. Evelyn could see the muscles in his neck tighten to ripcords at every mention of Ashworth's name. "You can't be serious."

"I'm no more thrilled about the concept than you are, Detective," Pierson told him. "But it's not just up to me, and besides, this isn't the time to discuss it. I can see you are all busy and you're going to be even busier once the press gets hold of this story."

"They already have." Riley nodded toward the parkway intersection.

"I know." Mayor Pierson waited until Rupert had rushed to the cameras and boom mikes like an ant to sugar, then turned back to Evelyn. "How's Angel?"

"Great." She felt Milaski fidget, probably from boredom. Or else he was getting the lay of the land and sensing a minefield. Despite a touch of guilt, she continued, letting the murder investigation languish while she played catch-up with an old friend. "Destiny must be growing up."

"Seventeen going on thirty-five, yes. She lives at Tower City mall and covers me with cell phone bills. She won't even let her mother kiss her good night anymore. In fact she broke her finger yesterday playing ball with her brothers and we're relishing the opportunity to baby her again." He shook his head ruefully. "Say, are you and Riley coming to the fund-raiser tonight? I'm sorry, you're—"

"Milaski. David Milaski. I'm in Homicide," he added, his voice respectful but not interested. He glanced at the riverbank as if he just wanted to get back to the investigation. Evelyn felt the same way, though not exactly for the same reason.

"I need the support of the law enforcement community if we're going to scare up some funding from the feds. Evelyn? Plenty of champagne and the best food in the city."

"You know I'd love to see you and Danielle." Had she really managed to keep the irony out of her tone? "But I'll be busy here for quite some time. It was nice to see you again." Over the silent snowfall, reporters' cameras clicked away as the prosecutor droned on. The jackhammer had stopped. The valley fell quiet, as if cocooned by snow. "I'm sure the ME will be in touch with you as soon as we have an ID."

"Thanks."

Pierson remained behind the tape as she fled down the slope to the body, seeking refuge in the company of a dead girl. There, that hadn't been so bad. They had only dated for two years in college, anyway. *Get over it, girl.*

When she looked back, he was gone.

With relief she squatted next to the body, pulled on a new pair of gloves, and touched the woman's ice-cold forearm, turning the palm upward. Her inner arms showed no signs of drug use. A peek under her outer clothing revealed a bra and panties. Tiny diamond earrings winked at them. She had a thin gold chain around her neck and a star sapphire on her right hand; no wedding band.

Milaski joined her, their knees practically touching. "Question."

She glared at him through the fading light, inwardly daring him to say one word about Darryl Pierson.

"You said she had a family and a job. How do you know that?"

She put Pierson out of her mind. "Okay, it's more of an assumption. She doesn't look homeless, undernourished, or riddled with needle tracks. Her hair has been trimmed, her unbroken nails are even, and her clothes aren't stained or full of holes. She isn't poor. She either has a decent job or a family to notice she's gone, and most young, healthy people have both. That's why it shouldn't take too long for an identification—someone, somewhere, will wonder where she is."

"That's all it takes, to be young and healthy? What happens when you're old and you drink too much?"

She gave him a look, half mocking, half compassionate. "Then you might be unfairly unmissed."

"Story of my life," he grumbled.

Several hours later Evelyn finally felt warm. In jersey pajamas and thick socks, she watered the limp plants in her living room and thought about

Darryl Pierson as the cat swatted at her ankles. Did any woman ever make peace with how she felt about an old boyfriend? A sort of apprehension permeated the memory, a sense that you either avoided a narrow escape or missed an alternate future that might perhaps have worked out better. The past didn't make her anxious, only the future she didn't choose.

They had met in her second year at Cleveland State. She had introduced herself by spilling coffee on his Honors English notebook. He said he liked her because she never pretended to understand what it was like to be black. She liked him because he could talk to her without staring at her chest. The courtship had been intense, the breakup swift and unexpected.

Darryl's background differed a hundred and eighty degrees from hers—not your standard poor-kid-from-the-hood-makes-good kind of background, but a *really* hard background about which he told her only bits and pieces. In the years after the breakup, she privately celebrated his success. He had gotten what he wanted by working almost fanatically for it, and he deserved the brass ring. It had worked out for the best, right? If she hadn't married Rick, she wouldn't have that special combination of DNA and cellular organelles that had become Angel. As if in response to the thought, her daughter breezed into the house.

Evelyn often asked herself what kind of a fantasy world she had been living in when she named the girl Angel. It had never fit her. Instead of a sweet-tempered ethereal blonde, she had inherited Rick's raven hair and penchant for mischief. Now she mumbled a greeting and pushed aside the mail on the kitchen table in order to reorganize her purse, a scrap of fabric only slightly larger than an envelope.

Rick, dark and stout, walked in as if he still owned the place, with Terrie at his elbow. She took in Evelyn's pajamas with a complete lack of expression. "We were at Rio Bravo. Rick wanted to go to the Flats, but I didn't think it was a good idea. No sense showing a sixteen-year-old everyone hanging out at the bars."

"Of course," Evelyn agreed as she avoided Nefertiti, whose claws made clear her desire for Evelyn's undivided attention. "We had a victim stabbed there last week."

Terrie blinked. "How awful. It must be so hard to see things like that."

No, Evelyn thought, *it isn't hard at all, because I'm a coldhearted bitch. Isn't that what Rick and Angel tell you? That I stole the house from him and how I make Angel abide by a—gasp—ten o'clock curfew?*

Rick made leaving motions. "Okay"—Terrie laughed—"we're going. Take care, Angel. Don't watch too much TV."

As the door closed, Evelyn turned to her pale and sullen daughter, watching her place each makeup item in its preordained pocket. *At least she's not into Goth,* Evelyn thought, thanking her lucky stars. Angel dressed neatly, in collared shirts and khakis so perfectly pressed that it never failed to amaze her mother how a disaster area of a bedroom could produce such an example of precision.

"How was school today?" Evelyn tried. "Did you have your math quiz?"

"Yeah."

"And what did you get?"

"Eighty-three."

"Mmm." Evelyn wanted to say, I saw a dead girl today. Just about your age. Life is short, so very short. Maybe you should be nicer to your mother. Maybe your mother should be nicer to you. But that was the easy way out, using her job to control her daughter.

"It was hard," Angel said defensively. "Can't we turn up the heat in here? What good is saving on electricity if we freeze to death before we get to spend what we've saved?"

A spontaneous statement. Encouraged, Evelyn opened her mouth to respond, but Angel flounced up the stairs, her light frame making thuds heavier than should have been physically possible.

Evelyn stared at the bottle of nail polish in among the letters on the heavy kitchen table. *Too much TV. And how many children have you had? Let's see, that would be none, wouldn't it?*

How easy was it to be the perfect mother if you had to do it only every other weekend? Terrie hadn't had to give birth. She hadn't had to sit through ten years of band concerts or held a bucket next to the bed when Angel had the flu. She hadn't paced the floor when Angel was out way past curfew or had nightmares about the SATs. Just go out to dinner every other weekend, and maybe a museum now and then.

Evelyn shook her head in disgust. Why did she resent Terrie more for liking her daughter than for sleeping with her husband? She sighed, patted the cat, turned out the lights, and threw on a coat to walk to her mother's house next door and say good night. At least she'd be warm there.

CHAPTER

3

THE GIRL SWAM UPWARD through the currents of her subconscious without concern or haste. She didn't particularly want to wake up; comfortable where she sat, she dreamed of a boy in her English class. But her stomach ached, she felt nauseated, and the peculiar heaviness on her feet pricked her curiosity.

She tried to open her eyes, but her lids felt too heavy to raise. Instead she wiggled the toes on her left foot. The wet, sticky sensation felt almost erotic, but at the same time it was just a few degrees too warm and she thought she really *ought* to deal with this, so she opened her eyes.

What she saw made no sense. She shut her eyes again and let the images mill about in her brain for a while. Maybe then they would form some kind of order.

She sat in a basement, or at least a neat room with gray concrete walls and floor. The view included a tool-scattered workbench and homemade wooden shelves, which held a myriad of items from cardboard boxes to a beach ball. It smelled . . . not pleasant, along the lines of a stale, animal sweat. She knew her scents. She could tell Opium from Tommy Girl from any kind of Chanel on her friends even when they'd showered after drill team practice, and she was never wrong. She was never wrong *period*.

Her legs, from midcalf to toes, were immersed in a five-gallon plastic bucket filled with heavy cool gray stuff. Her new Italian pumps were in the bucket with her feet and almost certainly ruined, which irritated her. Her hands were pulled way to the back of the cheap folding chair and this made her shoulders hurt. She tried to pull them forward but something wouldn't let them move. Now *that* was ridiculous. *No one* told her when she could or could not move her arms.

She opened her eyes again.

Same scene. For the first time it occurred to her to be afraid, and the sensation nauseated her further.

Shit.

She was in trouble. She was in *big* trouble.

Her muddled brain tried to regain some sense, some control. She had been at a party . . . Crosscut images of people and drinks and music came back to her, but she could not be sure if that had been tonight, last night, or some night forever ago.

Screw that, it didn't matter. She was here now, immobile, with one hand tied to the other by something hard and cold and rattling—like chains.

She wasn't only tied but *chained*? Somebody was going to get their ass whupped big-time when she got out of there.

If she got out of there.

Worry grew to panic. She began to wriggle like a worm on a hook, searching for a weakness in the links, a gap that would allow her to slip her bonds. The chains snaked up and over her, lying on her shoulders, but only the ones around her wrists were tight and her fingers were tingly and going numb. The rest of the chains were not as tight, but still prevented her from moving in any significant way.

Her attention swung to her feet. She tried to pull them out of the cement—for that's what it had to be, she wasn't so sheltered that she had never been exposed to wet cement—but one chain kept her knees primly glued to the chair seat. She kept her toes active while she thought, flexing the Italian leather up and down, and moved her knees as if she were doing a sort of aerobic exercise. *Hey, everybody, want to lose weight and look great? Try cementecize! Works off those extra inches in no time!* A chuckle that came too close to hysteria escaped her throat and she tried to call it back.

Too late.

Above her, she heard an abrupt thunk and a series of thuds, exactly as if someone upstairs had dropped a chair onto all four feet and was now crossing the floor. Toward the basement door. Toward her.

She tried to remember exactly what position she had been in when she regained consciousness, couldn't, and decided it didn't matter because her options were few. She couldn't move anything but her head, which she now let loll forward like a forgotten rag doll. It hurt her neck, but she willed herself to be absolutely still. She really *did* want to throw up, but she refused to think about it. She left her eyelids slightly ajar, just enough for a hazy view of the floor.

Whoever it was came from the steps and paused right in front of her, but still she couldn't see his—*its*—feet. Then he moved two shuddering steps closer.

Blue workpants stained with traces of light gray ended above scuffed brown shoes. They weren't Timberlands or Rockports. Some loser in generic shoes—now what?

Maybe playing dead wasn't the way to go. Maybe she should try to talk to him, ask what the hell he thought he was doing and by the way, would you let me go? I promise I won't tell anyone if you just let me go. *Yeah, right.*

On the other hand, maybe he was just waiting for her to wake up before he started in with the torture, standard serial killer stuff like Drano under the skin or cutting off her fingers. In which case it would behoove her to be a heavy sleeper. She tried to keep her breathing steady and found it impossible to breathe normally while her heart pounded furiously.

Maybe he wasn't a serial killer. Please, *please* let this whole thing be the revenge of some bimbo who didn't make Homecoming Court, just trying to scare her.

Maybe she'd just keep quiet until she knew for sure.

In the two seconds it took for these thoughts to flit in a panicked rush across her brain, he moved again, walking around behind her. The sight of his shoes frightened her enough, but *not* to see them felt infinitely worse. What if he didn't care if she woke up or not? What if he intended to kill her right now?

There was a clinking sound, which had to mean a chain was about to be lowered around her neck and tightened until—

He grabbed her arm. She couldn't help an involuntary jerk at his touch, as clammy cold as the cement itself, but kept her head down. He simply wiggled her arm a bit, not to hurt her but to check the chains and fasteners, pulling on each one. Her eyelids were squeezed together like a little child's, something she would be embarrassed about later but not right now.

The steps went away.

She heard him clumping up the stairs and waited for the door to shut before she drew a normal breath, and even that she did with the utmost caution, scared that one link of her chains might bang against another and alert him again.

Him? Who was he? Where was she? And what did he intend to do with her?

Then she saw the mark. The grainy surface of the cement in the bucket had been marred. He must have stuck a finger in it to test the hardness.

Again, she willed her heart to calm. When the pressure is on, her father always said, focus on the priorities. Forget about the problems you can't solve for the moment and concentrate on those you can. What do you need to do *right now*?

Get the hell out of here.

She started moving her legs again, wiggling her toes, moving her knees, trying to straighten her foot to a Barbie-like point. She did this for several minutes without knowing why, and then figured out what her body had known automatically: If she created a hole in the cement larger than her legs, then her legs would slip out of it.

Except that at least two of the chains ended in the cement. He had not only encased her legs but had literally chained her to this anchor.

And then she knew.

There was only one reason to put someone's feet in cement. She had seen *Billy Bathgate*. She had heard the slang. They drowned people with cement shoes.

It was ridiculous, too fantastic to contemplate. If you wanted to kill someone you blew them away from the window of a moving car, you didn't mess with stupid shit like this. No, they were going to leave her naked in Public Square or handcuffed to the men's room at Jacob's Field. She wiggled for all she was worth.

While she did that, she checked out the rest of the basement. She could see two glass block windows, no door. No way out except for the stairs.

The cement thickened, getting harder and harder to stir. It was like a nightmare where she was trying to run away from something awful but couldn't make her legs move. If she got through this, no lame-ass nightmare would ever bother her again.

Why only one guy? If this was a revenge deal, there should be a couple of people. Teenagers did everything in groups. There should be two or three girls giggling upstairs about how she was going to "get hers." A boy or man alone made no sense. Boys never got mad at her—frustrated maybe, but not mad.

The thought of her acquaintances calmed her; she felt comfortable in their world of intrigue and betrayal. This temporary composure evaporated when the upstairs door opened and the man returned.

She strained her neck again, letting her head hang until her long dark hair obscured her face. He moved past her to the workbench, where she heard a series of small movements. *This is unbearable,* she thought. *I'd rather be jumped in an alley, beaten up, anything so long as I could see my attacker and know what he wanted. What the hell did he want?*

Abruptly he grabbed the back of her hair and she struggled, twisting her head and trying to jerk away, but with his other hand he clamped something plastic over her nose and mouth and she was trapped. Still she struggled, her entire body writhing at his touch.

"I thought so," she heard him say. His voice was low, calm, utterly ordinary, and vaguely familiar.

When she finally inhaled, there was an overwhelming chemical smell that made her gag. She coughed and tried not to breathe, but her terrorized body couldn't hold out for long. She breathed in.

Then there was nothing.

Later. She was in a different place now, outside, and cold. She could hear the night birds chirping, then falling silent as they heard the sounds of metal and rubber wheels. Then a sensation of movement. Her feet were being pulled out of a car trunk and the open edge of it scraped her body. She protested at the painful burning along her hip, but the shout came out as a murmur. She had tape over her mouth.

He held her up, his body pressed against hers as he loaded the cement bucket onto a two-wheel dolly. Then he pulled on the chains down her back to keep her upright while he tilted the dolly back. Her knees could not support her. The chain around her neck bit into her larynx and her head ached as it bounced against the bar. The smell of vomit snaked through the air, and her throat burned. He wheeled her over the rough road as if she were a crate of oranges. *This is starting to suck big-time.*

The birds became a backdrop to the main noise, one that reached her ears just as the fishy smell reached her nose. They were near moving water. He was taking her to the water.

Shit!

Why was he doing this? Why?

They were not by the lake, but on some kind of a bridge. There were no lights, not even streetlights, and she could just barely see the surrounding trees. She could not get her bearings. Nothing about the area seemed familiar, but she had never been much for the outdoors. No walks in the park for her.

A giggle escaped. She was losing it.

Think, girl!

Her feet, however, felt loose in their cement holes. The chains hung on. Her hands hurt terribly. She tried to push the tape away with her tongue, but it extended all the way across her cheeks and wouldn't budge.

They stopped in the middle of the bridge and he pitched her body sideways onto the low, wide wall, not caring that the rough brick scraped the bare skin on her arms and face. Hell, he was throwing her away, why would he care about keeping her in good shape?

Her hands hurt, she realized, because circulation had been restored. Without the folding chair, the system of chains around her body and wrist had loosened.

With a terrific grunt he hefted the cement onto the wall, using the handle of the bucket. He straightened her legs, the bucket balancing on its side along the wall's top, the handle resting on her shins. He paused.

He was going to throw her into the water.

She was going to die.

She was going to die horribly in that frigid water.

Insane with panic, she began to scream, her voice coming out as a muffled series of pathetic grunts to which he paid no mind.

He pushed her shoulder back, turning her faceup. In the weak light of a quarter moon, a shadow formed his face, a grotesque empty hole where a face should have been.

"Please." Her words escaped the duct tape, loosened slightly by her tears. "Please don't."

Without warning, he pushed her over.

The shock of the water terrified her more than she could have imagined. It encased her in a tomb of ice, cut off all sound other than her frenzied heartbeat, and stabbed through her flesh straight to the bone. Not to inhale in response to the stunning cold took every ounce of strength she had.

She sank to the bottom as the chains over her shoulders pulled her down with the block. The pressure mounted in her ears and sinuses. Her lungs ached. She felt soft things around her—seaweed, fish, or her own hair. She knew she would die, but also discovered that her hands were free.

Insensible with fear, she felt her body function on its own: She slipped each wrist through the links, worked her feet out of the rigid holes one at a time, and pulled the chains off her shoulders as if shedding a negligee.

The loop around her waist held fast.

She pushed off the cement block and strained against the bounds, but the chains held on to her hips.

With pained fingers she undid her belt buckle and yanked her miniskirt down to her knees, managing to hang on to her panties. Then she lost a few more precious seconds working the chain down over her hips before finally kicking free. She didn't waste time with the tape over her mouth and swam upward, giddy with success. Except that she couldn't hold her breath any longer.

She tried to let it out, just a little, just to relieve the pressure, and swam harder. How deep could she be? Which way was up? She opened her eyes and saw nothing, freezing limbo.

Her lungs had held out as long as they could. She sucked in icy water through her nose, freezing her sinuses; she tried to cough through the tape, thinking, *I'm not going to make it.*

One hand reached air, only a few degrees warmer, and she burst through the surface trying to gulp air through her water-filled head. One hand scraped the slimy surface of a bridge pylon and she broke two nails grabbing for it. With the other she pulled the tape off her numb skin and coughed spasmodically, spitting out the water and sucking in lungfuls of the sweet, clear air.

The river moved along, but not fast enough to rip her from the pylon. She clung to the stone, trying to comprehend what had just happened. She had done it. She had escaped an icy tomb but still had to swim to the shore, visible only as a darker black against the charcoal gray of the water, and get to some shelter or a person who could help. And she had to do all that with no pants and no shoes and without freezing first, a feat that seemed less possible with every passing moment. She could no longer feel any of her limbs, yet they were still moving at her command. Maybe she could make it. The damn polar bear club did it, didn't they?

She struck out for the bank. It occurred to her that the man might not have left, he might have heard her furious breathing and splashing, but that was a chance she'd have to take. Anything to get out of the damn water.

The downstream current carried her away from the bridge—she had only to make her way toward the bank. But it was *so* cold. Her head slipped under the freezing water.

Then her foot struck bottom; the water had grown shallower. She stood. The current pushed her down and she crawled over the smooth rocks on her hands and knees. When the water faded to a foot deep she stood again and moved carefully over the stones in her bare feet.

For a moment the air felt good, warmer than the water by several degrees. But then a breeze came through and turned her flesh to ice. She couldn't survive out here for long, maybe not at all. She grabbed the branches of a bush and pulled herself up the incline, slipping a bit on the muddy bank.

She moved blindly, unable to hear anything over her own ragged breathing. She kept her head down to keep her eyes safe as she plowed through the undergrowth. Branches and thorns tore her skin but she barely felt it—the advantage of being numb, although the movement began to thaw out her hands. A monotonous droning sound turned out to be the chattering of her teeth.

Then the ground leveled out a little, became more horizontal. With another few steps she felt gravel, then hardness under her frozen toes. She had found a road. She stopped, unable to decide which way to turn.

When she became still, she could hear them.

Footsteps.

Steps with a slight crunch, as if someone were walking along the side of the road, partly in the gravel.

No!

He moved toward her, the feeble moonlight picking up a white shirt under a long jacket. But his face was hidden beneath a hood.

She turned in the other direction and started to run, as fast as her frozen, barefoot body would allow, scarcely more than a limping trot. She had covered perhaps five feet when he grabbed her by the back of her sodden T-shirt and tripped her. She hit the ground heavily and felt the biting sting of a scraped knee.

"What?" she shrieked at him with lips only half thawed, and he hesitated just for a moment as if startled by her voice. "What do you want? Who are you?"

"How did you get out of there?" he demanded, his voice full and loud and terrible.

"Leave me alone!" She struggled to her knees, her mind beyond reason. All she wanted to do was go home and be warm and safe. All she wanted to do was *live.* "Go away!"

He kicked her in the stomach as she started to stand, dropping her to her knees once more. "How did you get out of there?"

"Go away," she sobbed.

He straddled her back. She heard an almost gentle clinking sound and then the chain passed around her neck. He pulled the ends taut but not yet tight.

The touch of the unyielding metal shocked her mind into a new direction. "You can't do this." She fought one last time to get to her feet, tearing at the skin of her own neck as she tried to pull the chains away with her right hand. "Do you know what will happen to you?"

He said nothing.

"Don't you know who I am, you son of a bitch? I'm Destiny Pierson. *I'm the goddamn mayor's daughter!*"

The chain tightened.

EVELYN WROTE HER REPORT the following morning seated at her desk, with one eye on the small sign that read: *Non illegitimi carborundum est.* Don't let the bastards grind you down. As always, she resisted the temptation to cross out *illegitimi* and write in *Tony.* Her desk, a battle-weary metal job with impressive seniority, staggered under the weight of reports to be checked, instrument manuals, a Beavell Scientific catalog and a picture of Angel from when she was still willing to smile for the camera—before the divorce, in other words. Yellowing *Far Side* cartoons clung to the wall.

The trace evidence lab occupied half of the third floor of the ME's office, but that wasn't saying much. A single large room housed most of the equipment—the atomic absorption spectrophotometer to analyze gunshot residue, the Fourier transform infrared spectrometer (FTIR) for paints and fibers—and areas for preliminary DNA work. Two smaller rooms in the back were reserved for the rest of the DNA process. Boxes of microtubes and disposable pipettes were stacked close enough to the ceiling to violate OSHA regulations. Obnoxious smells from the first-floor autopsy suite wafted up the stairwells. The thermostat had two settings—on and off.

"Evelyn!" Tony Jessick bellowed from his office in a tone that would have intimidated Attila the Hun, at least until the great warrior had heard it forty-seven thousand times.

"Yo."

"Our girl's up next," her supervisor snapped from the doorway, a man to whom the word *rotund* didn't do justice. Short blond hair curved over Tony's head like fingers on a bowling ball. Behind heavy glasses his eyes focused on her, then the ceiling, the filing cabinet. His weight did nothing to slow his hyperactivity. Tony had a bottomless source of frenzied energy, fueled by the burning conviction that someone, somewhere, was talking about him. "How the hell are we going to get that stuff off her feet? Other than using a sledgehammer?"

Under his glare she snagged the last cup of coffee. "If she had decomposed a little more, her feet would probably slip out."

"The doc isn't going to wait."

"How about a Sawzall?" Evelyn suggested.

"Does that go through concrete?"

"I think they go through anything."

"Come up with something, Evelyn." Tony's supervisory style could be summed up in a few words: all of the authority, none of the responsibility. "The powers that be are really interested in this one. You don't produce some answers soon, you're out of here. I'll move Jason into your job as soon as his grant position expires."

A weak threat—Tony needed her too much, and Jason was brand-new to the field. But Tony had the instincts of a shark, with less compassion. She couldn't ignore the insinuation. If Evelyn solved the case, Tony would look good to the ME. If she screwed up, Tony would ladle her out like chum.

Evelyn spent the next hour renting a Sawzall from Home Warehouse (of course the county wouldn't *buy* it) and cringed over the nonsterile blade. With the help of two deskmen, made muscular by lifting bodies on and off of gurneys all day, she managed to get the cement off without removing any toes. This left her with four blocks of concrete, each cast with the impression of one side of a foot, with chains extruding from the top. Some of the dead girl's skin remained with the stone. Evelyn stored the sections away for further study and returned to the autopsy suite. Tony fled, having already spent too much time away from his phone. David and Riley had not shown up, but cops didn't always have time to attend autopsies.

Jonathan Tyler, the most recent addition to the ME's office and the only African-American doctor on staff, entered the room, yawning. Working full-time and studying for the board exams, he lived in a constant state of fatigue. "You got the cement off? Good job."

At least someone appreciated her trip to the hardware store. She joined him next to the stainless steel table. Autopsies didn't faze her, though friends had a tough time understanding how a woman who never forgot a birthday and loved Disney movies could work among scenes of the most violent depravity and yet remain unchanged. If asked, she said simply, "You get used to it."

While Jonathan cut through the woman's chest wall only inches away, Evelyn examined the woman's cheeks with a magnifying glass. A slight amount of adhesive residue but no bruising. How did the killer get his victim to sit still while he poured cement on her feet? Why hadn't she screamed, yelled for help? Had she been drugged, unconscious, or bound? There were discolorations around the wrists, but were they from the chains or a previous binding?

Then again maybe she *did* scream, and no one could hear her.

Jonathan removed the lungs and sectioned them, slicing through the red matter with a knife on a polypropylene cutting board that would have looked more at home in Evelyn's kitchen. She always expected lungs to look as they did on diagrams, gray colored and filled with bubble-like alveoli, but she couldn't tell lungs in real bodies from the liver or the spleen—just one more dark red, amorphous mass. Jonathan squeezed them like a kid with Play-Doh. "Plenty of water."

"Well, duh."

"Not *duh*," he gently corrected. "People can drown without aspirating water. A laryngospasm—chest-wall spasm—seals up the airways. It happens in about ten to fifteen percent of drowning cases."

"What if she had already died? Would she have water in the lungs?"

"Maybe yes, maybe no."

"Thanks a lot."

"But there is significantly less pulmonary edema when the victim is already dead."

"And in this case?"

"Lots of edema." He squeezed the lungs again to demonstrate and she felt her heart tighten, nudging her stomach. She hoped David Milaski *would* catch this guy.

"How can we find out if someone drowned her in the bathtub first and then got rid of the body? Diatoms?" She meant the microscopic silica-coated algae present in Lake Erie water.

"They usually equal drowning as far as I'm concerned. What makes you think she drowned in a bathtub?" Jonathan dropped sections into a plastic container of formalin. The fumes stung her eyes.

"I just want a reason to think she wasn't alive when she went into that river."

"Drowning in a bathtub would be easier?"

"Not having to sit there waiting for the concrete to harden would be easier."

"In this line of work it's not a good idea to have a vivid imagination," he warned.

"I agree. But in this case a little imagination is called for. We don't have anything else to go on."

"Unless we find out she died of a drug overdose, a heart attack, a cracked skull, or some bizarre poison, drowning is what we're left with. I'll make an educated guess that she drowned in the river we found her in until I can check for diatoms. Which I could do if someone would let me work."

"Okay, okay. Anything I can do to help?"

"Find out where she got the concrete sneakers."

Tony filled the doorway like a leftover Halloween costume, looking perturbed beyond his usual paranoia. "Evelyn."

She looked up.

"Hate to take you away from the sweet smells in here, but there's another one."

"Another homicide like this?"

"Well, that's just it. They're not quite sure."

CHAPTER

5

DAVID MILASKI CHECKED HIS watch as he settled into the passenger seat.

"Got a date?" Riley asked, cutting off a pickup to make the Chagrin Road exit ramp. He didn't even look back as a horn blared.

As if. "No. That's why I jumped at the chance to meet a real-live mobster. Or the chance to breathe in the charming atmosphere of this police vehicle. Have you ever tried a nicotine patch? I've heard they work wonders."

"I've heard that new Homicide cops who whine find themselves transferred to Property Crimes."

David dropped it. He did not come to this case with every advantage. Three years in Vice had perfected the cocky shell he showed the world, but it had not prepared him for homicide investigations. The purpose of a vice crime was profit. People sold drugs, sold their bodies, sold their guns—just business. In homicides, however, the motivations were much more varied. More slippery. More personal. He had a lot to learn. "Why are we going to see this guy?"

"I told you."

"Because his company is building a plaza one street over from where we found the body? Doesn't seem like much of a reason. Isn't this a little over-the-top dramatic for a mob murder?"

To his surprise, Riley agreed. "Yes. But I never miss an opportunity to get in Mario Ashworth's face. And you never know. Young Mario learned the family business from his mother's grandfather, the oldest, meanest bastard I've ever tossed a search warrant at in thirty years of police work. Maybe he's returning to some of the classic techniques."

"How long have you been acquainted with the family?"

"I've been in Homicide ten years. I knew of them before that, when I worked Narcotics."

Riley didn't ask for David's history, though David could have summed it up neatly: a disastrous choice made to join the Marines instead of attending college, followed by an equally disastrous stint in police Special Ops, followed by a decade in Vice. Forty years of age, unmarried, childless, proud owner of a dinette set, a rusting Dodge, and an eccentric golden retriever.

But Riley didn't ask, and David didn't volunteer. Riley gave the wheel a jerk and turned into an elongated driveway.

Mario Ashworth's house served as a monument to both his construction skills and his inability to keep a low profile. White pillars flanked the entranceway, one corner of the house bloomed with a latticework of balconies, and the grass remained green even under a dusting of snow. Two Mercedes and a BMW waited in the circular drive. Riley's battered Grand Marquis fit the decor as well as a Dumpster would have. Riley, however, didn't seem the least bit embarrassed. He bounced up to the oversize front door and rang the bell. Five times.

It opened to reveal a towering man with perfect black skin and a perfect black suit. The word *smooth* had been invented for this man. Although it wasn't even Thanksgiving yet, the foyer's gleaming marble tile and sixteen-foot ceiling already exhibited Christmas decorations. The huge man holding the door seemed no less intimidating with a twig of mistletoe hovering above his shining pate.

"Good evening, Marcus," Riley boomed. "We're here to see your boss."

"Do you have an appointment?"

"No. I have a badge." The man had obviously seen too many badges to be impressed by them. He shut the door gently and left them to wait on the doorstep like delivery boys, which David felt sure bothered Riley not at all. It didn't bother him much, either. A fancy house did not a righteous man make.

"Who was that?" David asked.

"Ivan Marcus. The right-hand man. You don't want to turn your back on him if you want to keep both your kidneys. He's left guys coughing up their own blood and been home in time to play Barbies with his daughter. Without changing either his clothes or his expression."

David resolved to keep that in mind as Marcus showed them into a small room off the main foyer. The dark colors, the rows of books, and a bowl of orchids on the edge of a mahogany desk all befit the house of a very rich man; only a haphazard pile of blueprints on the blotter and Mario Ashworth himself seemed out of place. At least a million dollars cycled through his organization every month and the guy—in a maroon sweatshirt, faded blue jeans, and faded blue eyes— looked like a frazzled soccer dad.

"Mr. Ashworth." Riley made it a statement instead of an inquiry. He dropped his lanky form into a leather armchair of butter-soft calf-skin, which even David could guess cost more than his monthly salary, and pulled out a notebook and a pack of cigarettes.

"No smoking," Ashworth said.

David remained standing, browsing the books and pictures haphazardly arranged on custom cherrywood shelves. Forcing Ashworth to divide his attention between the two of them might unnerve him, make him more talkative. He had read that in a textbook. Of course it might just tick the guy off.

Ashworth drummed a pencil on his desk blotter, fast enough to blur. He slumped back in his chair and stared at Riley a moment before speaking. "I'm very busy today, so let's make this quick. What do you think I've done now?"

"You and I are already acquainted, and this, by the way, is Detective David Milaski. I take it you often have visits from Cleveland PD?"

"About every other week."

David listened as he peered at a baseball signed by Babe Ruth. The guy had the great Bambino's signature sitting on his *shelf*. Next to it sat an ornate pewter frame bearing the picture of a young woman with dark hair to her waist. She perched on a wrought-iron bench in front of a flower-laden archway, and looked completely out of place there. Her rebellious look, tight clothes, and sultry lips would have been more at home in a brothel. A very classy brothel.

Meanwhile, Riley made a show of consulting his notebook. "Are you building a shopping plaza over on West Thirty-fifth?"

"Yes," Ashworth answered, his eye on David.

"Would you know anything about a dead body found there?"

"On my site?"

"Near there."

"How near? Five blocks over?" he asked, annoyance bubbling through the words.

"Near," Riley repeated.

"A construction worker? Some kind of accident?" The news channels would not break the story until five, so Ashworth could not have heard about the girl's body from TV. To David, the man seemed genuinely perplexed.

"No."

"Look, Officer—"

"Detective," Riley snapped. Marcus, seated in the corner, didn't move, didn't seem to breathe.

"Whatever. I have a lot of projects at the moment, and I don't know every single thing that goes on. I wasn't informed of any accidents—"

"Who is this?" David interrupted, holding up the photo frame.

"My daughter, Ivy. She's eighteen, too young for you."

Ivy. From the photo, her eyes confirmed her name. They bored into him, twining through his body, taking his lust for granted. "Where is your daughter?"

"She's not here. Would you put that down, please?" He turned back to Riley. "Just because I'm a successful businessman and you only make whatever scraps the taxpayers want to throw your way—"

"Are you sure you mind if I smoke?" Riley interrupted, with a sweet smile.

"Yes."

"Where is she?" David asked again, his persistence surprising himself and, it seemed, everyone else. Even Marcus turned to look at him with eyes so cool they seemed dead.

Ashworth threw the pencil down. "What the hell does my daughter have to do with anything? Just leave her out of it!"

"All I'm asking is where she is."

"She's on a driving tour of New England. We used to make that trip every fall, look at the trees, smell the ocean. What the hell is it to you?"

"Isn't eighteen a little young to be roaming the countryside?"

"Maybe in Podunk, Iowa, or wherever you came from. People with means grow up a little faster."

David felt a hot sting flush his cheeks, but he persisted. "The fall foliage is over."

"So fucking *what*?"

"So, Mr. Ashworth." David returned the frame to its precise orientation. "We really need to talk to your daughter."

The room fell silent.

For a moment Ashworth wavered, glaring at David with anger and just a fleeting glimpse of fear in his face. Silently he straightened his back and sat forward, setting his elbows on the blotter with care. "There is nothing about my daughter you need to concern yourself with. You got a problem with me, you talk to me. Leave her alone."

A shrill beep pierced the tense air. Riley glanced at his pager, frowning. "Well, Mr. Ashworth . . . thank you for your time."

As they drove away, Riley glanced at David. "Well, *you* made an impression."

"I always do. Usually a bad one."

"And what the hell would you know about the fall foliage in New England?"

"I can't tell from the picture—people look a lot different when they're dead—but what if we just pulled Mr. Ashworth's absent daughter out of the river?" He glanced at his watch again—two P.M. He tried to call the nursing home by five every afternoon. His father's doctor had stressed the importance of routine.

"I don't know," Riley muttered as they passed through large wrought-iron gates and turned onto a street lined by similar mansions. "We come in talking about a body that's now resting on a slab at the morgue. You'd think if he didn't know where his daughter was, he'd be a little more curious. A little more worried."

"Unless he put her there," David pointed out.

CHAPTER

6

EVELYN PARKED IN FRONT of Milaski's car and found his partner. Riley greeted her with a frown, either because he was hungover or because she didn't get there quickly enough to suit him. She suspected the former.

The scene appeared to be an instant replay of the day before, just in a different area of the park and with the main action taking place along the road; the bridge sat several hundred feet back. Instead of construction workers, at least ten police officers of varying rank inhabited the fifty feet of grassy bank between the road and the river. Evelyn pulled on gloves and cushioned the expensive camera against her parka. The temperature had gone up a few degrees since the day before and hovered around freezing, which did nothing to make the outdoors more comfortable and meant that potential precipitation would be a toss-up between rain and snow.

"This is weird, Evelyn," Riley began as he lit a cigarette, the brief match flame representing the only source of warmth for miles.

"Weird is what we do for a living."

"Don't mess with my head, it's too early for that. I mean, this is *weird*. We have a strangled girl next to the road. Okay, that's strange right there, because he could have just rolled her down the hill and who knows how long it would have taken to find the body. But he leaves her by the road."

"Maybe he pushed her out of a car."

"Let me finish. And by the way, you might want to stay away from David Milaski."

"Thanks, Riley, but I already have an older brother." Curiosity, however, got the better of her. "Why do you say that?"

"He's bad news. His last partner, Jack—never mind, it's a long story, but the kid's got quite a past to overcome and he's not making much of an effort. Just trust me on this one, okay? Now, about this victim," he went on before she could respond. "She's black, not white like yesterday, but she's about the same age and she's wet, soaking wet, more than just dew. Don't know about her face, we haven't turned her over yet, waited for you. Her hair is frozen like a block of ice. She's wearing nothing but a T-shirt, bra, and panties."

"Not good weather for that. You think she fell in the water?"

"I think she came *out* of the water."

"Oh," Evelyn said, in a tone usually reserved for tales of alien abduction.

"There's prints in the mud, coming up the bank. She had to tear through a number of bushes—scratched herself up pretty good—but the prints are definitely coming out of the water and going up the bank."

"She just decided to go swimming?"

"Or he threw her in," David Milaski said as he joined their huddle. Evelyn gave him a quick smile to hide her fresh scrutiny. So Milaski had a past with a capital *P*. Not her problem. She decided to ignore the weariness around his eyes and instead focused on his words as he said, "Maybe he pushed her in, but somehow she gets out of the water and he catches up to her again. That's what I don't get."

"What?"

"Why he didn't just kill her before he threw her in the first time?"

"She didn't freeze to death?" she asked, shivering, bouncing on her toes to keep the circulation going, part of a midwesterner's daily aerobics.

"He strangled her."

"This sounds completely different from yesterday's homicide," Evelyn pointed out.

"You haven't heard it all yet," Riley said.

"He strangled her with a chain," David clarified. Evelyn gazed at him with a slight frown and he went on: "A thin stainless steel link chain. And there's dried cement on her legs."

Evelyn's eyebrows stretched into her forehead.

"At least it looks like cement. Gray smears, clinging to her skin."

"Let me get this straight. You think he fitted her with a pair of cement shoes and she somehow *escaped* them?"

"That's what the evidence indicates," David said a bit pompously.

Evelyn's overloaded mind gave protest. "The other victim was chained to the cement. How did she get out of that?"

"I don't know. But he had a piece of the chain left over for finishing this one off."

Evelyn turned and looked at the river, deceptively peaceful in the frigid air, and she pictured what she had been trying hard not to picture. What would it be like to be trapped in a stone and dropped to your death by someone who had plenty of time as the cement hardened to decide to let you live? Would you hold your breath or would the icy water knock it out of you? Would you have a few seconds as you sank to the bottom, feeling the cold invade your bones, the only warmth provided by your burning lungs, time enough to give up all hope? Would the cold actually help, numbing your mind as well as your body? Or would it simply make the pain more intense? And what of that final surrender, that last spastic coughing death?

And what would it be like to escape that, only to die anyway?

"I want to see her," Evelyn said, with a set to her jaw that hadn't been there a moment before.

Riley said, "This way."

The body lay under a tree, but there all pretensions of peacefulness were shattered. She rested on her right side, slightly facing the river as if she regretted leaving its glacial protection. The ends of the chain hung loose; he had simply pulled each end in the opposite direction until she died, and discarded the weapon along with the body.

A young patrol cop wiped his nose on his sleeve, reddening a face that had not yet outgrown acne. "Here she is," he said to her. "The victim, otherwise known as just another dead bitch."

Evelyn wasn't offended by cop language—she'd heard much worse out of her own husband—but did get bored with it. She studied him as if looking through a microscope at what had turned out to be a quite disappointing specimen.

"I don't know if you're just trying to be tough in front of your fellow officers," she said in the voice of every child's most feared grade-school teacher, "but when you've been a cop for longer than a week or two you'll know that a setup like this is not just another anything."

His cheeks, which had been white with cold, now flushed to a healthy rose, and he invoked his right to remain silent for the rest of her visit.

The girl's arms and legs were covered with scratches, none very deep. Delicate diamond stud earrings still winked in the girl's ears—ruling out robbery as a motive—and her hair was enviable even with icicles forming in its curls. The short-sleeve, purple shirt had been woven with threads of silver so that it shimmered as it clung. Her left arm lay in front of her, her right beneath her torso. A lightweight osteopathic brace encircled her left hand. White medical tape still clung to it, in defiance of the river's currents. Evelyn's stomach clenched.

"Turn her over," she whispered.

The cops tugged at the ramrod-stiff body, the left arm stretching outward. Her eyes and tongue bulged in the usual aftermath of strangulation. The girl's sightless eyes gazed up at Evelyn, uncaring, no longer interested in the emotions of others.

One of the road cops said, "Hey, isn't that—"

"*No.*"

David grabbed her shoulders as she swayed. "What is it? What's the matter?"

She choked out the words from behind one palm. "It's Darryl Pierson's daughter. It's Destiny."

"The mayor's daughter?" David asked.

"The *mayor's* daughter?" Riley asked. "Oh, shit."

Evelyn couldn't think, couldn't react, couldn't, for once in her life, be professional. She could only see Darryl swell with pride when he had mentioned his daughter the day before. How could he hear she was dead? How could he bear it?

David put his arms around her as she listed into him, sobbing.

CHAPTER

7

THEY DROVE OUT OF the park, the bleak November trees forming a ghostly sentinel along the road. She watched them slip past her window in silence. So much had happened in a short time; it seemed like it couldn't possibly still be the same day. She had volunteered to break the news to the Piersons—the last thing in the world she wanted to do, a ghastly task that had never before been hers, but she owed Darryl at least that much. However, the chief of Homicide insisted on a more official route and contacted the mayor's right-hand man, who had also been a friend of the family for twenty years. Evelyn felt intensely relieved, and guilty because of it.

She had remained at the scene to supervise the removal of the body, averting her eyes from the curious glances of the other cops and the body snatchers. There was no precedent for Evelyn freaking out over a dead body. Someone would be on the phone to Tony within minutes, providing coffee-break fodder for him and Jason for at least two weeks.

There were no clues to the killer: Grass around the body hindered footprints, and no tire tracks or any other evidence came to light. Divers were sent into the water, in case, as fantastic as it seemed, she had somehow escaped the deadly weight that had murdered the other still-unidentified female.

Then the chief of Homicide called Riley to say that the mayor wanted to see Evelyn and they should hustle her over there right now, because this case would probably determine everything about the Cleveland Police Department for the next ten years or however long this guy remained mayor. Let's stay on his good side.

What would she say to Darryl? Why was she this horribly upset? She hadn't given Darryl a thought for months at a time, and yesterday had been the first time in years she'd seen him other than on a TV screen. She did not still love him, and when it came right down to it she had never even met Destiny.

Maybe because Destiny was his daughter, and Evelyn had a daughter as well. It so easily could have been Angel.

The coffee threatened to come up.

"You okay?"

"No." She took a deep breath, worrying her Egyptian mummy key chain as if it were a talisman. "I don't know what to say to him. I never do this, this isn't part of my job. This is *your* job."

"I don't think he asked for you because of your job," David said in a strained tone. "I think it's because you're a friend."

"Yesterday was the first time I'd seen him in person in about seventeen years."

He stopped for a light, the red color reflecting in his face. "Then—"

"We knew each other in college. We were . . . friends."

David paused as if he meant to proceed cautiously. "I'm sorry. I didn't mean to pry into your personal life. I thought it was some political conflict."

"In a way, maybe it was." She watched the snow alight on the windshield. "But it's been a long time, and we both got married. Perhaps we made the right decisions."

"Is his wife from Cleveland?"

"She's from Chicago. Her parents have a piece of almost every radio station built since the turn of the century. They make the Forbes list every year."

"Oh, I see."

"Yes," she said. "So do I."

The mayor's house nestled in understated wealth on the border of Cleveland and Cleveland Heights. November winds had left the greenery largely untouched. The driveway, already filled with cars, curved in front of the house. David parked behind a champagne Rolls-Royce and turned off the ignition.

"You're not alone, you know."

She glanced at him quizzically. He flushed and looked away, as if already regretting having said anything at all.

"About second-guessing past decisions," he explained. "I know all about that."

The inside foyer seethed with well-dressed black men, all of whom stared at the two. The mayor's personal assistant, Will Brown, introduced himself in order to show Evelyn upstairs. David was to wait in the kitchen. She glanced back from the landing. He hadn't moved, his eyes still on her. Feeling oddly comforted, she continued on.

On the second floor Evelyn found herself tiptoeing, hoping she had managed to scrape all the mud off her shoes. She half expected to hear Mrs. Pierson keening her loss, but the upper floors were silent. She felt a deep pang of sympathy when she thought of Danielle, a mother who no longer had a daughter.

Will escorted her into what was obviously Darryl's private office, a large room where utilitarian filing cabinets were crammed alongside his passions: books, original paintings, and African sculptures. He huddled behind his desk as if marooned in an unfamiliar place.

Evelyn took a deep breath and sat a few feet from him on an antique straight-back chair that creaked at even her slight weight.

"Darryl."

He turned to look at her, a person different from the man she had met the night before, from the boy she had known in college. His eyes were hollow, without vitality. She couldn't speak, just stretched out a hand, which he took and squeezed.

"Don't say you're sorry," he said, his voice stronger than she expected, although it quavered every few words as the pain rolled through. "I can see it in your face, and I'm going to hear that phrase from so many people in the coming weeks that I don't think I'll be able to stand it."

"Okay," she said, not trusting herself to say more.

He let go of her hand. "Tell me," he said, words carefully precise, "was my baby raped?"

She hesitated only a moment before saying, "I don't think so. I can't know until the autopsy"—then caught her breath when she saw him wince at the word—"but we saw no indication of it in the first case. Therefore I think it's unlikely." She finished with more confidence than she felt.

He didn't ask about the first case, and she wondered if the chief of detectives had told him of the similarities between his daughter's case and that of the other girl. Would it be more comforting to know that it didn't happen just because her name was Pierson? Or more galling that it might be a completely random crime?

"I need to know how this happened. I need to know who did it and see him punished. I *have* to, Evelyn."

She knew now why he asked for her. He could deal more easily with anger than with pain. Why not use the investigation as an excuse to put off grief for another day? "We'll find out, Darryl. He had to leave clues."

"You have to catch him, Evelyn," he said, his gaze unwavering. "Promise me you will."

"Darryl, I'm a forensic scientist. I'm not the investigating officer, I'm only part of the overall effort."

Darryl lurched from his chair and collapsed on one knee next to her, taking her hand in both of his. It would have been a comical gesture had it not been born of such obvious agony. "Promise me."

She never made promises. They seemed too risky, too big a chance. What if you couldn't deliver? It was better not to disappoint, not to open yourself to the guilt of having failed. "You don't know what you're asking," she whispered.

"Just promise me you'll find him. You don't even have to catch him or convict him. Just tell me who he is."

"I'll do my best," she tried, knowing he wouldn't be satisfied with that. Darryl had never been satisfied with half measures.

"Promise me."

It seemed to her that his face held all the pain of every parent's fears, of every demon that haunts in the small hours of the morning when you listen for their foot on the step, of every life cut too short, leaving a bewildered agony in its wake. "I promise."

And then the shrill beep of her pager cracked the air; startled, she pulled her hand away. Darryl barely noticed, just returned to his seat, his current objective accomplished.

"I'm so sorry," she said, looking at the digital display. Then she looked again. Her home phone number glowed at her. She had left her cell phone in the car.

She had been reluctant to come; now she felt reluctant to leave. "Darryl, is there a phone I can use?"

He nodded as if his neck hurt and he had to move it slowly, and got to his feet as if his body felt the same way. "In the hall." He put his hand on her elbow to guide her and said, "Thanks for coming, Evelyn. You didn't have to."

"Yes, I did."

"You'll keep me posted?" he said, with an insistent squeeze to her elbow.

"Of course," she said with less certainty. He turned to face her.

"I know everything's supposed to go through the ME, but this is different. This is *my* daughter. Don't bother with channels. Just call me whenever you know anything. Anyone here will put you through."

"Darryl, I—"

"I know," he said. "I'm asking you to take a risk, but I'll keep everything you tell me confidential. No one will know." He held her gaze, sounding more like the Darryl she had known. "I wouldn't ask you to toss your job down the tubes. Just tell me everything. I'll make damn sure no one ever knows where it came from. I just have to know, Evelyn. You can understand that, can't you?"

She nodded.

"I have to be with Danielle, now," he added, and the thought brought tears to his eyes. "God, I— and the boys are so confused, they just keep asking where their sister went. Here's the phone. You can find your way out?"

"Yes."

"Thank you, Evelyn." He grasped her shoulder, and for a moment his face began to slide into grief. Then he choked out, "Thank you," and left her alone.

In the hallway she picked up the receiver on a beautifully crafted phone on a beautifully crafted desk and without thinking dialed 9 for an outside line. What a crazy life to have five lines on your home phone, to have to grieve with a near-total lack of privacy.

Angel answered. "Mom?"

"Yeah, hon, what's the matter?"

"Where are you?"

"I'm at the mayor's house." Evelyn mentally skipped over the whining note in her daughter's voice. "What is it?"

"The mayor's house? What are you doing there?"

"Why did you page me?" she snapped. "What's wrong?"

"Mom." Now Evelyn heard the tremulous overtones. "I need you to come home. I feel really sick."

DAVID WAITED FOR EVELYN in the car, cold but more comfortable than he would have been inside, surrounded by Cleveland's elite. The smell of all those expensive suits made him woozy. The last time he had been in the presence of that much delicate tailoring he had barely avoided going to jail.

Maria Hardin had been one of his truly bad decisions, but as many times as he looked back, he couldn't imagine making any other. A well-kept hothouse flower with jet-black hair and bottomless eyes, she had faultless skin over a frame of iron. Her marriage to his Special Ops commander didn't even slow him down.

Though his father still fumed over David's decision to throw away college to join the Marines, his military training got him into Special Operations. True, he had exaggerated his armed forces experience— while the world churned over the Iran hostage rescue and the Grenada invasion, David spent most of his career at a desk at Fort Bragg—but he figured he could keep up until he learned more. He listened to the other guys, read all the manuals, and pulled off a spectacular hostage rescue in his third week. It seemed as if things were finally going his way. Then one of the guys threw a party and David met Maria.

She did nothing to indicate that she made a habit of seducing her husband's subordinates. They simply had a short conversation about hibachi grills, and he was completely, consummately lost.

He pursued her with a single-mindedness that curtailed his job training and worried his coworkers. Men who barely knew him felt compelled to take him aside and try to talk some sense into him. He didn't listen. He hardly heard them.

When he finally convinced her to make a surreptitious visit to his apartment, he called in sick and spent the whole day cleaning. He washed and folded laundry that hadn't seen a machine in weeks. The windows were spotless. Even his retriever, Harry, got a bath, which the dog clearly considered over-the-top. David stood in the living room, wondering if he had enough time to repaint, when the doorbell rang.

She stepped into his apartment for the first time. "I shouldn't be here."

David had always believed, *had* to believe, that Maria felt torn. At least she said as much to him, that she could no more stop herself than he could.

"I do love you," she said four weeks later during a stolen ten minutes at Tower City mall. "But I love him, too."

"I wish you didn't." It would be their last private moment together.

Several days later three inept bank robbers dressed in Halloween masks tried to make a withdrawal from the downtown National Bank. A teller tripped the alarm before the first one reached the red ropes. They collected the money in a floral print pillowcase and ran outside to see four police cars, lights blazing, the sidewalk blocked, and made a hasty retreat back into the bank.

David found himself on the roof with Maria's husband, visible to office workers in a few neighboring towers but hidden from the road. Rod monitored the radio traffic. The police officers on the street reported that customers were lying on the floor in the front area as the negotiators attempted to call the robbers on the assistant manager's phone.

"What now?" David asked over the rising wind. The sun warmed his back but not his heart. Worry prickled the back of his neck.

"Now we wait. There's nothing we can do for the moment. By the way," Rod said casually, turning, "how long have you been fucking my wife?"

David never found out how he knew, whether Maria had told him or someone else had. But he saw no doubt in his supervisor's eyes, and even less in the semiautomatic SIG-Sauer P226 in his right hand. It had fifteen rounds of 9-millimeter Luger full-metal-jacket cartridges and Rod could fire the entire clip in less than eight seconds. David stood very still, both dignified and ashamed by the sympathy in his own voice. "I'm sorry. But I love her."

"Did you really think you'd ride off in the sunset and I'd just let you go? Be a big man about it?"

"I—"

"I hate to tell you, but I ain't that big. Nobody's that big. Not over someone like her."

"I know—"

"Did you know," his supervisor said, as if addressing a class of rookies, "that nine-millimeter bullets, properly loaded, travel at a rate of four thousand feet per second? And if one hit your body it would pass straight through, so long as it didn't get stuck in the skull, the spine, or the pelvic bone?"

David's pores began to weep sweat.

"I mean, we're in the middle of a shootout situation here, and unless I miss my guess—"

"Rod—"

"—those morons down there can't go out, so they'll come up. All sorts of bullets could fly."

David heard a bang and some muffled thuds, and then all three bank robbers tumbled through the stairwell door, blinded at first by the bright sun after the dim bank. The unlucky soul in the lead landed at Rod's feet; the other two ducked back down the stairwell.

Rod aimed, but not at the robber, now sprinting for the fire escape. It might appear that way from a distance, but the gun's muzzle pointed at David's chest. It could be done. Rod could get away with it.

All of this shot across David's brain in the split second it took for him to throw himself across the tar paper. The SIG-Sauer spit out a single round and the guy didn't make it to the fire escape.

David saw a red stain spread across the man's chest. He stayed where he was. Let Rod explain how he "accidentally" shot David when he was on the ground. Let the secretaries see.

Rod looked from the dying man to David and back again. Considering.

When he looked again, his eyes weren't quite as feverish. "Well, congratulations. You've stopped an armed robbery in progress."

They never spoke again, never mentioned Maria, never coordinated their stories. David told the well-dressed review board members that the man had tried to escape—even though they hadn't even said "Stop!" and the guy probably would have wet his pants if they had. It must have been the same story Rod told because there were no repercussions. But it had been a bad shoot and he knew it, Rod knew it, and whether David chalked it up to paranoia or a good understanding of how much cops gossip, he had the firm belief that every other cop on the force knew it, too.

He never returned to the Special Ops team. Before his mandatory postshooting leave expired, David transferred to Vice as a detective, a brilliant move in its way. The other cops, even those that knew of the affair, had to question why Rod would recommend promotion for the guy who banged his wife. Maybe they were wrong and David was innocent. *How* Rod had done it, David couldn't guess. He must have called in some favors. A lot of favors.

David never saw Maria again. He never told her what had happened, doubting, in the harsh light of day, that she would even believe him. He debated whether he should leave her alone to rebuild her marriage or if he should warn her that her husband's jealousy, reasoned or unreasoning, could put her in danger. The point became moot when Rod, opting for an early retirement buyout, sent Maria ahead to a luxurious Florida condo and David was left with nothing but a torturous longing and a job he didn't deserve.

And now came Evelyn, an intriguing combination of attractiveness and resourcefulness. She could help him solve this case with forensic information, but how much use could she be if she spent all her time holding the mayor's hand? Obviously she still loved the man, but David had held her while she cried and he couldn't get the burning feeling to leave his arms. If still inclined to make impulsive, stupid decisions with his life, he had better learn to see them coming, and he could see this one from several football fields away. He would have nothing to do with Evelyn, either personally or professionally. He would finally, as his father had begged him, learn.

He looked at his watch.

CHAPTER

9

EVELYN CROSSED HER ARMS and wondered why emergency rooms had to be kept at near refrigerator-like temperatures. She supposed it kept germ growth down, but did that balance the inadvisability of taking people who were already sick and freezing them to death?

"How do you feel?"

"Crappy," her daughter said, her voice a pained hush. "Just like the last five times you asked."

"Sorry."

Angel curled up under the white sheets as if she couldn't get warm, doubled over in pain. She had left the house without makeup and didn't seem to care that her hair stuck out all over, two facts that worried Evelyn more than the doctors and nurses coming and going without telling her anything.

Evelyn felt helpless and resented it. "How long have you been sick?"

"I've been feeling kind of punky for a couple days, but it wasn't anything much. Just today I started to feel really bad."

Evelyn and Angel were walled off by hanging curtains patterned in a pale blue; activity in the rest of the room manifested itself in the form of scurrying feet, voices ranging from unintelligible whispers to the hard, piercing shriek of a baby, and the faint ebb and flow of sirens. Evelyn had been staring at the wall, decorated with mounted boxes of gloves and oxygen hoses, for two hours.

"What were you doing at the mayor's house?" Angel said, her voice not much more than a whisper. Evelyn hoped her daughter just didn't want to disturb the nurses and actually had the strength for more volume, but it was an idle hope. Angel never minded disturbing people.

"Just work stuff." Evelyn brushed a raven-colored strand off Angel's flushed cheek. She didn't want to tell her about someone else's dead daughter, didn't even want to raise the specter of death. Evelyn had two diametrically opposed approaches to the subject. On the job, death was commonplace, a normal part of the life cycle. But when it came to her family, she could not bear the thought of it. If this created some wear and tear on her psyche, too bad. "It's not important."

"Sorry to interrupt you."

"It wasn't anything fun, believe me."

It had to be appendicitis. It wouldn't be a tumor. Why would it be a tumor? Their family had no history of tumors. But what about Rick's? Maybe Angel had an ulcer. Maybe the divorce had so traumatized her that she had an ulcer. Would it be reported to Children and Families if parents gave their kid an ulcer? It would be a form of abuse, wouldn't it?

"Mrs. James?"

"Yes!" Evelyn snapped to attention. "Yes!"

The doctor, a preppy kid with *D. Sweeney* on his name tag, someone who didn't seem old enough to drive, looked at her oddly. Evelyn found it encouraging that Angel combed her hair with her fingers as well as she could, never too sick to notice a decent-looking male.

"Angel has acute appendicitis," he said to no one's surprise or relief. "It's going to have to come out, I'm afraid."

Evelyn watched fear seep through her daughter's features until it robbed her skin of color, but all Angel said was "Okay," with a grimness that made Evelyn realize how much her daughter resembled her—stoic, keeping her emotions hidden where no one could taunt her with them. Characteristics Evelyn had always been proud of, though now she doubted herself. Had she set an example of strength for her daughter? Or repression?

"I'm going to do the surgery, and Dr. Cho will be the anesthesiologist."

"Dr. Carry is her regular doctor," Evelyn fussed as the situation slipped completely out of her control, and finally realized it had been all along.

"Yes, we'll inform her pediatrician," the young doctor said kindly, and went on. "The charge nurse tells me this is all okay through her insurance. We should be all set."

Angel said nothing.

"Wh-wh-when will you be scheduling this for?" Evelyn's words tumbled out and made no sense to her, though the doctor seemed to understand.

"Now."

"What?"

"I'm sorry I didn't make that clear, Mrs. James. Angel's appendix has to come out right now. I know we'd prefer to wait until at least tomorrow morning, but even that would be a great risk. No, we'll start as soon as she's through pre-op. Don't worry," he said, suddenly bursting into a cheerful, have-no-fear bedside manner. "I've done this at least forty times and I've never had a problem. Angel, when did you last eat?"

"Lunchtime," Angel whispered. "I ate a little bit of a hamburger. But I didn't want anything after that. I had a glass of milk at home, but only a few sips."

Dr. Sweeney made a note. "The nurse will take you to pre-op, and he'll show you where to wait, Mrs. James."

"They're going to cut me open, huh?" Angel said after the doctor left, turning over this plan in her mind and deciding how to feel about it.

"People have had their appendixes out for the past hundred years, honey," Evelyn told the girl with confidence she didn't feel. Never let kids see you scared, something she had learned from her mother. The debate about emotional expression aside, she knew that if she took it in stride, Angel would, too. "It's a simple operation. Nothing to worry about."

"I'm not worried."

"I'm sure the doctors know exactly what they're doing." *Despite the fact that I've never laid eyes on this medical staff before, I'm going to pretend that I have complete confidence in them.* "You'll be just fine."

"What choice do I have?"

"Well," Evelyn said, "you really don't. It has to come out. If it bursts, you'll be much sicker."

"I know."

"There's really nothing anyone can do about it."

"I know."

"It's best that the doctors take it out."

"I *know*, Mom."

"Don't worry, Angel. You'll be fine."

"I *know*."

Please, God, don't let anything happen to my daughter.

The privacy curtain flew back with a theatrical flair and a young man in cow-print scrubs stepped into their space. "Hi!" he said. "I'm Nurse Neal. Which one of us is having our appendix out today?"

Evelyn frowned.

Angel giggled.

He consulted his clipboard with mock seriousness, then beamed at the girl in the bed. "And you must be . . . *Angel*." He drew out the vowels with exaggerated interest, prompting another giggle. He pulled a sphygmomanometer off the wall. "That's quite a name. A *movie* star's name. Are you a movie star?"

"No," Angel whispered. Her grin slipped into a grimace of pain, but quickly went back to a grin, and she willingly offered her arm to the blood pressure cuff.

Evelyn smiled for Angel's sake and took her daughter's other hand. "You're the nurse that's going to take her to pre-op?"

"That's me," he said, pumping. "Jimmy Neal. Nurse Neal. Pre-op's on the third floor east, then she'll go to operating room four. Just go to the third floor west nurses' station and ask for the surgical waiting room. It's a really nice room and they have free coffee, in case your nerves aren't jangled enough."

"Mom's favorite stuff."

"Your blood pressure is perfect, *Angel*." Again he exaggerated the name, and it began to grate on Evelyn's nerves even though she knew he was being kind. "Miss Movie Star. My aunt was an actress. The pinnacle of her success was a Garfield aluminum siding commercial. Her shoeprints are in cement outside the Hanna, but that's only because she was bal—um, dating the manager." Under Evelyn's icy stare he changed the subject. "Time to go. You can walk with us, Mom. Please remember to take all your personal belongings with you when you leave and keep hands and arms inside the vehicle at all times."

They made a slow-moving procession to the elevators and Evelyn watched as the overhead lights reflected from Angel's upturned eyes. Her daughter seemed elaborately unconcerned, but then that was Angel's favorite affectation. She had to be nervous but probably wasn't afraid. It would never occur to someone her age that she might die; youth believes itself immortal. She wouldn't think, as Evelyn did, of how important an empty stomach could be to the administration of a general anesthetic, maybe that half a hamburger would come up into the oxygen mask while Angel was in recovery and no one would be watching her and she could choke on her own vomit. She could have an allergic reaction to the anesthetic, the antibiotic, or any one of half a dozen other substances that would now be introduced into her body. Perhaps the appendix had already burst—no, it would have stopped hurting if it had—

Nurse Neal interrupted her thoughts. "How's Mom doing?"

Evelyn bit back a retort. "Mom's been better. How long has Dr. Sweeney been at this hospital?"

"Want to run a criminal history on him, Mom?" Angel asked.

"Criminal history?" Nurse Neal's cheer faltered for a moment as he concentrated on angling the rolling bed into a double-long elevator. "Are you a cop?"

"No. I'd just like to know something about him. I only met the man an hour ago."

"He's terrific. He does tons of surgeries, never had any surprises. The nurses love him." He stabbed the lighted button labeled *3*. "He's been here about a year and a half."

"Great."

"Don't worry, Mom," the nurse said in a voice too loud for the confined space. "Angel will be just fine."

"Easy for you to say." Evelyn stopped herself from adding, *She's not your daughter*, but her glare said it all. Nurse Neal cut the banter and Evelyn kicked herself. She found her daughter's hand again and squeezed. For the first time since she had turned twelve, Angel squeezed back. Evelyn's eyes grew damp. The elevator doors opened.

"What about Dad?" Angel asked.

Shit!

"I'm sorry, honey," Evelyn said in anguish. "I should have called him right away."

"It's no big deal."

Believe me, I'd rather give him a miss. "No, he has to know. I don't know if he'll be able to get here in time, but I'll call right away."

"He doesn't have to come."

He does if he's any kind of father. It was Terrie that didn't have to come, but she would show up with a bouquet of flowers, a basket of snacks, balloons, and a teddy bear. *Please, God, let her be out of town or something.*

"Here's pre-op," Nurse Neal told them, as if it were the entrance to Disney World.

Evelyn jumped. "So soon?"

"Bye, Mom," Angel said, withdrawing her hand.

Don't say good-bye! It's not good-bye! "I'll be right out here, honey," Evelyn called, embarrassing them both as panic overtook her voice. The gurney slipped through the doors and the nurse turned to give Evelyn one last too-bright smile that he must have meant to be comforting.

"Don't worry, Mom," Angel's voice floated back to her. "People have been having these out for a hundred years!"

Why doesn't that make me feel better?

The doors swung shut and her daughter was gone, among strangers.

CHAPTER
10

AT LEAST TERRIE DIDN'T answer the phone. Rick, predictably, saw no point in sitting in a hospital waiting room. "I'll come by and see her when she's home."

"It's up to you," Evelyn said, walking a fine line between not wanting him there for her own sake and at the same time wanting him there for Angel's. "I just thought you might want to be here when she wakes up."

"She'll be fine."

"I know." *It's only your daughter and it's only major surgery, but hey, I wouldn't want you to miss an episode of* The Sopranos.

"I'll give her a call later."

"She'll probably be here until tomorrow sometime, if not longer."

"Maybe we'll come by tomorrow, then, if she's still there. What hospital are you at?"

"Riverside."

Relieved and again feeling guilty because of it, Evelyn tried to page through an outdated issue of *Glamour.* She gave up and paced the waiting room, carefully avoiding eye contact with the other inmates. They all had the same forced calm, the same lurking worries; she didn't want to talk about hers and didn't want to hear theirs. She called her mother instead. She was the only person Evelyn wanted and needed for moral support and whom she had left at home to save her the stress of a hospital wait.

As always, she thought about work, finding it easier to imagine the bloodied corpses of strangers than any *ER*-inspired medical nightmares involving her daughter. They had two dead girls pulled from the river—one unknown and one very well known. Where could their paths have crossed?

At eleven, someone shook her awake from an uneasy dream in which Angel appeared in the lobby of the ME's office in Dickensian garb, brandishing a bloody scalpel and telling her, "What were you worried about? People have been having their appendix out for a hundred years," and Evelyn looked up through bleary eyes at Nurse Neal.

"All over, Mom." He showed an indecent amount of energy for that time of night. "She got the star treatment. The nasty appendix is out and all is well in the state of Angel."

Relief flooded through her. "Thank you," she said before following him down a too-bright hallway, but added under her breath, "And don't call me Mom."

Angel seemed impossibly pale, almost translucent, but her eyes flickered open intermittently and she managed a debilitated smile in response to her name.

"It's all over, honey. You're just fine."

"I told her that already," Neal said.

Evelyn shot him a venomous look and he had the sense to leave.

She spent the rest of the night in an orange vinyl chair next to Angel's bed. She woke with a deformed neck and could take comfort only in her daughter's peaceful face and the knowledge that any guilt trip she could lay on Rick for not showing up would be an amateur effort compared to what Terrie would do. *How could you let your daughter lie there all alone? She needed her daddy!*

For the first time, Evelyn gave Terrie some careful thought. Maybe she had a really lousy father and she needed Rick to be seen as the perfect one. Maybe she had a perfect family and wanted to live up to it. Maybe she needed an ideal relationship with her husband's child because she had no intention of having any of her own. Maybe, and more likely, she was one of those young, childless, never-before-married women who think they have all the answers to both situations, who had observed all her friends and knew exactly what they were doing wrong.

Maybe anything, Evelyn sighed.

Her pager went off in mid-doze, making her glad to have a cardiac care unit close by. When her heart stopped pounding, she called the number.

"I'm sorry, Tony," she said. "I didn't notice the time or I would have called." She explained about Angel.

"When are you coming to work?"

"Probably tomorrow."

"Probably? We need you here today. They're doing the autopsy on Destiny Pierson. The place is full of cops and the press is all over the place and—"

"My daughter had her appendix out," Evelyn explained patiently, knowing that Tony truly had no clue what Angel's appendix had to do with her mother's job. "I have to stay with her."

"You said she was okay. Can't you come in for part of the day? We need you here."

"So does she. I'm sorry, Tony, but this can't be helped."

"This is the biggest murder to hit this city since—"

Patience evaporated. "I don't give a shit," she said, and hung up.

"Such language, Mom," Angel murmured.

"Tony would drive a saint to swear. And in case you haven't noticed, I ain't no saint. How do you feel?"

"Fine," Angel sighed. "Mom?"

"Yes?"

"Are you going to start dating again?"

"*What?* Where did that come from?"

"I had a dream about you." Angel's voice sounded so low and sleepy that Evelyn had trouble catching the words. "You can, you know."

"Thanks for your permission." Evelyn laughed. "But no thank you."

"I mean it." A flicker of indignation strengthened her whisper. "Melissa's mom doesn't want to date anyone because she thinks it will screw Melissa up, but Melissa says it's making her crazy. The sexual frustration is getting to the woman."

"Well, it's not getting to me." Evelyn held her daughter's half-closed gaze. "For the first time in seventeen years my life is my own, and I like it that way, thank you very much. Don't you worry about my love life."

"Isn't there anyone you can date?"

"Go to sleep."

"Someone at work?"

"No—oh."

The telltale hesitation had the same effect as a shot of adrenaline. "Who?" Angel demanded.

"Nobody."

"*Mom.*"

At least the subject kept Angel amused. "There *is* this new Homicide detective—"

"Is he nice?"

Evelyn gave a burst of laughter loud enough to wake up the college student with the broken leg in the next bed.

"What's so funny?" Angel demanded.

"Nothing, honey, really. It just kind of struck me. When I went out with boys, that's all your grandmother would ask me: 'Is he a *nice* boy?' Well, first she would ask is he Catholic, and *then* she'd ask if he was a nice boy. But never anything like where did he live, what did his father do for a living, did he have a car—just 'Is he a *nice* boy?' "

"Grandma's got her priorities straight."

"Yes, she does."

"So date this cop."

"He hasn't asked me, dear, nor does he seem likely to. Besides, work relationships are problematic. And Tony would hassle me over it."

"But you don't give a shit about work," Angel reminded her slyly, and slipped away again before she could protest.

The problem was, Evelyn *did* give a shit. If she didn't get some results soon, Rupert would lean on Tony, and Tony held her job in his chubby, nervous palm. More than that, it was Darryl's daughter on that cold slab, and she wanted to be there to see it through. A great deal of work remained. Destiny's clothes had to be removed and dried in sterile surroundings; careful photographs needed to be taken of the body's injuries; and like all obsessive workers Evelyn didn't want to leave those tasks to her perfectly competent coworkers. She wouldn't be happy unless she did them herself. She had promised Darryl she'd do everything she could and she'd meant it, and now she'd miss the first day of the investigation.

But it was *her* daughter in this cold hospital bed, and that was that.

Evelyn stooped over a water fountain, watching Rick and Terrie approach. The woman had restricted herself to a modest bouquet, a stuffed bunny, and two candy bars, both of which slid out of her arms as she asked how Angel felt. Evelyn told them what the doctors had said.

"Take this in to her," Terrie said, handing half of the loot to Rick to give the appearance of a doting father, though even a doting father would never have picked out the sickly sweet teddy bear he now clutched in one hand. "I'll give you two a minute."

A backache prevented Evelyn from feeling sorry for her ex-husband, who obviously had no idea what she expected him to do during this intimate father-daughter minute. But he dutifully disappeared and Terrie turned to Evelyn, who couldn't help but compare Terrie's fresh face to her own oily skin and lank bangs. But then, she consoled herself, Terrie hadn't spent the night in an orange vinyl chair.

"This must have been awful for you," Terrie said with an annoying amount of bubbliness.

"It wouldn't have been as bad if I could find a cup of coffee around here that's not seven hours old."

"I'm sorry we didn't come last night, but by the time I got home, Rick insisted visiting hours were over and the hospital wouldn't let us in."

Rick always had a logic behind his convenience, Evelyn mused. He loved his daughter greatly but within reason, whereas Evelyn felt the whole point of love was that it lacked reason. Evelyn merely nodded at Terrie, too worn out for biting repartee.

"I knew she had to be sick when she was with us, from her pale skin," Terrie went on, tapping her heels on the industrial-gray tile floor. "Did she have a fever?"

"I don't know."

"Didn't you check?"

"Why would I check?" Evelyn tried to keep the irritation out of her voice. She had the strong feeling that any antipathy toward Terrie would be revealed later to Angel, from Terrie's point of view and with the good stepmother in the starring role.

"Because she was sick."

What? Now I'm expected to be an adoring mother, a soulmate, and *a human thermometer?* "She didn't tell me."

"After dinner she told me her stomach hurt and she felt cold." Terrie nibbled at an already worn nail, a sign of imperfection that Evelyn pounced on and savored. "But then she can talk to me more easily than you."

Terrie paused, and for once seemed to realize she had been slightly less than tactful, but decided her concern for Angel took precedence over discretion. "I mean, you're her *mother*—"

"Exactly."

"And she doesn't feel that you want to listen to her," Little Miss Perfect Child Psychologist went on. "It's kind of a weak spot in your relationship. She's such a sensitive child."

Evelyn looked at Terrie's vacant blue eyes as a wave of fury passed through her. She'd had it. She had been up all night, was sore, tired, in trouble with her boss, and worried sick about her daughter. At that moment she could murder over a cup of coffee, let alone the suggestion—no, statement—that she was an abysmal, coldhearted bitch of a mother.

"Yes, she is," Evelyn said. "Imagine how such a vulnerable child would feel if she found out her father had shacked up with you long before our divorce."

She regretted the words as soon as they hit the air. Even the satisfaction of seeing the blood drain from Terrie's face didn't make up for the icy sense of foreboding that invaded her cells.

"Did you tell her that?" Terrie asked in a horrified whisper, all bubbles gone.

"I would never tell her that. She's such a *sensitive* child." Evelyn brushed past the other woman, not gently, and reclaimed the orange vinyl chair next to her only child as if all the armies of the world couldn't oust her from it.

For a moment she thought Terrie might spend the rest of the visit in the hallway, but the sturdy younger woman entered with a burst of cheerfulness for everyone except Evelyn, whom she ignored for the next fifteen minutes while she spoke to Angel in the "you poor kid, that must have been awful, why didn't you tell us you were that sick" vein. At first Angel gave little response to the gushing, as her stitches had begun to hurt and her tolerance was frayed. But after the nurse introduced a little morphine into her IV, Angel relaxed and told Terrie about her pain and fear in much more detail than she had told her mother.

Maybe Terrie's right, Evelyn thought in horror. *Because I keep my feelings to myself, does Angel feel she has to do the same or I won't re-*

spect her, think her weak? Am I by example creating a wall between us? Or is she just telling Terrie these things because she knows it's what Terrie wants to hear, in that peculiar chameleonlike way that so many women develop?

Then she glanced at the TV screen, which had pictures with no sound, and saw a bouncy anchorwoman talking away with a blown-up picture of Destiny Pierson in the background. She felt an ache of sympathy for Darryl, but didn't turn the sound up. Even though the news would have no personal meaning for her daughter, she still didn't want Angel to know that another teenage girl had died on the same day her life was, however briefly, threatened.

THE NEXT MORNING SHE left Angel at home, safely ensconced with her phone, her cable TV, her overly indulgent grandmother, and her school assignments (which would almost certainly be ignored), and plunged back into the maelstrom the murders had created around the ME's office. Vans from the four local TV channels clogged the parking lot and the front steps were filled with representatives from CNN, Parents of Murdered Children, Block Watch, and Black on Black Crime Prevention.

"Excuse me." She pushed by the same bleached-blond anchorwoman she had watched on Angel's hospital TV as she joined the line of employees running the gauntlet.

Someone clutched her elbow. "Here," department intern Jason announced to the group at large. "This is Evelyn James. She will answer all your questions." He melted into the crowd before she could stick out a foot and trip him.

Eager faces, microphones, cameras, and very bright lights not only invaded her personal space but decimated it. She knew she resembled a deer in the headlights of an oncoming train. Not just any train, the high-speed kind. The reporters nearly salivated as they shouted questions.

"Was the mayor's daughter raped?"

"Was her body mutilated?"

"Is it true there were racial epithets carved into her skin?"

I work with dead bodies, she thought, *and these people are giving* me *the creeps.* She thrust her shoulders back, lifted her chin, and looked the biggest camera directly in its cold lens. "All inquiries should be directed to the medical examiner, Mr. Stone."

Having delivered the party line, she pressed through the crowd, which extended into the lobby. The wizened receptionist, Mrs. Anderson, had been forced to light a cigarette and let the halo of smoke clear a space around her desk.

"Where you been, missy?" she queried. "Hell of a time to skip town. Not that I didn't think of it myself, but Greyhound won't give tickets on credit anymore."

"My daughter had her appendix out. Where's Jonathan?"

"Tony's bellowing for you," the receptionist noted with satisfaction, and tapped long nails on the chipped countertop. "Has been since yesterday morning. You'd think the exercise would work off some of the fat in his neck, but no, he looks just the same, like a basketball on a tire."

Evelyn's coworker Marissa squeezed past the crowd, ignoring the pleas of reporters the same way she ignored men who shouted from passing cars, and plucked her sheaf of messages from between Mrs. Anderson's bloodred nails. The young Hispanic serologist had the face of a model and a thousand-yard stare. "Hey, heard about your daughter. How'd that go?"

To Evelyn's surprise, she put her arms around Marissa and let the woman give her a tight hug. "It was awful. They wheeled her into surgery and I just wanted to die. Even though I knew it was stupid. People have had this done for a hundred years."

"But for a hundred years, it wasn't *your* kid. And that makes all the difference. Then you have to jump back into this zoo."

"I didn't even make it to the door before Jason threw me to the wolves. That kid doesn't like me," she went on in a rare moment of petulance. "And I have been nothing but nice to him."

" 'Cause he wants your job, honey," put in Mrs. Anderson. "His position now is through a federal grant. Once the money's up, so is he."

"Come on. He's a kid. He doesn't even have his degree yet."

"His *master's*," Marissa said seriously. "He's got a bachelor's. Once he gets his master's, he'll have something over you."

"Oh." As Evelyn digested this, a weak tornado of worry began to swirl in her stomach. She couldn't lose her job. Particularly not to some pimply geek like Jason, but under any circumstances, *she could not lose her job.*

The moment of panic passed, and she continued to protest: "But he has no experience. And tossing me to the reporters is just his idea of a joke."

"Don't be naïve," Mrs. Anderson snapped. "You put a fox in the henhouse, don't be surprised when you lose some eggs."

"Yeah, but––" Evelyn searched for another objection. "He's still totally green. Does he really think that Tony will think that he can just waltz in and do all the work?"

"He will if you keep taking off for family emergencies. People like him, with no families, don't understand that. Besides, Tony doesn't care about work, he just wants someone to bullshit with." Marissa spoke with conviction and, Evelyn had to admit, accuracy. "He's got you and me, his hos, to do the real work."

Evelyn had to laugh. "I think I should object to being referred to as a ho."

"I sure as hell object to being *treated* as one."

"Okay, okay. Anybody know where Jonathan is?"

"He's at viewing, probably," Mrs. Anderson volunteered. "You know, where they all stand in a circle around the dead bodies, listening to the case histories? No way to start the day, I always thought.

You want I should tell Tony you left the country? It's guaranteed to put him in intensive care. I'll send flowers."

"I'll be up in a minute. I just want to get with the doctor first. Isn't this a nonsmoking building?"

"You can't scare me," the woman said with absolute certainty. "I raised kids."

Evelyn dove back into the crowd and fought her way to the rear of the building, where a deskman who would have looked more at home in a Browns uniform guarded the doorway.

"Morning, Greg."

"They keep tryin' to come back here," he said, referring to the visitors. "Don't know why. They'd probably puke if they did."

"Death fascinates people."

"Makes them puke, too. You be careful if you leave the building, them vultures harass people until they say something, and the ME said nobody makes any statements but him if they want to keep working here."

"I'll be careful."

She found Jonathan standing over a cancer victim, writing fastidious notes on a preprinted form. "How is your daughter?" he asked without preamble.

"She's fine, thanks. Everything went okay. Did you do Destiny?"

A smile surfaced. "There's several ways one could take that question, but if you're asking if I did the autopsy on the Pierson kid, yes, I did."

"What did you find?"

"Hang on." He prodded the unfortunate man on the gurney. Normally Evelyn found his unflappability comforting, but this morning it was all she could do to keep from tapping her foot. A stench washed through the dock, of decaying flesh, fecal matter, body odor, and industrial-strength cleaner, but it smelled like that every day and she took no notice. She *did* notice a news crew in the parking lot, their camera snatching some footage every time the overhead door in the loading dock opened, their van planted in a space labeled *For Authorized Vehicles Only.*

Jonathan finished and she followed him to his office, one cubicle out of a room he shared with three other pathologists. The available shelf space had been filled with medical texts, *Unnatural Death* by Dr. Michael Baden, and a picture of his parents and brother. "Sit."

Evelyn sat.

He opened a file, and she could see the standard form bearing the outlines of a female body. Jonathan had filled in every injury or mark on the skin. There were more present than any young girl should have to suffer, but they were all minor compared to the dark red line around the neck.

"She was strangled with the chain around her neck, no surprise. The links left distinct marks. Her skin wasn't waterlogged, except for her left hand, which lay in a puddle, so any swim right before her death was a brief one."

"But—"

"But," he went on, "she had some water in her lungs, and a culture showed bacteria consistent with river water. It did not come from a bathtub."

"So she got a mouthful of water, but she didn't drown."

"She definitely didn't drown. She was pretty healthy up until he tightened the chain."

Evelyn shuddered.

"You okay?"

"Yeah."

"You don't usually get the willies." His brown eyes saw, as always, so much more than the surface. "Something about this case getting to you?"

She hesitated. "I spent yesterday in a hospital with my sixteen-year-old. I guess there's just too many dead girls around all of a sudden."

"Oh."

She felt a qualm about keeping her personal connection to the victim from him but didn't want to get into it. "Were there any other injuries?"

"Besides the broken finger, she had scrapes, bruises, mud and dirt on her hands, a broken nail. It's all minor. It could be from our perp and it could be from fighting the elements, clawing her way up that bank."

"Sexual assault?"

"No sign of it, but then the water could have washed a lot away. We took swabs, so Marissa should have the results this morning. But there were no signs of injuries. Maybe he got her skirt off and then she bolted."

"I hope so."

"You sure you're okay? Maybe you should have taken another day off."

She smiled at him. "And miss getting on the six o'clock news? Not on your life."

"Yeah, that's you. Such a ham."

"I'd better find Tony before he pages me. Thanks a lot."

Evelyn went up the back staircase but turned away from Trace Evidence, knocking instead on the door to the Toxicology Department. Tox had twice the staff as Trace and much more organization, but then their jobs were more easily regimented. On a regular basis, they tested three items from each body: blood, urine, and stomach contents. The staff rotated among the instrument stations every few months to avoid burnout, and they were even allowed to have a radio.

Once admitted, she wound between benches filled with small plastic jars of samples from autopsy, clipboards, and scattered tools to a corner desk tucked in between the HPLC and the compressed air tanks. The hard-packed liquid chromatograph hummed as it separated controlled substances—legal and illegal drugs—from bodily fluids. Ed Ferullo, pale, ponytailed, as rotund as Tony but frighteningly smart, crammed another few words on a yellow legal pad and pointedly ignored her.

She amused herself for a moment by checking out the latest comic strips, which covered the wall, window, and HPLC, and even extended onto the gas tanks. Underneath these flapping pieces of paper, textbooks, a true-crime novel, and what looked suspiciously like a Harlequin romance were stacked in a perfect pyramid in one corner of his desk; in the other corner sat an Egyptian sarcophagus (one-eighteenth scale) and several manila folders with illegible labels. Ed ensured his privacy by making sure that no one but him could read his writing. Evelyn picked up the romance.

"I didn't know you cared for these, Ed."

Without changing his position in any way, he said, "Idiot woman poisoned a character with a campfire made of oleander branches. I am writing to tell her that the stupid *smoke* won't do it. She had to poke the sharpened branches into the little weenies or oysters or whatever her star-crossed lovers are eating."

"Glad to know you're keeping the world safe from inaccuracy in romance literature. I have a question."

"Did you know," he said conversationally, storing his legal pad and pen in a precise configuration on his desk blotter and staring out his obstructed window as he spoke, "that Cleopatra was not Egyptian?"

"Yes." It was an interest they shared; possibly, she thought with relief, the *only* interest they shared. "She was descended from Alexander the Great. Although since they had gone through quite a few generations, she must have been *partly* Egyptian."

"Perhaps." He remained silent, either pondering the last pharaoh's ethnicity or waiting until he made Evelyn fidget with impatience. "What is your question?"

She pulled over a stool and perched on it, discovering too late its lack of structural integrity. She hung on and swayed to one side. "I have two girls, both apparently snatched and subdued without much of a struggle, at least not a struggle that did them much physical harm. They weren't knocked out with a head injury, yet they must have been immobile for several hours at least."

"Your cement-shoes lady."

"And Destiny Pierson. Is it possible that they were drugged somehow?"

"No, not possible. No one ever uses drugs in this world."

"Can you check for drugs? Or chemicals?"

"If you read the lettering on the door as you came in, lady, you know this fine unit exists for no other reason than to test the life fluids of those who have departed this plane of existence, for drugs and other illegal substances."

"I don't mean to try your patience, Ed." Talking to him required a delicate dance and a good amount of groveling. But if he paid off, it would be worth it.

"Then you're doing a good imitation."

"I mean, can you flag their specimens and test for things you don't normally test for? Not just narcotics but the date-rape drugs, stuff vets use on animals, anything that would cause sleep, relaxation, or unconsciousness? Please?"

He sighed. "How many times do I have to explain this? This is real life. This"— he pointed at the HPLC—"is not the Bat Computer. We can't pour in alphabet soup and have it spell out a message. If you want me to look for something exotic, you have to tell me what I'm looking for."

"I'll try to find out. I know I'm asking for a miracle."

"That's okay, you can ask," he said with relish. "Because you're not going to get one."

She played her trump card. "You know, in the old detective novels they knocked people out with some chloroform on a rag. Clamped it over the delicate heroine's mouth, one breath, and out she goes."

He opened his mouth, closed it, opened it again. "That's silly. No one does that anymore."

"I know."

"Besides, it would leave burns on the skin. And the victim would promptly throw up, conscious or unconscious. And where would he get it? I mean, unless your killer works in a chemistry lab."

"Just a thought." She paused discreetly, and then added: "Of course, he could mix bleach and nail polish remover and distill it."

"Easier than that," Ed snapped. "Just mix bleach and methyl ethyl ketone—otherwise known as paint thinner—and suck the precipitate from the bottom. Easier than distilling."

"The bucket had been full of chlorine tabs for a swimming pool. Could he dissolve those and use it for the bleach?"

"No! Pool chemicals can be made up of a bunch of different chemicals, which are not the same thing as plain old household bleach." A gleam, just a pinpoint, had developed in his eyes. "Well. I'll take a look at the samples on the two females in question, and see what I can get out of the HPLC and that antiquated piece of junk called a mass spec. Just to make you happy."

She gave him a brilliant smile. "Thanks, Ed."

Evelyn stepped back through the hallway, feeling like an executive who had negotiated an indecent number of stock options on the eve of an IPO. If the girls had been drugged at all, it might turn out to be a mundane sedative, but now that she had gotten Ed interested, he would leave no chemical compound unturned.

Two steps into the lab and Tony bellowed her name from his office door. She found him backed into his favorite chair and armed with coffee; the phone cord, wildly twisted, gave mute testimony to the chaos of the past day. He looked at her almost desperately.

"Where the hell have you been? Ever hang up on me again and you're fired," he added absently. "Jonathan did the autopsy on the Pierson kid."

"I know, I just talked to him."

"They still don't have an ID on that first girl, but Riley's got some bug up his butt about it and says he needs you this morning. You've got to go over the Pierson clothing first, though, and you'd better find every single fiber and hair on it because if this case doesn't get solved fast we're all going to be swaying from spikes. The prosecutor came out here this morning—but of course you weren't here—and the mayor called here personally. I talked to him, but he asked for you. Now why did he ask for you?"

Bright blue eyes with an animal intuition peered at her. Tony might be annoying, but he wasn't stupid. And he had a prodigious instinct for pain, embarrassment, and scandal. She reminded herself, like a mantra, that Tony had hired her fresh from her second round of college, after she'd applied to every other crime lab in the area. No matter what, she owed him. So she answered calmly. "We knew each other at college."

"Oh? Friends?"

"More or less," she said, dismally aware that her casual tone would only raise his suspicions. "We hadn't seen each other for years until the other day. The press are ravenous over his daughter. Incidentally, Jason all but physically threw me at them this morning."

"Whatever. We have to assume that the same guy who got Pierson killed that first girl. You've got to find some trace evidence to connect them."

She nodded, knowing that to argue that she had no control over the existence or nonexistence of evidence would be pointless. Tony didn't believe in inconvenient facts.

"So get her clothing done this morning. What did you get on the first girl's clothes?"

"Nothing yet. It had to dry before I could check for fibers."

"I'm sure it's dry by now," he said, heavily sarcastic.

"But since then it's been one thing after—"

"Get that done this morning. If there's any hairs, get them to Marissa for DNA. And get everything on Pierson done super-rush-rush. Riley will be here in half an hour."

"In other words, I need to be in three places at once?"

"Exactly." He grinned, as if admitting his lack of reason made it okay, then bellowed "Marissa!" with window-rattling force.

Marissa stalked in, her outstanding looks managing to radiate the mood of someone who hadn't had enough sleep and regretted last night's Oreo binge. *"What?"*

"Any sperm?"

"Not last night, thanks for asking."

"I mean on the Pierson kid!"

"No."

"No, no sperm, or no, you don't know?"

"No, no sperm. Nothing, nada, zip. No acid phosphatase, either." A positive acid phosphatase test indicated the presence of semen. As the serologist/DNA expert, Marissa analyzed the samples of bodily fluids Evelyn collected from the evidence, the victim's clothing, and the crime scenes. She spent her days both without leaving the lab and in proximity to Tony, and swore to Evelyn that the combination made her claustrophobic. "I suppose we don't know how long she was in the water?" she asked Evelyn.

"Not long enough to drown, which would have been quick at that water temperature."

"So it could have been washed off, but not likely. Any semen in the vagina should have still been there."

"Well, that will give her family some comfort," Evelyn said.

"No sperm on the first girl, either," Tony thought aloud. "We've got a serial."

"But she was submerged for a day or two," Evelyn protested. "In her case it could have been washed away. We can't know for sure."

"Two pairs of cement shoes? Yeah, I think we know for sure."

"But we don't know for sure that Destiny had cement—"

"If you'd come to work instead of staying home playing with your kid, you'd know some things," Tony said. "Divers found the cement bucket that Destiny had been in—under the bridge. So yes, I do know for sure."

CHAPTER
12

EVELYN PRODDED THE RECALCITRANT stone as if the outer surface might flake off and reveal a hidden treasure. Something like the killer's driver's license would be nice. "Another chlorine bucket. Same brand as the other one. How did she get out?"

"Don't know," Jonathan said. "I wish we could ask her. But it couldn't have been too tough, her legs are in pretty good shape and there's no skin left on the cement."

"How'd she get out of the chains?"

"I repeat, I don't know. They're wound around each other just like in the first girl, but only Destiny's wrists show ligature marks, so the rest of the chains couldn't have been very tight."

"I'm glad they got divers out there. Usually something like that takes a week to authorize."

"This is the mayor's daughter, Eve. If calling out the National Guard would help, it would be done. We will spare no expense," he added grimly. "This is top priority like nothing's ever been top priority before."

"I get the feeling you're trying to tell me something."

"I'm trying to tell you to watch your back. This case is a career maker or a career crash-and-burner. If we don't get this guy, you might end up Tony's sacrifice to the angry gods. Or the angry city council."

"Yo, doc." The deiner, or autopsy assistant, poked his head into the exam room. "Hate to interrupt you two an' all, but there's a suicide here and a suspicious death on its way."

"No rest for the wicked."

"Speak for yourself," she groused. "My father said it was no rest for the *weary*."

After she had collected gunshot residue from the suicide victim's hands and sent the unlucky soul to Autopsy, examined the suspicious death and found nothing suspicious about it—but no one had wanted to get close enough to tell after the body had spent several days decomposing—finished her cup of cold coffee, and fended off two reporters who had somehow gotten past Greg, Riley appeared, looking only slightly less wrinkled than the corpse. "Come on, time to go."

"Well, just let me red-tape this stuff—"

"We're in a hurry, Evelyn." The odor of cigarettes wafted off his clothing, stronger even than the rotting-flesh smell currently filling the hallways.

"You and everyone else. I can't just drop—"

David appeared in the doorway. "Evelyn—"

"What?"

"I heard about your daughter," he said. "How is she?"

Evelyn's face melted into a smile. "She's okay. Everything went fine. Where are we going in such a hurry, gentlemen?"

"To see our resident mob boss."

"Which one? Ashworth or the other guy I hear about now and then—Garcia?"

"Ashworth."

"A social call?"

"We picked up one of his guys on a drug charge, and he's told us some interesting things about the Big M. Such as a lot of talk about that girl in the river, and the fact that his daughter dropped out of sight last week and Daddy isn't saying word one to anybody about where she went."

"Incidentally," Evelyn asked as they passed the Museum of Art lagoon, "why am I here?"

"Don't get metaphysical on me," Riley muttered.

"I mean, why am I coming along? Interrogating mob bosses is not my job."

"Well, I thought you might want to give it a whirl. It can be a lot of fun, especially when they make comments about sending their goons after your wife and kids someday while you're at work."

Evelyn snuggled deeper into her parka. The backseat of the Grand Marquis felt warm enough to bake croissants, but still she was cold to the bone. "I don't think I *want* that to be part of my job. How about I wait in the car?"

"You've seen our dead girl cleaned up. We haven't because we missed the autopsy and we can't get the photos because your developer has gone on the blink again."

"Second time in six months. But we're going to go digital next year, so the ME doesn't want to put a lot of money into it."

"I want you to take a look at a picture of his daughter and see if she might be victim number one. I also want you to check out his carpeting fibers. I know all you can do is eyeball the color, but—"

"Fibers?"

"Fibers that match what you found on the two dead girls." He shot an impatient glance at her in the rearview mirror. "Tony said you had fibers."

Evelyn silently sentenced her boss to the inner circles of the Inferno. "Tony gets a bit ahead of himself. Honestly, Riley, I've been in this business ten years and I've *never* attended an interrogation. What's going on?"

She could see only his eyes in the rearview mirror, but they looked murderous. "I need a reason to get a body search warrant. If we could just compare his DNA, we could either eliminate him or arrest him."

"I'm not going to know for sure just from looking at a picture of this girl—"

"I don't need sure, just an educated guess. Besides, this guy has had cops at his heels all his life. We don't impress him anymore. Just having an unknown factor like you in the room might throw him off guard. I need *help*, okay, Evelyn?"

A strained silence lasted for over ten minutes before she changed the subject. If Riley wanted to drag her along while questioning a suspect, she didn't mind. It might be interesting. "By the way, have you been able to trace Destiny's movements? The paper said she attended her father's fund-raiser, but what then?"

"That's a good question." David turned to talk over the back of his seat. "Apparently the Piersons left the dinner and went home. Destiny intended to go out with a girlfriend, Laurie."

"On a school night?"

"She said they had to 'study.' It seems that Danielle is pretty indulgent and Destiny got good grades, so they cut her a lot of slack. Besides, Destiny had an attitude, according to the kitchen staff, who know everything that goes on in that house. She didn't take the word *no* very well. She didn't fight it, she simply ignored it. Typical rich kid."

Evelyn bit her lip.

"Well, she and this Laurie had no intention of studying and hit a teen club on Prospect. They met up with some other schoolmates, boogied, probably drank a little—nothing serious according to Laurie. She insists neither of them were high. No one gave them a problem, no creepy guys followed them around, nothing. Just another night among the young and wealthy. Then they decided to walk to a Denny's two blocks away and get something to eat. Somewhere between the Beat Club and Denny's, Destiny disappeared."

"And no one saw this happen?"

"There were eight kids in various stages of mild intoxication strolling along on a dark night. As they walked they spread out over half a block or so, and not one of them distinctly remembers where Destiny fell in this line. Laurie walked with two girls and assumed Destiny was somewhere behind them. A boy said she might have been bringing up the rear. He had been talking to her when they left the club, but then he had a small argument with another boy and they started bouncing around, throwing shadow punches at each other. He lost track of Destiny, whether she was in front of them or behind them. We talked to all eight kids, and I'm sure they're covering up some drinking and smoking, but they all had the same story about Destiny. No one noticed she was missing until they'd already sat down in Denny's and ordered."

Riley shook his head as he turned a corner. "Kids."

"They didn't go back and look?"

David spoke. "They'd already ordered."

Evelyn sighed and wondered uncomfortably what Angel would do in the same situation.

"Actually, Laurie, who isn't quite as stupid as she sounds at first, grabbed one of the boys and made him walk back with her. They ran, because they didn't want to miss their food, but they did go a little way into each alley they passed and called her name. They stuck their head into the club, which had wall-to-wall people and a bouncer who didn't speak English. So they just went back to Denny's and convinced themselves that she'd gone back to the club. She had been chatting up a boy there, and they thought maybe she'd gone back for him and stayed."

This time Evelyn shook her head.

"It didn't matter anyway," David said to her. "This guy took Destiny and went. He knew what he was doing."

"What about the boy at the club?"

"We haven't found him. The kids described him as a white boy, older than them, dressed 'plain,' which means he doesn't know his designers, nice enough. He started talking to Destiny about cars, and they seemed to hit it off. But two of the kids said this boy had already left when they started out for Denny's. Three others didn't think he had. The whole place is lit only by colored dance-floor lights and the music is so loud you couldn't hear a bomb go off, so who knows?"

"So this kid could have slipped something in her drink." Evelyn could think of several date-rape drugs.

"Possibly. No one remembers if she drank anything with this kid. The two boys had a short conversation with Destiny before they started their argument, and both insist that she did not seem at all drunk. She made some joke about the Terminal Tower being a phallic symbol, and walked and talked completely straight. How fast does that stuff take effect?"

"Very fast. What did Laurie think?"

"She noticed the kid, but didn't think he was worth much attention. She can, and I quote, *tell* when Destiny is majorly hot for someone. She only mentioned him as a possible reason for why Destiny would suddenly disappear. Destiny didn't have her car and no one else from their group left. So in her teenage mind she came up with the safest explanation she could. I think little Laurie got really scared really fast and didn't want to face it. So she convinced herself that Destiny simply got another ride home."

"She didn't tell anyone the girl had disappeared?"

"She's a teenager. She didn't want to call the Piersons and say, 'By the way, is Destiny there?' and get her friend in trouble."

"What did the Piersons do when she didn't come home?"

"Destiny planned to stay over at Laurie's and go to school from there. She did that often—Laurie lives within walking distance of the school. The school called when she didn't show up for class but got an assistant, who, again trying not to get the boss's kid in trouble, checked her room and car and asked all the staff before he went to Danielle. At the same time Laurie bit the bullet and called the Pierson house, and very shortly after that, we found the body and it all became moot. No one had even told Pierson that Destiny was missing before they told him she was dead. Danielle had tried to keep her baby girl from getting Daddy angry."

Evelyn sighed and pictured a household in chaos, the panic growing until stopped short by grief. She closed her eyes.

"You okay?" David asked. "I bet you didn't get a lot of sleep last night."

Riley gave her a dark look, a warning look.

Evelyn remembered his advice but answered anyway. "I think my spine is permanently deformed. So where does Mario Ashworth come into all this? You think this guy killed his own daughter?"

"I don't know what to think. But he's connected to the scene, she matches the description of the dead girl, and by several reports, she's missing."

"I don't know. That girl didn't look like a rich girl."

Riley snorted. "She was *dead*."

"The rich are different even when dead. She ignored her cuticles and her eyebrows needed plucking. Rich girls are usually better maintained."

Riley shook his head but didn't argue. David looked pensive, as if wondering just how much maintenance a pair of eyebrows took.

They pulled onto the long driveway.

"Wow." Evelyn took in every detail of the marble, the balconies, the perfectly rounded hedges. "I'm in the wrong line of work."

Ivan Marcus answered the door, appearing just as the detectives had described him—like a block of granite, but less friendly.

Raised voices spilled out into the hallway toward them. Someone was angry.

"Mr. Ashworth can't be disturbed," he said before Riley could open his mouth.

The voices fell silent, and in another moment the man in question emerged defiantly from a doorway to the right. "Well, well, Cleveland's finest. This really tops off a perfect day."

A girl slid through the doorway while trying, electron-like, to maintain a maximum distance from him. She had dark hair, stage-quality makeup, and a body in lush bloom under a scoop-neck sweater.

"Cops," she said coldly. "Good. Maybe you can get Daddy to tell you what he *really* does for a living."

Riley and David stared with horror at the girl, now stalking down the hallway. Riley recovered first. "Miss Ashworth."

She stopped, pirouetting on one foot with primitive grace.

"Where have you been?" Riley asked her.

She smiled the lazy smile of a cat at rest under a birdhouse. "Rehab. Nowhere I haven't been before. They have a room with my name on it at Riverside. Daddy, of course, doesn't approve of my frequent-flier status." She continued on her way, leg muscles flexing under tight black pants, and disappeared into the rest of the house.

Evelyn sized up Ashworth, whose face resembled a storm cloud about to be upgraded to tornado. She promptly forgot her desire to hide out in the car. "Am I the only one who finds it ironic that kids who are so big on honesty are the same ones who won't tell you where they've been all evening?"

The clouds parted. "You sound like you have some of your own."

"A sixteen-year-old. Girl."

"Is it easier when you're a woman?" he asked with an earnestness that surprised her.

"No! Having hormones in common only gives them inside information. They know what buttons to push."

His shoulders relaxed. He was an attractive man, she couldn't help but notice, with dimples and an athletic build. His shoulders loosened with a grateful smile, as if he had found an old friend in a crowded foreign airport. It seemed odd to her, but if he chose to forget which side of the law she came from, she wasn't going to point it out.

"Come in." He turned and led the way into his study. "What can I help you with?"

Riley settled in a leather armchair and stumbled over his words. The reappearance of Ashworth's daughter had clearly thrown him off stride and now he had to come up with another reason for their visit. Evelyn didn't bother, just handed over the autopsy photograph of victim number one's face.

"We've had two young women killed in the past week. Obviously your daughter is accounted for, but since we're here, could you take a look at this? I'm sorry it's a rather unpleasant picture, but . . ."

He looked at the picture. And looked again. A slight compression of his lips, a set to his cheek, and Evelyn knew that he knew exactly who the dead girl was. *Wow,* she thought. *Got it in one.*

Silently he passed the photo to Marcus, who had materialized at Ashworth's elbow. Marcus also viewed the girl's face, but his own revealed not the slightest flicker of muscle or an unguarded glance. He merely looked at his boss, and waited.

"You know her?" David asked.

"I think she may work for me," Ashworth said. "Or have worked. Her name is . . . something unusual, started with an *O* . . ."

"Ophelia," Marcus said. "Ophelia Ripetti. Everyone called her Lia."

"Called by who?" Evelyn pressed, then amended, "Whom?"

"Her family. Her friends," Marcus said, and every word from his mouth rolled like a freight train through an underground tunnel, sonorous, heavy, and reluctant.

"Were you her friend?" Riley asked.

Marcus ignored Riley's implication. "We met her once," he went on. "She worked as a bookkeeper at our southeast office. It's on Emory Road in Warrensville Heights. She has been working there, I believe, five years, with a satisfactory record. That is all we know about her. I'm sure our construction manager there could give you her home address."

Evelyn found the use of the word *we* curious, and wondered if Marcus meant Ashworth and him, or the Ashworth upper management as a whole. Or if he meant himself only and had taken a page from Queen Victoria, though he didn't seem the Victorian type. She looked at Riley, who again seemed lost. He must have been dying to take Ashworth away in handcuffs but had no legitimate reason to do so. "You have over one hundred employees, yet you seem to recall a lot of detail about a girl you only met once."

"I remember everything," he said simply and frighteningly.

"Are you acquainted with our mayor?" David asked.

"Darryl Pierson?" Ashworth asked in surprise.

"Yes. That mayor."

"I've run into him here and there. I heard about his daughter, it's a great tragedy." He looked at Evelyn as he spoke, as if only she could appreciate his sincerity. Oddly he *did* sound sincere, but then she had never spoken to a crime boss before. Perhaps they all had that particular talent.

"Mind telling us where you went after that fund-raiser the other night?" Riley asked.

"I came home." Ashworth's voice and his color rose. The black man took a discreet step back, as if to avoid a splash by an approaching car. "What the hell does that have to do with Pierson's daughter? I know it's a habit of yours, Riley, to blame every murder in the city on me, but this time you're further off base than usual. Why would I want to hurt Pierson's daughter? I've never met the girl. I wouldn't know her if I passed her on the street. Why would I want to go around killing girls anyway?"

"I know," David said. "You're a businessman. But what if it *was* business?"

Ashworth calmed. "Get out of here and do some real police work. Some nut's out there killing girls and you're wasting time with me, hoping I'll make your job easy for you. I won't."

He turned and exited through a back door, one not hidden but so cleverly camouflaged that they hadn't noticed it. The room fell silent. They were left alone with Ivan Marcus.

"This way, gentlemen. Ma'am."

Riley moved with great reluctance. "We're going to need Miss Ripetti's information."

"I'll tell the southeast office manager to expect you."

They left.

"Ophelia," Evelyn said as soon as her car door had slammed shut. "That seems appropriate."

"Why?"

"Suitably dramatic." The car had cooled off and she rubbed her hands together. "Poor doomed Ophelia, wet tendrils of hair flowing around her pale face."

Riley stared at her via the rearview mirror. "You got a weird kind of imagination, girl."

"So I've been told."

"It's not the same thing at all," David argued. "Ophelia went mad because her man dumped her. I don't think this girl committed suicide."

"True. So now we have to find out everything about Lia. And more important, why no one missed her."

"No, the first thing we have to do is go to a funeral."

"What?" Evelyn asked with great misgiving.

"Destiny's funeral. It's at eleven, and I want to check out the crowd. The old myth about killers attending their victim's funeral is usually a myth, but in a case this weird, it wouldn't surprise me. I'm sorry, but we don't have time to drop you off first."

"But—"

He cut her off. "It's already ten-fifty."

David said nothing.

Evelyn spent the rest of the trip trying to get her curls to behave and buttoning her full-length coat to hide her sweatshirt. If she looped her scarf around with some sort of fashionable flair, she might carry it off but not happily. Darryl had asked her for help on the darkest day of his life, and first she took a day off and then showed up for his daughter's funeral in Reeboks. If he ever needed a reason to be glad he married Danielle instead . . . She gave up and pulled out her cell phone to check on Angel.

CHAPTER

13

THE FUNERAL SERVICE TOOK place in a seventy-year-old Baptist church on the near east side. The cavernous main room overflowed with people, mostly African-American, dressed for elegant mourning and waiting quietly when Evelyn and the two cops took the last three open spaces against the back wall. Competing brands of cologne wafted upward, where lightbulbs in wrought-iron fixtures did their best to dispel the gloom cast by eternally overcast Cleveland skies. She could see Darryl in the first pew, head bent.

Only two days had elapsed since Destiny's murder, long enough to turn her funeral into an event. Wedged between Riley and David like a sardine in a tin, Evelyn felt very short and very white. At least she was warm. No one else wore Reeboks, and her bright blue parka stuck out among the somber black overcoats like a stripper at a PTA meeting. Too many had dressed for an important corporate function, as if this teenage girl's funeral served as nothing more than a step in their career networking plan. Darryl's political life could not be separated from his personal one, even for one day. But Danielle's family

sat with her—their subtle but potent wealth made their identity obvious—and the pews across the aisle were occupied by Destiny's entire
school class. All the girls cried, and even some of the boys. *Kids are
so emotional at that age,* Evelyn thought. But then they had known
Destiny the best and must have been very important to her. *As Angel's
friends must be to her,* Evelyn thought, *and how much do I really
know about them?*

She broke from this uncomfortable line of thought, startled by a
face across the pews. At the same time, the preacher took to the pulpit
for an opening prayer.

David heard her gasp, and leaned down. "What is it?"

"See that guy over there?"

He looked up. "Which of the two hundred guys over there are you
referring to?"

"Brothers and sisters," the preacher intoned. "Oftentimes when I
am called upon for a funeral service, I have a hard time coming up
with something to say about the deceased. Speaking ill of the dead is
frowned upon, and the truth is, most people are quite ordinary."

"The one standing next to the guy with the purple tie. White guy,
about five-eleven, gray coat."

"But in this case, there is so much one can say about Destiny Pierson that I scarcely know where to begin. A young woman, with all the
energy and enthusiasm that youth confers, and then some."

"The one standing under the second window from the left?"

"Yes."

"She had her mother's beauty and her father's popularity, and
brains that made Darryl admit he had no idea where she got them."

The crowd gave a low chuckle, except from one or two people
who turned to glare at Evelyn and David. The cop didn't notice.
"What about him?"

"Well, he—"

The glares escalated to psychic threats of gagging and eviction,
and Evelyn muttered, "He's Nurse Neal."

"What?"

"I'll explain later."

The cemetery matched the church—neat, fashionably antique, and crowded, but much colder. Appropriately gloomy weather walled off the sun behind heavy clouds, while a bitter wind off the lake added insult to injury. Ladies held on to their hats and men hunched into their overcoats. Evelyn wished desperately to be somewhere else—preferably somewhere warm—because she wasn't there as a mourner or even a friend. She might have arrived there by accident, but now she intended to ferret out the slightest fact that might help the cops solve this murder. She had loved Darryl once. She owed him that much.

Nurse Neal topped her list of avenues for investigation. The stocky, sandy-haired boy had disappeared from the service before she could speak to him, but to her relief had shown up among the gravestones. While the sad procession of people emerged reluctantly from their vehicles, she approached him, Riley and David within earshot.

He seemed more surprised to see her than vice versa. "Oh, hi!" he said, making a haphazard gesture with his index finger. "Appendectomy, right?"

"Yeah."

"Angel, right? Who can forget that name? How's she doing?"

"Fine, thanks. What are you doing here?"

"I took care of her." He seemed unfazed by the question. "Destiny Pierson, I mean."

"Took care of her?"

"Yeah, at the hospital. They put her and her broken finger in my unit. Last week," he added, as if that final detail explained it all. She watched him, perplexed, and under her scrutiny he went on. Occasionally he sniffled, wiping his nose with the sleeve of the trench coat. It had a coffee stain on the right sleeve and a torn pocket. She saw, with mixed feelings, that he wore Reeboks.

"I worked Pediatrics that week. I'm a floater at the moment because surgery is a little overstaffed, so I'm always all over the place. They kept her for observation in case of thrombosis—which means they milked the case because her parents had money. I liked her. She would order everyone around like she was the Queen of Sheba or something, but the way she did it made you laugh instead of get mad."

Evelyn had done her best to ignore him during Angel's appendectomy, frankly hadn't wanted to look at him, and doing so now did nothing to help her dislike of him. He seemed on the surface to be a kind, caring man, and though that part of him rang sincere, it couldn't counteract the somehow bizarre set to his frame, the thick neck, the uncertain flutter of his hands, the way his eye movements didn't seem to be perfectly coordinated. A whole series of almost indiscernible maladjustments put him somehow out of whack.

"So you came to her funeral?"

"Yeah, I feel bad for her, dying and all." She noticed he spent more time looking at the assembled guests than gazing sadly at the casket. "There's her father and mother over there. That guy next to the mother is worth over two billion. Incredible."

"Do you know how she died?"

"Yeah." He looked at her oddly. "She was murdered. It said so in the paper. Big headlines."

"Do you always come to funerals of people you only met once?"

"Sometimes people can really affect your life—even if you only met once," he said with jaunty confidence, peering at a group of city council members.

Dimly aware that the graveside service was about to begin, she couldn't take her eyes from Jimmy Neal. Lust? Loneliness? Or madness? What brought him here?

A young man with eyes the color of Hershey bars stepped up to them, hands jammed into his pockets. "Jeez, Jimmy, do we have to stay for this whole thing?"

"I want to." He gestured to Evelyn. "This is my cousin Max."

"Had you met Destiny, too?"

"No. Jimmy just dragged me along. Jimmy doesn't do anything alone." He shivered and gave his cousin an unappreciative look. "He's kind of needy that way."

"Hey, I go with you to visit your dead," Neal snapped. "You can come see mine. How did you know Destiny, Mrs. James?"

A pause. "I'm a friend of the family." The service began and she moved closer to the preacher, not daring to disrupt another of his sermons.

The weather had thinned the crowd, and for the first time she could see the mourning parents. Darryl's hollow eyes stared at his daughter's coffin as if his soul lay inside, leaving his body lost on the frigid hillside. Danielle sat beside him; her beauty had deserted her like a fair-weather friend. Her skin looked chalky, her hair completely hidden by an unfashionable black hat. Only the perfect bone structure could not be disguised.

After a mercifully brief graveside service the crowd scattered to their warm cars. David went after Neal and Riley collared another man he said he knew. Evelyn shivered and hoped they would hurry. The wind pierced her long coat and her feet were slowly freezing in the slushy grass.

"Evelyn."

She turned. Darryl stood beside her, with a face so haunted it frightened her.

"I'm so sorry, Darryl," she said. "I know you told me not to say that, but I don't know what else to say. I know—" Then she *did* stop herself, knowing that she couldn't possibly know how he felt and hoped she never would. "Angel is sixteen. I keep thinking—" *It could have been her.*

"Look at us. Angel and Destiny. Aren't we a couple of optimists." His lips curved in a faint smile, and for a second his eyes were the old Darryl, the same boy who wrote hilarious limericks and had secret, wickedly apropos nicknames for all his professors.

She smiled back. "I hadn't thought of that, but yes, we are."

"Were." His smile evanesced. "Have you made any progress?"

"I'm so sorry. But I spent yesterday with Angel, she—"

"I know. Will told me. My personal assistant. Of course I understand—but have you gotten anywhere?"

She told him how the divers found the cement—he already knew that, too, Channel 3 had the report of an intrepid reporter who had camped at the scene—and added: "We're trying to get some information about the first victim, and maybe who attended that campaign fund-raiser the other night. Destiny is top, top priority, Darryl. I can assure you of that at least."

"I believe you." He sighed, gazing at the field of gravestones, apparently unaware of the soft flakes of snow dusting his head and shoulders. "There's something else, Evelyn."

"What?"

He turned to her. "I know you think I tossed you aside because Danielle's family had money, but that's not how it was."

She felt her breath whoosh out of her. "Darryl—"

"I did love you, Evelyn."

"This really isn't the time to talk about this," she said desperately.

"Yes, it is. My daughter's dead. All the games I've played in my life, and what did they get me? My daughter's in her grave at sixteen. I'm through with games."

Evelyn held his gaze as she searched for words. "It—it probably wouldn't have worked out, anyway. I wouldn't have been a very good mayor's wife, and even in this day and age, interracial marriages—"

"I made a million excuses." His voice grated harshly against the cold air. "They were all shit. I had a million reasons, and most of them were shit, too."

"So did I, Darryl," she assured him. Out popped a question she never thought she'd hear herself ask. "Do you love her?"

It startled him. His face returned to something like normal as he thought about something other than Destiny for the first time in twenty-four hours. "Danielle?"

"Yes. Danielle."

He paused just for an instant, then said without smiling, "Yes. Yes, I do."

"Then that's all that matters."

He took her hand, pressing it gently, and they rested for a moment in a temporary calm. Then a man, the same person who had escorted Evelyn to Darryl's study, approached them. "Darryl."

He looked up, still holding Evelyn's hand. "I'll be right there, Will." To Evelyn he added, "You'll keep me informed?"

"Yes," she promised, still without knowing what she meant by it.

The men walked off, and David appeared at her side. The snow continued to fall, and his face reflected the cruel clouds.

"*How* informed?"

She felt blindsided. "What?"

"I had a bad feeling about him asking you to come to the house. So you're going to be his inside girl?"

Fury began to burn in the pit of her stomach. "His daughter's dead. He wants to know how the investigation is going. You can't blame him."

"I don't blame him for asking. I *will* blame you for talking. All we need is to have every lead show up on the six o'clock news. I already lost one partner that way."

"Hey—"

"All *I* need is to have you report each move I make to the mayor, so that every delay, every avenue that doesn't pan out, is all laid to my incompetence. This is my *life* here, lady."

"Paranoid, aren't you?" she said as forcefully as she could while keeping her voice low. She glanced around, but the mourners sought the shelter of their cars and no one was paying any attention to them. "I am not going to tell him anything about the investigation other than what I *can* tell him."

"And who determines that?"

"I do. And you do. And Tony does. In case you haven't noticed, I don't work for Darryl."

"But you didn't sleep with me or Tony."

She leveled him with a look women learn from their mothers. He took a deep breath, obviously trying to bring himself under control. "Look, I know you want to do an old friend a favor. I would feel that way myself. But if you leak tips to him, he could publicize them, so our suspect disappears or moves on. Or even worse, he could go after the guy himself, which could get all sorts of people hurt and completely screw up the chances for successful prosecution."

The allegation that she might do a favor for a friend didn't bother her. The idea that she was too stupid to realize how much damage it could do made the embers in her eyes erupt into flame. "Do I look like a total idiot to you? You think I don't know that?"

"I'm just saying—"

"*I'm* just saying that I feel real sorry for Darryl, and I feel especially sorry because I have a daughter myself who's the same age. But if you think I would *ever* put my job on the line for an old boyfriend or any other man, then you're a moron who has no business being a homicide detective."

She stalked off in a swirl of coat and scarf.

IT RELIEVED DAVID WHEN Evelyn refused to join them on the trail of Ophelia Ripetti, though Riley seemed to regard her as some sort of talisman. At her insistence they dropped her at the ME's to work on Destiny Pierson's clothing and continued southeast. At least Riley wouldn't report their movements to the mayor's office, David thought to himself.

The souring of their acquaintance hurt, surprisingly, but it couldn't be helped. He had one last chance to resurrect his career and could not let some naïve ex-girlfriend of the city power structure stand in his way.

Though Evelyn never struck him as naïve. Kind, yes. Not naïve.

If Riley had noticed their tiff or the waves of frost that emanated from the backseat of the car, he said nothing. But David knew the older detective had caught the exchange. Riley noticed everything and stored it away in the jowls of his mind like a clairvoyant chipmunk.

"I caught up with that male nurse," David said as a conversational gambit. "He seems to be more of a celebrity hound than a psycho. He didn't ring any bells with me."

"Mmm."

"And little Ivy Ashworth is alive and well."

"Mmm," Riley growled as if he considered her continued existence a personal affront.

"They gave up Ophelia without argument."

"Because they knew we'd find out anyway. Makes them look cooperative. They do that a lot."

"They?"

"The mob."

The more David learned about the murder, the less he felt it had anything to do with organized crime. This murder process required too much time, too much intimacy. It felt personal. But he kept his thoughts to himself, trying to learn from the older man. "You've been following his career for a while."

Riley steered the car onto a gravel parking lot. The southeast office appeared to be little more than a shack, a dilapidated brick building hidden from the road by weeping willows. Crumbling steps led to a single door. A discreet sign read: *Ashworth Construction.*

"I worked Organized Crime for seven years before I came to Homicide." Riley's words came out slowly, as if he took no pride in them. "My partner, one smart son of a bitch named Edwards, dug away at a couple of soldiers until he found a cautious little protection ring going on. Ashworth was hardly old enough to drink, but he had, shall we say, an arrangement with our supervisor. Couldn't prove it, of course." He opened the car door and stepped out, crunching the gravel with more force than necessary.

David fell into step beside him. "What happened to your supervisor?"

"Nothing. Retired with full pension a few years after I left. Like I said, we couldn't prove it."

"Is Edwards still with Organized Crime?"

"He's dead."

David looked up, nearly tripping over the bottom step.

"At least I think so," Riley amended. "We never found his body." He jerked the door open and entered. David followed.

The inside of the Ashworth Construction office building hid its flaws with more success than the outside, but with even less sense of decor. Light gray walls surrounded wooden desks old enough to have served in the last world war, covered with papers, blueprints, and ashtrays. The air smelled of dampness, cigarettes, and vanilla candles. They heard a few soft footfalls as a man lumbered in. Jeans and a plaid flannel shirt barely covered a bulk that exceeded both detectives combined. His eyes were sharp and calm.

"I'm Murfield, the supervisor." He obviously knew who they were, either because Marcus had called him or because he could spot a cop four blocks away on a rainy night.

"Mr. Ashworth sent us here," Riley said, which produced no more response than their presence. He held out the photograph of Ophelia Ripetti. "Do you know this girl?"

Murfield took the photo in one massive hand and gazed at it, unsurprised. Marcus had definitely called. They could have skipped the funeral, but it would have made no difference. Phone lines were faster than Fords.

The large man studied the picture as if truly pissed off by what he saw there. "Yeah, that's Lia." He shook his head. "Poor kid. What happened to her?"

"She was murdered. What did she do here?"

"Bookkeeper. That's her place there." He pointed out one of the many desks, and made no objection when David crossed to it and sat down. All three men knew he could demand a search warrant, but Murfield chose not to waste the time. David started to search its contents methodically, almost gently, showing respect to the dead, hoping to soothe Murfield and impress Riley at the same time.

The man walked Riley through their current jobs, what accounts

Ophelia would have worked on. There were a number of projects, including the plaza near the bridge where she had been found and the proposal for the new ME's office. David found a condom, still wrapped, and Yahoo Maps! directions to the art museum.

"She have any conflicts with anyone here? Any office spats?" Riley went on.

Murfield's eyes blazed, either at the inference or at the sorry son of a bitch who would kill a young woman. "No. Everyone liked her— a really sweet kid."

"How sweet?"

"What do you mean? She was a nice kid and did her job. That's all there is to say."

"Did she have a boyfriend here?"

"She went out with some guy, but nobody I knew."

David picked up another pile of forms. Apparently Ophelia took care of vendor accounts and payments, but the columns of numbers meant nothing to him. He'd need a forensic accountant to find any evidence of wrongdoing on her cluttered desk. Riley would thrill to examine Ashworth's accounts, but they'd never get a warrant without a more compelling connection between Lia's death and her work. And where did Destiny fit in?

"She express any dissatisfaction with her job?"

"No."

"With her boss?"

"No."

"With you?"

"I am the boss. She didn't have any problems here. *We* wouldn't have let any harm come to her."

The distinction wasn't lost on Riley. "Who is *we*?"

"Well, you cops are supposed to protect people, ain't you? How come there's some nut running around killing little girls like Lia?" There would always be nuts killing little girls, his voice seemed to say, and he felt genuinely frustrated about it.

Lia Ripetti had only two personal items on her desk: a photograph of herself and a young man, taken on a balcony overlooking a raging ocean, and a shot glass from Los Alamos, New Mexico. David peered at the young man.

"So she never missed a day," Riley said.

"Hardly ever." His face contorted with thought. "Last week she stayed home sick."

"Sick?"

"Food poisoning. We had a grand opening at the new wing of the South Side Mall. Damn caterer served rotten potato salad, sent a bunch of people to the hospital. Never touch the stuff myself. She felt really lousy for a few days, but came back on Thursday and Friday."

"How'd she get this job?" Riley asked.

"She had bookkeeping experience, and Mr. Ashworth said to hire her because he knew her dad."

"So Ashworth took an interest in Ophelia?"

"Lia. No one called her that Shakespeare name. I don't think she ever met Mr. Ashworth. He just knew her dad. I got work to do, you got anything else?"

"And she didn't stumble over any inconvenient figures, in the books she took care of for you?"

"I know what you think," Murfield said, resolutely calm. "But I'm telling you, Lia was one of our family, and we wouldn't have let anything happen to her." His cheeks were flushed and he looked Riley in the eye, telegraphing the truth through his sincerity. "And when you find the pervert who did it, you bring him to me and I'll make sure he don't become no damn *recidivist*. You understand me?"

"I got it," Riley said.

After Murfield gave them Lia's home address, the two cops left and sat in the parking lot for several minutes waiting for the car to warm up; they had been inside for only ten minutes, but the temperature inside the car had fallen well below freezing, in direct violation of all physical laws.

"You believe him?" David asked.

"I don't know. One thing you got to remember about these guys—they're real good liars. They've had a lot of practice."

"I don't think he's lying. Organized crime doesn't kill people this way. Too flashy."

To his surprise, Riley did not argue. "I know," he sighed. "But we had no other leads and it gave me an excuse to yank Ashworth's chain."

"Yeah."

"On the other hand—"

"What?"

"Ashworth knew her."

Lia Ripetti had lived in an apartment building in the suburb of Solon that matched her office and, they learned, her life: a simple, dependable structure that provided security and comfort. The superintendent collected their search warrant and let them into her apartment at the end of the third-floor hallway without comment, as if he had long ago learned not to ask questions when he didn't really want to know the answers. The one-bedroom suite with an eat-in kitchen had been decorated in early American garage sale but not without a whimsical charm. Colors and textures fought for prominence; perhaps Lia craved stimulation from her home that she wasn't getting from her life or wanted to express herself through her choices. Did the killer come here to get her? Did she let him in?

David noticed the delicately stitched quilt over the sofa, the few matching pieces of elegant bone china dinnerware, and the soft peach towel hanging from the bathroom rack. Lia had chosen her luxuries carefully, and they were things to touch, to use, not items just to look at.

Interesting, but it didn't point him to a killer. He found himself wishing Evelyn *had* come along. She endangered his focus, with her crystal eyes that might see through him, but he needed her help. *Damn.*

The heat in the apartment worked a little too well, enough that the two detectives removed their coats after a few minutes, and then their jackets. A few photographs were tucked in a drawer, but only of Lia herself. Her address book did not indicate a social butterfly. While David glanced over her extensive collection of books, he heard a sound at the open door. A hefty young man in baggy jeans, his face cluttered with freckles and shaggy red tendrils, took one horrified look at the two cops and bolted down the hall.

"Hey!" David followed. Riley heard him and emerged from the bedroom at a run. They pounded down the hallway and David caught up with the man just as he reached the stairwell. They exploded through the fire door, David on the young man's back. His chin hit the cracked linoleum with a noise like a pistol shot.

"Shouldn't wear such long pants," David said as he cuffed him. "They slow you down. Come on, get up."

"What's this guy's story?" Riley asked.

"I don't know, but he knows Lia. His picture is on her desk at work."

"The plot thickens."

Their prisoner let out a muffled roar. When David pushed him into an armchair in the dead girl's apartment, he saw the guy's chin beginning to purple and tears running down his cheeks, intensifying the freckles. *Oh, boy,* David thought. *Here it comes. Make my day and confess, son. We'll both feel better. Especially me.*

"She's dead, isn't she?" The kid's voice reverberated from deep within his oversize body.

"What?"

"Lia. She's dead. That's why you guys are here, isn't it?"

"What makes you say that?" Riley said cautiously.

"Why else would you be here?" he asked, hopeless and sarcastic. "The minute the super told me cops were in her apartment I knew something had to be really wrong."

David and Riley exchanged a look. David dug the photograph out of his coat, now draped over the sofa. "What's your name?"

"Mason Durling."

"Well, Mr. Durling, I'm sorry to have to ask you this"—he held out the photo of the woman they had already identified and watched carefully for Durling's reaction—"but is this Lia Ripetti?"

The man didn't so much weep as howl. He stomped his feet and contorted his body, as much as he could with his hands locked behind him, then descended into a wave of sobs. David exchanged another glance with his partner and took a deep breath to wash away the sharp stab of disappointment. The kid was either innocent or a complete wack job.

When the noise began to subside, David tried again. "Mason. Mr. Durling. Are you okay?"

"No. No, I'm not okay! How can Lia be—" He burst into another round of sobs.

"Mason, we need to talk to you. How about if I take off the handcuffs and get you some ice for your chin? Okay? Then can we talk?"

With a visible shudder, the redhead made an effort to control himself. He nodded, lips compressed.

"Okay, I'm going to take the cuffs off. You need to stay right where you are, you understand me? I'm sorry you're upset, but we need to talk to you, and we are both armed police officers, you understand?"

"I understand."

He gave no resistance as David unlocked the handcuffs, and meekly accepted a bag of ice wrapped in a kitchen towel. David sat opposite him and wiped sweat from his cheeks. These kinds of calisthenics wouldn't have bothered him in his younger days. Riley stood, an armed barrier between Durling and the door.

David opened his mouth, but Durling interrupted. "Who killed her?"

"What makes you think someone killed her?"

"Come on!" he exploded in frustration. "You wouldn't be searching her apartment if she died in a car wreck. Who killed her?"

"We don't know."

Over the ice bag, Durling gave him a look of utter disgust. David tried not to take it personally. "That's what we're trying to find out. First of all, why did you run away just now?"

Disgust turned back to sadness. "Because I knew when I saw you what you were going to tell me. I didn't want to hear it. I didn't want to know." He shook his head, rough bangs skirting across his forehead. "I just didn't want to know."

David had his doubts about this explanation, but went on. "What is your relationship to Ophelia Ripetti?"

"Lia. She's my girlfriend. We've been going out for about four months now. I planned to maybe propose at Christmas. I was thinking about it, anyway." Again the shake. "I should have thought faster."

"When did you last see her?"

"Friday. We had dinner here, just pizza. Then I went back to my place about ten. I live downstairs, that's how we met."

"Kind of early for a Friday night."

"I work Saturday. And Lia was leaving."

"Leaving?"

"On vacation."

"There's a suitcase on her bed," Riley said.

"She was going to Atlantic City for the weekend. She liked it there."

"Without you?" David asked.

"I just started a new job, I don't have any vacation time. It didn't bother Lia to do things alone. She's had to since her folks died in a fire."

"Any brothers or sisters?"

"Nobody. Just one aunt who's dead now, too. She didn't have anybody in the world," Durling said. His face, perched on its ice pillow, looked almost objective about Lia's sad history. "That's why it was so important for her to have me, man."

"She had Mr. Ashworth," Riley said.

"Who?"

"Her boss, a friend of her parents?" David prodded. "He got her hired at his firm because of it. Mario Ashworth."

"I know that's the name of the place she works at, but she never mentioned him."

"She must have been only seventeen when she started there."

Durling shrugged. "I guess. She had to work, her parents didn't leave much. She lived with an aunt for a while after it happened, but got her own place as soon as she could."

"How did she feel about her job?"

He shrugged again impatiently. "It paid the bills. She got along with everyone there. What's that got to do with who killed her?"

In the next fifteen minutes they established that Lia, twenty-two, had no conflicts with anyone and no one would mean her harm. She had no ex-boyfriends that he knew of—he didn't ask, she didn't tell—and had not expressed any concern or fear of anyone or anything in the months before her death. When Riley suggested that perhaps they had had an argument on Friday night and that's why she had packed, he got another disgusted glare and Durling said that Lia had planned the vacation weeks before and had reservations at a hotel on the beach. He had not reported her missing because he assumed she had gone to Atlantic City. He hadn't noticed that her car still sat in the garage (which David had learned from the superintendent) because each tenant had a separate, closed garage and he had had no reason to look in Lia's. He had no idea how Mario Ashworth had known Lia's parents but knew that her father had been an accountant. Lia wanted to be one as well but lacked the funds for college. Lia would not have let anyone into the apartment except himself or the super. The super, Durling added, might be a little lax on maintenance but that didn't make him a pervert. Besides, the super had been out with his wife and daughter at a relative's wedding on Friday night, because he and his middle-aged daughter were singing loudly and miserably off-key when they returned about two A.M. and passed his, Durling's, apartment.

Durling himself grew up in Solon and currently worked at Home Warehouse. When asked what Lia had been wearing on Friday night, he described the clothes she had been found in, although David didn't tell him that. She had been wearing shorts, Durling explained, because her thermostat didn't work properly and her apartment always got hot—not too bad if you sat still, but she had been bustling around with dinner and packing. She cracked the window to be able to sleep at night. She had complained to the super, but when it came to anything other than collecting rent the man was chronically slow.

When the detectives ran out of questions, Durling began to ask his own—namely, what were they doing to catch the guy? Their answers were nowhere near as satisfactory as his had been, and he plainly resented it. They finally got rid of him by directing him to the ME's office to identify and claim the body.

Once he had left, David and Riley looked at each other, suddenly afraid to touch anything in the apartment.

"He took her out of here," Riley said.

"If she had left of her own will she would have put warmer clothes on. He grabbed her after Durling left—if Durling is telling the truth—and before she went to bed. But without raising a fuss, unless one of the neighbors tells us differently, and without much violence, unless he came back later and cleaned up."

"If he had come back later, he should have taken her suitcase and her car. He could have dumped it at the airport or something and she would go down as a young lady who got tired of her life and left it behind."

"We've got to get Forensics out here." David felt oddly pleased at the idea. "We're going to have to tear Evelyn away from Destiny's clothing—again."

CHAPTER

15

"WHAT IS THAT STUFF you're using?" David asked Evelyn two hours later.

"Mag powder."

"What's that?" They stood on the fire escape outside Lia's living room window, shivering in the cold and looking for fingerprints. He knew he topped Evelyn's shit list, but he needed her too much to stay on her bad side, or so he told himself. The truth was, he really wanted her to like him, case or no case.

He'd just be real careful what he said around her, that was all. He could not lose another partner, another case, another last chance.

"You can't use black powder on wet surfaces—the carbon dust sticks to water. However, the outside of this window isn't exactly wet, it's frozen, especially since the super turned off the heat to this apartment. It's just possible to develop frozen prints with magnesium powder, a black powder with magnetic shavings in it. Since it's applied with a magnet and not a brush, I can control how much gets on the print better than I can with black powder. If any areas are wet I can dispose of the mag powder without ruining the wand. Nothing ruins a black powder brush faster than water."

"I hope you find something." David sighed. "We need a break. Either she knew this person—which she could have, we've only begun to investigate her life—or she didn't know him and yet he managed to get into her apartment without leaving any sign of forced entry."

"There's just one problem."

"Yeah. According to Durling she left her bedroom window open, and it is cracked a few inches. So how did this guy hang in midair to get into a window that's ten feet from the fire escape?"

"She could have left both windows open."

"The window leading to the fire escape is locked from the inside. He could have gone in and shut it behind him, but then he couldn't have come back this way. I think he took her out her own door. She's right next to the stairwell and it lets out into the back parking lot. He goes out, down, out. It's the middle of the night and there's no one around to see him."

"He'd have to be pretty strong to toss her over his shoulder like a sack of potatoes. He couldn't have dragged her, she'd have more bruises."

"What did she weigh, one-ten? One-twenty? It wouldn't be too hard." He leaned on the tenuous railing, thought better of it, and continued to watch her.

In his line of work he met both women who worked with or hung around cops because they liked being around men and women who came on with a tough-as-nails persona to keep men from scaling the walls they had carefully constructed. The first type were usually available for the asking; the second type, well—a little persistence always crumbled the walls, exposed the vulnerability, because those women didn't really want to be tough as nails. Evelyn didn't fall into either category. There was no technique to make her either need him or want him, no strategy he could apply. Did he want her to want him? He couldn't waste important time thinking about it.

Evelyn finished with the powder. "Either the rain we had on Sunday took care of any prints or there weren't any here to begin with. I've got nothing." She packed up her print kit and started down the fire escape. Their feet made the iron steps ring as David followed, holding tightly to the banister.

David said, "I haven't run into too many perps who are neat enough to close the window behind them. Maybe this guy came in the front door."

"You think she knew him?"

"According to Durling, she isn't the type to let a total stranger into her place, especially late at night. If we take away him and the superintendent, that leaves someone from work."

"From what you told me of her supervisor, Murfield, he doesn't sound like a likely suspect."

"No, but supposedly she would never have let anyone she didn't know into her apartment." With gratitude he put his feet on solid ground.

"Mmm."

"You sound skeptical."

"Not skeptical. I just always found it worrisome that the Boston Strangler said he never forced his way into an apartment. He always convinced the women to let him in. He said he never knew what to say until they opened the door, but he'd always come up with something." She shivered, and not from the cold. "Scary."

"Well, that's according to Durling, anyway."

Evelyn turned to face him, her eyes the exact shade of the overcast sky. "You don't believe him?"

"I don't know yet. He's still the most likely suspect—and he works at Home Warehouse."

"Plenty of cement and steel chains."

"If I bring you samples from where he works, can you compare them?"

To his surprise, she laughed. "I haven't done it before."

"There's always a first time."

"Well, no, there's not." She settled her butt on the series of steps leading into the apartment building, looking over the snow that gleamed over the trees like frosting, sighing as if she hadn't had enough sleep in the past few days. "Not in Forensics. Before there's a first time, there's a vast collection of samples, comparisons, and self-tests. I can't pick up a type of evidence I've never worked with before and say, 'Gee, they look the same to me.' "

"Why not?" he asked, only half seriously.

"Because every chain in the world might look identical, for all I know." She blew on her fingers through leather gloves.

"So you have to look at every chain in the world?"

"I need what is called a representative sample. I have to make a sincere effort to collect a cross section of available chains of similar size and shape, then look at them all and see if I can tell them apart."

"Doesn't sound too bad."

"It depends. They may all be so similar that I can't tell them apart. They may have distinctive links, but we can't be positive he bought the chain in this city. We can't be positive we aren't missing a mom-and-pop hardware store somewhere that carries other types. We can't be positive the judge will allow it in. After all, when we do quantifica-tion trials for DNA or gunshot residue trials, we do ten thousand sam-ples, a lot more definitive than gathering ten or twelve types of chain from the local hardware store."

"I stand corrected. It does sound bad."

"Welcome to the scientific method."

He held out a hand. "Come on, get up. My mother said that sitting on cold cement will give you hemorrhoids."

She cocked an eyebrow. "Oh yeah? Well, my mother says that sit-ting on cold cement will give you a kidney infection."

He hauled her to her feet until their noses were a mere four inches apart—just a joke, a laughing situation, but it surprised him how des-perately he enjoyed it. He broke away before the proximity went to his head. "Either way, you don't want it. Come on." He held the door for her as they reentered the comfortably warm building. She avoided the elevator and insisted on the stairs. "Claustrophobic?"

"Getting my aerobics for the day."

They entered Lia's apartment. Marissa had arrived and now neatly sketched the shape of the room and the placement of the furniture.

"I'm going to take the bedding when I'm done with this," she told Evelyn while checking David out. He noticed her scrutiny, but if she had come to any conclusions, her face kept them well hidden. He didn't know if he passed or didn't pass her muster, whether she considered him a possible suitor for Evelyn or herself, or if he simply wondered if he could solve such a high-profile case. He wondered himself.

"Why?" he asked. "The bed had been made with the suitcase on top of it."

"Maybe there's a second boyfriend," Marissa theorized. "They have sex and she makes the bed and starts to pack. All I know is, Tony will chew my ass if I don't collect it."

"He got her out of here without a noisy struggle or screams," Riley pointed out. "All her neighbors were home and no one heard a noise. That indicates she knew him, or somehow he knocked her out before she could fight back."

Evelyn studied the linen closet.

"Want to borrow the vacuum cleaner?" David asked.

"It could be that I just watch too much TV, but assuming she left here not willingly but unconscious, he might have wrapped her in something. The bedspread and the shower curtain, the two obvious choices, are still present. There's sheets and blankets here, but no way to know if one is missing."

"Did you say there were fibers on her clothing?"

"Everyone has fibers on their clothing."

"What kind were on hers?"

"I don't know."

Riley lit a cigarette, confident that Lia could not object. He took a tin from his pocket to contain the ashes rather than leave them at the scene. "What do you mean, you don't know?"

"I mean I've spent the last forty-eight hours at cemeteries, hospitals, and crime scenes. I barely got back to work before you guys pulled me out here. Where do you think I'd have time to look at Lia's clothing?"

"Can't you work past four-thirty? You know, put in a little over-time?"

Evelyn gave him a look that could have boiled water. "My daughter's at home recuperating from surgery. I don't give a damn about overtime."

True to her word, she stubbornly left work at the usual time and spent the evening with her mother and daughter. But the next day she succumbed to the accursed work ethic and arrived at the ME's office two hours early, hoping that with no one but the deskmen about she might actually get some work done.

"You look like you ought to be on a gurney," Greg, the deskman, told her.

"Thanks a hell of a lot."

"No prob. You see Jason on the news?"

"Never turned it on."

"He stuck his face in the camera, gave this firm, pro-fesh-en-al smile, and said he could not comment on an open investigation."

"Well, that will make the ME happy."

"Yeah. But he still got on the news, didn't he?" the deskman said. "Something weaselly about that boy."

Evelyn flicked on lights as she made her way to the examination room. The building sat around her as still and silent as a—well, as a morgue. Time to work. The killer's next victim might have cement hardening around her feet at that very moment.

Lia Ripetti's knit pink shirt had dried to a stiffness that quickly collapsed under Evelyn's probing fingers. The label said Ralph Lauren and it had eye hooks all the way down the front. Two were missing and one hung loose, as if the shirt had been pulled but not with any real violence. Slight brown-purple stains were scattered around the right shoulder area. They could have been there for some time; after all, she had worn the shirt only to work around her apartment.

The Lee denim shorts were size 8 and faded, with nothing in the pockets but an unwrapped Life Saver candy and a Kleenex dried into a misshapen lump. The shorts had a bleach spot on the right front thigh and a green stain on the left buttock, perhaps a grass stain—who would be out rolling around in the grass in this weather? Evelyn dutifully noted all these facts on a sheet of paper. Lia had also been wearing a pair of white cotton panties and an underwire sports bra, and Evelyn briefly noted their size and brand. Then she got out the tape.

She taped the clothes with 3M standard clear packaging tape, placing a strip of tape down on the clothing and lifting up, repeating until the front of the shirt and its sleeves were done. She placed the tape on a sheet of clear acetate paper, something normally used by artists. Then she repeated the process until she'd covered the surface of each item, including the underwear, inside and out. She put the sheets of acetate in a clean nine-by-twelve manila envelope, rebagged and resealed the clothing and put it back in storage, then wiped the table off and re-covered it with fresh brown paper. Ideally she should move to another room entirely to avoid cross-contamination, but that wasn't an option, given the cramped conditions of the building. Then she got Destiny Pierson's clothing from the drying room.

She thanked her lucky stars that both girls were so scantily dressed. Usually winter deaths meant she had to work through several shirts, a pair or two of pants, underwear, socks, boots, gloves, hats, scarves, and heavy coats. In her opinion nothing weighed more than a man's leather coat except a man's *wet* leather coat.

What Riley had referred to as a T-shirt was actually a Halston creation in lightweight purple polyester with subtle gold threads. Simple but elegant. There were no holes, but the fabric had several snags in the back, as if it had been up against something rough. There were no stains, at least none that she could discern against the dark fabric. She taped the shirt inside and out, without much confidence. Both sets of clothing had spent some time in the river, which greatly reduced the possibility of finding anything significant. The girls had to have been transported there by car, but the water could have washed away any carpet fibers. What an involved, complicated, cumbersome way to kill someone, she mused; impossible to do without a great deal of victim-killer contact, which would deposit all kinds of trace evidence from the killer and his location to the victim's body. Then he throws her in the water and it all washes away.

Destiny's bra, a Chinese-red crushed-velvet Victoria's Secret Miracle Bra, brought a smile to Evelyn's face. Every sixteen-year-old's dream. Angel had one in white—the product of an entire week's paycheck from her afterschool job at the miniature golf place. Evelyn had not been able to teach her daughter how to wait for a sale.

Destiny's panties, like Lia Ripetti's, were plain white. The miniskirt she had reportedly been wearing had most likely traveled several miles upstream by the time they found the body. She had no coat. Not even a teenager would go barhopping in a Cleveland November without a coat.

"You're in early," Jonathan said from the doorway.

"Catching up. I haven't had a chance to look at the clothing until now. Jonathan, somebody got both these girls without a cry, without a struggle. What does the tox screen show?"

"Nothing."

"Nothing at all?"

He leaned on the doorway, looking as tired as Evelyn felt even though the day had just begun. "Ripetti came up clean. The Pierson kid had a slight amount of alcohol—either from the bar or from a glass of fund-raiser champagne."

"You didn't go to that, did you?"

"I wasn't interested in being the ME's token black pathologist," he said simply, then smiled. "Besides, I had a date, and I'd rather spend time with her than the city council members."

"Did the two girls have any head injuries?"

"Some superficial bruises, like the rest of their bodies."

"So if he didn't knock them unconscious or gag them hard

enough to bruise their faces, how did he overpower them so quickly and quietly? Will the tox screen check for Rohypnol?"

"Not normally, but we pulled out all the stops on this one, so they checked for all the date-rape drugs. Nothing."

She gave him a disappointed look. "Then we have a real mystery."

"You love mysteries."

"Don't be so sure," she sighed, and repackaged the panties.

She started to roll up the brown paper when she felt something under her foot. A white wad sat on the brick-colored tile. She thought several curses to herself as she picked it up.

Unnoticed, the Kleenex from Lia Ripetti's pocket had fallen off the table as she examined the shorts. She had already sealed the shorts and would have to reopen the bag, put it inside, and reseal it. Furthermore, it had been in the room when she examined Destiny's clothing and so could possibly have cross-contaminated evidence; plus she might never have noticed it and it could have been swept up by the janitor and lost, and losing evidence did not occur at the ME's office no matter how dingy and disorganized the entire building seemed. The more she thought about it, the worse it got. What if the Kleenex belonged to the killer and contained his nasal mucus, and he had stuffed it into Lia's pocket . . . why? As a show of contempt? Because his clothes had no pockets? What if it came from his house or car, and he had given it to Lia?

Enough already, she thought. *You made a bad mistake but it's fixed now. Just repackage it and stop worrying.*

Before she did that, however, she pulled over the magnifying light and a fresh piece of brown paper and took a closer look. The surface of the wad seemed no more interesting than expected, so she took it firmly in both hands and broke it open like a petrified egg.

Something metal winked at her.

She set it down and walked away. She poked her head into the next room, an all-black cubicle with all the attractiveness of a cave, and called "Zoe!"

A thud echoed as the petite staff photographer put down her

morning coffee and emerged from the darkroom, a mazelike tunnel hidden behind the studio. She followed Evelyn with a camera and a running commentary on the opinions of the *Plain Dealer*'s film critic, tossing dark curls in indignation. ". . . like the movie was supposed to be great art in the first place. This thing? What is it? Looks like Kleenex. This guy doesn't like anything unless Bruce Willis is in it anyway."

"It is Kleenex. I think there's something in it."

"Want the other side?"

Evelyn flipped the lump over.

Click. "I mean, it's Jane Austen. What did he expect? A car chase in Act Two?"

Evelyn separated the lump into two parts to reveal a round piece of metal, obviously a gold ring. Zoe took another photograph of this painstaking excavation and continued her review of the review. Zoe spoke almost constantly, to herself, to no one, to anyone present—a habit disconcerting to newcomers until they discovered that her eternal comments were interesting, observant, and often scathingly funny.

Evelyn worked the rest of the tissue off. A deep green emerald gleamed from a delicate but sturdy setting of eighteen-karat gold. Zoe and Evelyn were silent for a moment with the respect any woman shows for a good piece of jewelry.

"Nice," Zoe said. *Click.*

"Yeah."

"Why did she wrap it in Kleenex?"

"I wish I knew."

Zoe returned to her den, ruminating now on both emeralds and boneheaded movie critics, while Evelyn pondered the question. Lia had been packing and probably cleaning, and could have put it in her pocket to keep from scratching or dirtying it. Or it was something she wanted to pack and shoved in her pocket temporarily? But why wrap it in Kleenex? If she was going to that length, why not just put it in the suitcase? Why not just wear it? She had been wearing only one ring when she was found—plenty of fingers left. Did she do it after the killer kidnapped her, afraid he would steal it? But why this ring and not the star sapphire she had on her right hand?

The magnifying lamp revealed nothing but *18K* and *Corelli* stamped into the band. There were some tiny scratches along the setting but not on the stone. It appeared to be a relatively new, expensive purchase. Or gift—from the looks of Lia Ripetti's apartment, there wasn't a lot of money left over at the end of the month to buy emeralds. Lia had believed in small luxuries, so she could have saved up for it. But why keep it in her pocket and not on her hand?

Perhaps she didn't want Durling to see it and shoved it in her pocket when he arrived for dinner. Or perhaps he had given it to her, and out of sentiment she protected it and not her other ring from the kidnapper. But David said that Durling had planned to propose at Christmas. Why buy her an expensive ring when he needed to save for a diamond on a Home Warehouse salary?

As usual, her mind became frustrated with too many questions and too few answers. She wrote a brief description of the ring, made a druggist's fold of brown paper for both the ring and the Kleenex shreds, and sealed the edges. Then she took the envelopes of clothing tapings and went upstairs to call David.

16

FOR A MOMENT DARRYL considered leaving. Playhouse Square hardly seemed a low-profile spot to meet, even on a weeknight, but after looking around the diner he decided to wait. Two partners with more money than sense had created Hanna's in the early 1980s, during the renovation of the surrounding once-opulent theaters, to be Cleveland's answer to Mann's Chinese Theatre. Named after industrialist and senator Mark Hanna, whose funds had been vital to the area around the turn of the century, Hanna's Diner was designed to spur Cleveland forward on its eternal quest for the glamour of L.A. or Chicago. As any sensible resident could have predicted, of course, the Hollywood crowd did not cooperate and the squares of cement in the sidewalk outside held hand- and footprints from local minor celebrities and a few singers from the Cleveland Opera, and one or two dotted prints of Cleveland Ballet stars' toe shoes. After the boiler explosion in 1983, which killed a waitress, a cook, and three customers, the partners rebuilt and carried on until a dot-com disaster wiped out the last of their optimism. The new owners kept Hanna's open, barely, and now theatergoers hurried past its dingy windows on the way to more fashionable lakefront eateries. Darryl relaxed. His fellow patrons seemed more interested in their beers than in him.

At least it gave him a moment's peace from both the well-meaning mourners and the critics who felt he did either too much or too little for "his people." Or Cleveland. Most of the country considered Cleveland to be second only to Buffalo as the armpit of the nation, but he loved his town. Its citizens might like you or might not, but they never left you in doubt. He didn't want to be anywhere else—except maybe in the governor's mansion in Columbus, of course, though that would come with a new cast of hundreds to be dealt with. This thought, which usually invigorated him, now left him exhausted.

Mario would know how to control the city council. Mario would know how to shake the funding loose. Mario always knew what to do.

How Darryl had missed him.

He warmed his hands around an Irish coffee and watched his old friend approach the table and sit across from him. Mario hardly seemed different from the dirty eight-year-old who had collided with him one summer day. Each had been running from a beating of one kind or another. From that day on, they ran together, and eventually convinced their tormentors to seek greener pastures. "Thanks for seeing me."

"Like what, I'm granting an audience? It's you who wouldn't see me, in case you've forgotten," Ashworth said without rancor, as if to establish the facts in case Darryl had developed a bad case of selective perception over the years.

He hadn't. "I know. Believe me, I know. I had to make choices to get my life where I needed it to go—"

"You had to disassociate yourself. It wouldn't do for the city councilman to have ties to organized crime."

"Or for you to have your best pal on the other side of the law."

They paused and looked at each other, but not for some sign of absolution. It had never been necessary and wasn't necessary now. Perhaps they had been closer than brothers, but they were both survivors, first, last, and always.

"Thanks for coming to the funeral yesterday. I saw you there."

Ashworth grinned, the exact grin he had had at eight, with smug pleasure in doing something reckless and getting away with it. "Did you? The cops didn't. At least they didn't corner me afterward, which means they didn't."

"You haven't lost that knack of being invisible when you want to be." A trace of a smile tugged at Darryl's lips. It vanished quickly.

"I'm sorry about your kid, Darryl. Really sorry."

Darryl just nodded. He had reached the point in his grief where words no longer helped.

"I don't know what I'd do if something happened to Ivy. And you know what? It probably will, because she's wilder than wild. My boy's great, real smart kid, but sometimes I think Ivy should inherit the business. She scares *me*."

"She's a handful?"

"She's exactly like me in that she likes to take risks. But I never took *crazy* risks, I always put self-preservation first. Like how I never fought Harry Vincenza, even though I could have beat him, because he had that group of cousins, uncles, and all and it just would have opened a can of worms that I didn't want to waste time dealing with."

Another half smile. "Destiny could scare me sometimes. She was irrepressible. She never had to think of her own safety, someone else did that for her. Maybe that made it easy for someone to snatch my baby off the street."

Ashworth said nothing. There were no words for that kind of pain. He turned his face away, giving Darryl a moment, and focused instead on a photo of a pretty, vapid-looking woman who laughed as she placed one stiletto pump into wet cement outside the restaurant. The kind of woman his grandfather went for. A man very like his grandfather stood next to her, with one meaty hand on her rear end. One of them had autographed the photo, adding the sentiment *Make your own dreams. Just like Darryl and me,* he thought. *We made our own. The trick is to keep them from turning into nightmares.*

"Of course she might not have had a chance," Darryl went on. "And her attitude had nothing to do with it. I just don't know. In my mind I've gone over every single person I know, looking for some clue, for something to make me see a political motivation. Every scenario I come up with seems ludicrous."

"Nobody's leaning on you? About a vote or a zoning law? An appointment?"

"Nothing worth killing over. Not that I'm universally liked," he added with a rueful smile. "I have as many enemies as I have friends, I know that. That's politics. But no matter how much I hate certain people, I just can't see them killing my daughter over a political issue. Besides, what's the point if I don't know who did it or why?"

Ashworth stirred the cherry in his Manhattan. "Well, like my grandpa always said, ask why first. Why is always more important than who or how. No one's blackmailing you, holding something over your head? You're not pressuring anyone else?"

Darryl took no offense at the question, no more than if Ashworth had asked where he might have dropped his wallet. "No. Nothing."

"What about you personally? Having an affair with anyone? Is Danielle?"

He flinched at that one, but only at the thought. "No."

"You sure?"

"Positive."

"No other family problems? Former girlfriends, boyfriends? Does Danielle have an ex-husband? Anyone, in other words, who might have some deep hatred for either or both of you?"

"No."

"What about Destiny? She break up with a boyfriend lately? Steal some girl's boyfriend?"

"The police asked me all this," Darryl pointed out mildly.

"The police haven't found him. If you want me to apply my resources to find this guy, I need some facts to start with."

Darryl hesitated.

"That *is* why we're here, isn't it?"

"I've got no right to ask." He hadn't spoken to his best and only friend in years, and he spoke now because he wanted something. He did it because he could. Loyalty wasn't just a word to Mario, it was a way of living. "She was my baby, Mar. The only daughter I'll ever have. I can wait, but I can't not know. I can live with her death—I know I can—but I can't live with the thought that this guy might never be found, never be caught, or never be punished. As logical as I've always been about my career, I'm not willing to be logical about this. I'll find this guy if it takes every penny I have, and if the courts can't kill him I'll do it with my bare hands. And if it costs me my career, so be it. I can live with not being governor. I can't live with this."

"It won't bring Destiny back, you know. You still have to live without her for the rest of your years whether you want to or not. Throwing away your life won't bring her more peace than she's already got."

"No, it won't. But it will bring it to *me*. And Danielle."

That said, Ashworth turned businesslike. "We can keep you out of it anyway. Now, back to Destiny. Any boyfriends?"

"She had too much strength for most boys," Darryl said proudly. "And they were intimidated by me. Mostly they just hung out in a group. There weren't any falling-outs that I know of, but I'll ask Danielle. The other thing that worries me—both worries and relieves me—is this other girl. The other drowned girl. She had nothing to do with us, so maybe he picked Destiny at random. If he snatched this other girl off the street . . ."

Ashworth nodded. "She worked for me."

"What?"

"She worked at one of my offices. I didn't know her."

So there *had* been a connection between the two girls, and that connection was Mario Ashworth. In the next instant he dismissed the fact as a coincidence, even before Mario went on.

"I know it's weird. She kept some books, nothing big. She didn't know anything that made her a danger. None of my boys did it, that I'm sure of. They're as baffled as anyone else. And angry."

"Evelyn didn't tell me that."

"Who?"

"An old friend of mine works at the ME's office. She didn't tell me they'd even identified the girl, or that she worked for you."

"They didn't know until this morning. I think, for some bizarre reason, they thought she might be Ivy—the first dead girl, I mean. I ID'd Lia from the picture. I met Evelyn." He paused, making connections. "Oh. *That* Evelyn."

"What do you mean?"

"The one you dumped for Danielle."

"I didn't dump her." Had he? How much of the attraction had been Danielle's stunning looks and how much Danielle's stunning stock portfolio? All he knew now was that he'd love Danielle even if she'd grown up in a trailer park. And that was all he needed to know. "How did you hear about that? We'd already—"

"Yeah, you'd already dropped me," Ashworth said cheerfully. "But I kept up with current events. So you have a pal at the ME's office . . . that might come in handy."

Darryl shook his head. "I'm not sure. We've been out of touch for a lot of years. She promised to keep me informed, but I think when it hits the fan she won't risk her job for me."

"Mmm. Evelyn and me, both cast aside like something the cat coughed up—and both of us castees still willing to help out the caster," Ashworth pointed out with a wide grin. "Are we loyal or just stupid? Relax, man, I'm just ragging you. Anyway, if she doesn't help we'll find another source. There's always a disgruntled or frustrated employee willing to talk in order to make something happen for themselves."

"Besides," Darryl backpedaled, "the ME's office probably doesn't know much. What about the cops?"

"I've got a few on my payroll. I'll see what they can produce. How do I get hold of you?"

Darryl pulled out his card and scribbled a number on the back. "This will be either me or Will. You can leave a message with him. He doesn't know who you are, but he won't ask."

"Okay." Ashworth sobered. "I'll do everything I can, Dare."

"Thanks. Thanks a lot."

Ashworth started to fidget, in the universal language of someone preparing to leave. But Darryl hadn't finished.

"About the new ME's office—"

Ashworth stilled. "Yes?"

"I'm going to offer you a bribe." Darryl's lips twisted in their secret smile. "And I will ask you not to be insulted; I know you would help me out of friendship, but I'm asking a lot and I want to show my . . . gratitude."

Ashworth waited, flushing with the beginnings of anger despite Darryl's plea.

"Find who killed my daughter and I'll see you get the contract."

Ashworth laughed, anger apparently forgotten, then shook his head. "Wow, Dare. You've conspired with the mob and subverted the public interest in the same day. You really have been knocked for a loop."

Darryl shrugged. "Remember Gram used to say 'in for a penny, in for a pound'? Besides, I can do it with a clear conscience. I've looked at the other bids and their past projects. You do the best work for the money. You should get the contract."

"What about—"

"The city council does make the final decision, so no, I can't make any guarantees. But I've got a good council. They'll put a lot of weight on my recommendation."

"They'll do what you tell them," Ashworth translated.

"The council will listen to my advice," Darryl retranslated. "And my advice will be to do what's best for Cleveland."

"I could point out how many similarities a political enterprise and a criminal one have in common. But I won't."

"I'd appreciate that."

They left Hanna's together. No one noticed.

"GO AWAY," SUSANNAH SHINE demanded from a staging area behind her fortress of manila folders. Piled around the edge of her desk, they formed an impressive wall complete with flying buttresses, and she clutched an egg salad sandwich in one hand as if lining up a shot. A single desk lamp did little to dispel the industrial-gray gloom of the basement office. "Can't I even have my lunch hour in peace?"

"At least you *get* a lunch hour," Evelyn whined back, and closed a door reading *Missing Persons* on the frosted glass window. "I'm spending mine here."

"No you ain't, either. You go bother some other low-paid civil servant. You know all search requests have to be submitted in writing. No exceptions."

"I know, but I'm in a real hurry on this one—"

"No one jumps the line. First come, first served. All children are equal in the eyes of the Lord."

"I understand perfectly. I'm just going to use your computer, really. I'll be quiet. You won't even know I'm here."

"Huh." Susannah brushed crumbs off a black spandex top, already pushed to its limit by an oversize bosom. Kind but inaccurate people described her as a large woman when *huge* was more like it. But most of her hugeness came from muscle, bone lengths in the ninety-ninth percentile, and extra height added by good posture. When in motion she had the bearing of a queen and the attitude to match; the combination left her unmolested by all but the most hardy. Or types like Evelyn, who had figured out her secret.

Evelyn sat at a computer monitor that appeared to predate Windows and disturbed the blank screen to start up the search feature. The computer worked at its top speed, laboriously grinding gears and sounding like a box of tacks caught in a shredder. Evleyn absently tapped a foot and waited for the question.

It wasn't long in coming.

Evelyn heard the tortured groans of the desk chair wheels as the Missing Persons administrative assistant pushed it back so she could see Evelyn's computer screen. "What you got?"

"Just some girls."

"What kind o' girls?"

"Dead girls."

"That ain't what I call useful information. You come from the ME's office, all your girls is dead."

Evelyn pivoted to face the woman. Susannah worked at four times the speed of the ancient computer system, with greater accuracy. "The girl they pulled out of the river. And the mayor's daughter. We have all the earmarks of a ritual crime, which means he probably did it before, and if he did it before and we didn't find any victims, that means they're still under the water. That means somebody probably reported them missing. Maybe there's some clue here, something that these two girls and maybe some missing ones all have in common, something that could lead us to him."

"I didn't think missing persons was your job," Susannah pointed out.

"It isn't. Tony would rant if he knew I was here."

Another tortured squeak of the wheels, but the woman remained within her battlements.

"But I have to try to help," Evelyn added, "before this guy kills again."

A sigh heaved from inside the spandex. "What age?"

"Let's say between fifteen and thirty."

"Color?"

"All."

"Just women?"

"Yep."

Susannah quickly pulled files from the stacks, apparently at random, but Evelyn had no doubt that when she opened each one it would contain information on a missing woman between fifteen and thirty. The castle walls began to sway but didn't yet fall.

Evelyn abandoned the computer. "I can't figure it out, Susannah. Whether you're just insatiably curious about every last man, woman, and child on this earth or if you're just anal-retentive, like a crossword puzzle fanatic. You won't rest until you find a match for each one of these files. You might not want to leave that sandwich unattended, either. I am sorely tempted by an empty stomach and a great love for egg salad."

Susannah didn't even look up from her search. "You won't eat it, too many calories for a skinny thing like you. I work here because I care about all these lost children of Jesus. Praise the Lord."

"He should praise you. But I still think you're a compulsive puzzler. No one could do this job for purely altruistic reasons. Stuck in this cave, working on hopeless cases—"

"Oh, yeah? You work with dead people, why you do that?"

"I'm not saying there aren't similarities," Evelyn admitted. "I'm just saying that curiosity is a great motivator."

"Curiosity killed the cat, that's what it did." Susannah thrust about thirty pounds of paperwork into Evelyn's midriff. "The copier is over there. And don't come back here crying about no toner."

"YOU LOOK LIKE CRAP," Riley said.

"Thanks."

"I meant that as an insult."

"I know," David said. "But I have an excuse. I spent last night in Records."

"With the sexy night clerk?"

"Without the sexy night clerk."

"She's quite an Indians fan, you know," Riley added, tightening his tie, an overflow of color in wrinkled silk.

"I didn't get a chance to ask. I searched missing persons files for the past year."

"Why didn't you just ask Susannah?"

"Who?"

"Never mind. You think we've got more bodies sleeping with the fishes?" If impressed with David's initiative, he did a masterful job of concealing it.

"There's three girls that are between the ages of twelve and thirty, two white and one black, two from the near west side and one from Euclid. Actually there's four more besides them, but two were prostitutes who probably moved on to warmer pastures and two were wives who probably moved on to friendlier pastures. The last two took clothes and personal items with them."

"Don't be too quick to eliminate the hookers. A lot of serial killers start out with hookers—they're so easy to pick up."

"I copied their reports to keep handy, but I thought I'd start with these three."

"Start what, exactly? If Missing Persons doesn't have any leads, what are you going to do? Drag all the rivers?"

"I'd love to, but convincing the dive team to check all the bridges in Cuyahoga County in the middle of November—"

Riley nodded, almost with empathy. "Like talking the church choir into providing music for an orgy."

"About that, yeah. No, I thought I'd just check their backgrounds, see if they had anything in common with Pierson and Ripetti."

"Find anything?"

"No," David admitted. "They didn't live in the same neighborhoods, go to the same schools, the same churches, or the same hairdresser as near as I can tell. The missing girls were a twenty-year-old paralegal, a twenty-five-year-old chef and mother of two, and a nineteen-year-old graphic artist. Thalia Johnson, Christine Sabian, and Blair Danilov, respectively. They were average girls with average living conditions and no police record. They don't have anything in common with each other, much less our two homicides."

Riley had a chance here to say something encouraging, and he let it go by like a bad pitch.

"You still look like crap," he said.

David sat in his car and stared at the house. The neat brick bungalow rose above a manicured lawn scattered with snow, two soccer balls, and a Big Wheel. On the front seat next to him lay a report detailing the skeleton of a human life: husband, Roberto Sabian; wife, Christine Sabian; and two daughters, Kim and Kathy, aged three and eighteen months, respectively. Christine Sabian had disappeared on July 24. Maybe she was at the bottom of the river. Maybe she'd gotten tired of the working-mother treadmill. Maybe David sat here only because he didn't want to go back to his empty apartment.

He got out of the car and walked up to the front door; moving around brought the chill in his bones to the surface. The temperature hovered around twenty-eight, damp and cool, but not what a Clevelander would consider *cold*. Heck, winter hadn't even really begun yet.

Roberto Sabian opened the door with a baby on one hip, his Arrow shirt partially untucked, a tuft of black hair gone awry. The interior of the home held a living room ankle-deep in toys, and a table set with three places where there used to be four. The father looked at David with a peculiar mix of apprehension and impatience. The little girl looked at David as if he might have a new toy on him.

"What?" Sabian said.

David identified himself, but he doubted Sabian heard anything he said after the word *police*.

"Is there news? Did they find her?"

"I'm sorry, Mr. Sabian, there isn't. I don't have anything new to tell you." He could see the man's thoughts as if he had spoken them: *Then what the hell are you doing here?*

"Then what the hell are you doing here?" Sabian demanded, making no move to allow David in. "Don't you guys know what you do to me every time you call or show up? I die a thousand deaths, wondering what you're going to say. That she's dead, that you found her body, that she's got amnesia and has been wandering in Arizona . . ."

"I can imagine—"

"No." Sabian's voice sounded as bleak and harsh as a desert landscape. "You *can't* imagine." The little girl sensed his pain, and her eyes filled with tears. She huddled against her father, turning her back on the cold air from the open doorway.

"I'm sorry," David said again. "I'm investigating some other disappearances, too, and I just wanted to ask you a few questions. I know it's painful."

It seemed for a moment that Sabian might shut the door in his face, might refuse to let yet another stranger poke at his festering wound, but then he stood back to let David enter. "Come on in. I'll answer a thousand questions, a million, if you can find Christine."

David picked his way through the living room, careful not to step on the herd of plastic ponies occupying the carpeted area. Soft lavender paint covered the walls with a floral paper border near the ceiling. White recessed shelves flanked the fireplace on either side, stocked with framed photographs and books that dealt with either food or decorating. The photos were of Sabian and, David assumed, Christine, sometimes with their children and sometimes without, but always together. He picked up a posed portrait of the couple, with the standard cruise-ship tropical background. Christine had straight brown hair hanging to her breasts, a pert nose, and a smile that deepened her dimples.

"We took that on a cruise." Sabian set the girl down. She immediately took off for another part of the house.

David put the picture back and noticed a group shot that featured Christine and her two daughters in matching summer outfits. It had obviously been a hot day, perhaps shortly before she disappeared in June. The woman's house served as a character witness, testifying that Christine Sabian had been a happy, devoted wife and mother. But pictures, David knew, could lie.

"What other disappearances?" Sabian asked.

David turned, and followed the man into the kitchen and took a seat at the table, avoiding several carefully constructed piles of macaroni and cheese scattered along the tabletop. "I have been reexamining some other missing person reports. I'm just shooting in the dark, really, trying to see if there are any connections between the women."

"You think you got a Ted Bundy?" Sabian cleared the dishes from the table and scraped them with short, violent strokes, before stacking them in the dishwasher. He did most of this without taking his eyes off

David. Obviously Roberto Sabian was not still very often or for very long. "Somebody killing women?"

He asked it so casually, as if he had considered it as just one more possible explanation instead of a nightmarish scenario that kept him from drawing an easy breath, all day, every day.

He had to have heard about Destiny Pierson and Lia Ripetti, but did not connect it to his wife, nor did David want him to. So he hedged. "That's a possibility. I'm just throwing out the standard questions, hoping something will fall into a pattern. Did Christine have any medical problems?"

"None. Never sick a day in her life."

David thought of Nurse Neal and asked on a whim: "Where were your girls born?"

"Westlake Hospital."

His mind changed direction again. "And who would look after them while Christine worked?"

"Christine's mother. Sometimes a high school girl from down the street." Sabian added detergent to the dishwasher. He must have answered all these questions before, but he hadn't been joking when he said he'd do so again. "Chris worked for a catering service, so most of the time she had to work at night. Usually I could get home before she had to leave, so we didn't need anyone else."

Just themselves, cocooned into a happy web. "That must have been tough, working different shifts."

"Like, maybe we were having trouble, so I killed her or she ran away?" Sabian translated without rancor. "It's okay, that's been implied by everyone from the first cop that took the report to the checkout girl at the supermarket. I'm immune." He could take accusations, innuendo, insults. Just get his wife back. "But it isn't true. Chris didn't work every day and tried to avoid weekends. We weren't desperate for money. She worked because she loved it, and because she was good at it."

The eighteen-month-old girl must have informed her older sister of this new person in the house, and now they crept down the steps to peer through the banisters, to view this strange animal. David smiled at them.

"Girls," Sabian said. "Go upstairs." When they made no move, he thundered, *"Go!"* and the tiny feet echoed as they flowed upstairs on a wave of giggles. Sabian looked at David. "They keep asking me where she is, where's Mommy? God, they must ask five times a day. Five hundred for the first few weeks."

Sabian had been a handsome man until tragedy, stress, and worry had taken him directly from his mid-twenties to middle age. He picked up a few pieces of mail from the counter, looked at them without recognition, and tossed them down.

Maybe the life of a lonely, frustrated bachelor wasn't so bad, David thought. It had to be better than Roberto Sabian's unique personal hell. "So she liked her job?"

"Yeah. She worked for Kopecki's since before we met. She would develop new dishes for them, oversee the real fancy stuff. People would work there just to learn from her. Chris came up with the honey-mustard-rosemary chicken that you see at every shindig these days. The girls and I are losing weight without her," he added, a half-hearted attempt at humor.

"Any problems there? Any conflicts with other people?"

"Nah."

"Any hobbies? Clubs?"

"Who has time?"

"Did she like to go dancing?"

Sabian smiled, amused, then wistful. "Maybe at weddings and stuff. I've never been much of a dancer." He moved to the sliding glass door behind the kitchen table and closed the curtains. David wondered if he ever sat down.

"And you're an attorney?"

"Henderson, Pollack, and Shine. We do mostly contracts, corporate stuff, nothing exciting."

"No problems there in the past year?"

"We're attorneys—if there isn't a problem, no one needs us. But were there any large conflicts that someone would kidnap my wife over, no." He sat, finally, in a hard wooden chair across the table, but then squirmed, shifted, tapped his fingernails, and pulled at his collar so many times that David wished he'd stand up and pace some more.

Stifled exclamations escaped from the steps.

"Girls!" he shouted with a voice more like a loud roar than a shout, emphasizing by bass, not treble. Another stampede trampled up the steps.

"And before you ask, no, Christine did not have any boyfriends, and no, I do not have any girlfriends. Our marriage could not have been more solid. Chris knew that if she got tired of me she could get a head chef job at one of those overpriced places downtown, make a ton of money, and have her own groupies. But she didn't care about that. Our home, me, and our girls were most important to her." He looked at David, his righteous indignation foiled by exhaustion. He had probably made that speech more than once and no longer had the energy for it. He wanted her back, and every minute that went by brought him closer to the knowledge that it wasn't going to happen. So he kept moving, trying to make each minute last as long as possible, and the effort was wearing him out.

"What are these other disappearances that you think might be similar to hers?"

"Frankly," David said, not wanting to mention that they were murders, not disappearances, "I wasn't sure they were similar, and now that I'm here, I don't see that they are." Christine Sabian had been only a few years older than Lia Ripetti and Destiny Pierson, but she had already moved into another stage of life, anchored by a career and a family. David couldn't see a single thing the three girls had in common except that they were young and pretty. "I'm sorry to disturb you again," he said as he got to his feet.

"Disturb all you want," Sabian said. "Just get my wife back."

David couldn't meet his eye. "By the way, have you ever heard of Ashworth Construction?"

"Yeah, they built the stadium."

"I mean, have you ever worked for them, or Christine?"

"Nah, never. Why?"

"I'm not even sure myself. Like I said, just shooting in the dark."

A brushing sound escaped from the dark staircase behind him.

"Girls!" Another boom, another pounding retreat. Sabian stared up into the darkness of the upper floor. "I don't really mind that they keep asking me where she is," he said, his eyes unfocused, his voice diffused. "What really frightens me is that one day they'll *stop* asking."

David escaped into the cold air and gunned his car with a little too much verve, gazing through a frosted window at Roberto Sabian's house. He had hoped for some insight into the guy who had kidnapped Destiny Pierson and Lia Ripetti, and had learned nothing except that people could sink in the pain of uncertainty and drown.

His watch read seven-ten and he still hadn't called his father. He put the car into drive and said aloud: "Note to self—next spring, beg, cajole, or force the underwater team into diving at every bridge. Find that woman's body so this guy can get closure, remarry, and go on before his misery settles into his children like some kind of creeping mold."

CHAPTER

19

EVELYN SIGHED WITH CONTENTMENT. She and a cup of coffee were tucked away in a corner of the main lab room with her beloved comparison microscope. An ancient Zeiss, it had two separate stages with one eyepiece, so that two slides could be viewed side by side or even superimposed. By turning her chair she could use the new Nikon stereomicroscope for quick screening work. She had a stack of tapings to look through, and no suicides or homicides waiting for her ministrations. That most rare of luxuries, uninterrupted time, stretched ahead of her.

Of course she should have known better. She had just placed the first sheet of tapings under the stereomicroscope when Jason grew up at her elbow like a less-than-magical beanstalk.

"Tony wants a progress report," he told her.

"Okay." The only two responses acceptable to Tony were *yes* and *okay*. It didn't matter if she fulfilled the request, particularly since he tended to forget 95 percent of them, just so long as he felt in control.

It had taken Evelyn four years to learn this vital Trace Evidence Department survival technique.

"He wants to know where you are with fibers."

"Okay."

"What are you doing?"

"Just looking at what I've got," she said. Having to talk while working slowed her down, but teaching and training were part of her job. "These are the tapings from Lia Ripetti's shirt," she went on, explaining that she would examine the hairs and fibers and remove any of interest.

"How do you know what's of interest?"

"Any hair that doesn't look like hers, any animal hair, because she didn't have a pet, any large fibers—like there's a big green one here, and she didn't have any green in her clothes, her apartment carpeting is beige, and her car interior is blue."

"What do you do then?"

"I pull them off and mount them on a slide. If they're synthetic, I'll cut off a tiny bit first and run it through the FTIR—the Fourier transform infrared spectrometer—to confirm if it's nylon or polyester or whatever."

"You're not supposed to drink coffee in the lab," he added, not pleasantly.

"I know." Against all lab standards, Tony couldn't break the habit of moving around with a coffee cup permanently clutched in his fingers, and Evelyn would be damned before she'd follow a rule that the supervisor wouldn't.

Jason disappeared as effectively as he had arrived, and she turned her attention back to the green fiber. The trilobal shape, twenty-five micrometers wide, almost certainly derived from carpeting or upholstery. Under the microscope the three-lobed shape looked like a curving road with a tunnel running through the middle of it. She pulled it off the tape and cleaned the adhesive residue from the fiber with xylene, a powerful solvent that smelled good, yet produced insidious headaches.

Fibers were much easier to work with than hairs. Hairs didn't come in as many colors as fibers and could be compared only visually. Lawyers didn't like them—too many ambiguities—and juries found hair testimony less than compelling. Just trying to get hair as long as Lia Ripetti's mounted on a glass slide required an exercise in patience, and Evelyn felt relief when no human hairs other than Lia's appeared on the tapings, making it all a moot point.

There were, however, two black hairs with spade-shaped roots, short and easily identifiable as those of a dog, most likely a Doberman. The phone rang.

"Mmm?"

"Evelyn?" David asked.

"Yeah. Sorry, a dog distracted me. Who has a dog, by the way?"

A confused pause. "Beg pardon?"

"A dog."

"Well," he said, "*I* have one."

"A Doberman?"

"No, a golden retriever. Uh, what's—"

"Good, you scared me there for a minute. I mean who among our suspects owns a dog, because I found black dog hairs on Lia's shirt."

"Oh. I see. Unfortunately the only halfway decent suspect we have at the moment is Durling, and he has neither a dog nor a motive as far as I can tell."

"Mmm." She transferred another fiber to a glass slide.

"Anyway, I called to touch base with you—"

"Touch base? You've been hanging around Riley too long."

"*Tell* me about it. What have you come up with?"

"The dog."

"That's it?"

"What do you think?" Evelyn protested. "I have a Bat Computer or something? All the fibers in the world aren't going to help until you bring me a suspect, anyway. There is one thing, for what it's worth— I went over to Missing Persons to see if there are any other missing women in this city."

Another pause. "Really," David said, his voice surprisingly unen-thusiastic. "Me, too. I spent most of the other night in Records."

"Why didn't you just ask Susannah?"

"Because I . . . never mind. So what did you find?"

"I came up with three who fit the profile of our victims, what vague mess of a profile we have so far."

"Really."

"Three: Sabian, Johnson, Danilov. How about you?"

She heard a sound suspiciously like a manila folder skidding across a desk. "So much for impressing you with my investigative abilities."

"Who am I that I need to be impressed?" she asked simply.

Another pause. It seemed that David Milaski could not assemble his thoughts. The answer hit her suddenly and shattered her cozy in-nocence: The man was *interested* in her. This produced an instant flush of pleasure, followed by a rush of panic. The thought of dating again terrified her. Having to dress up and make conversation with a total stranger? She shuddered.

Of course, he wasn't a *total* stranger . . .

"Okay," he said suddenly, interrupting her mental chaos. If he had romance on his mind, his voice hid it well and sounded downright cold. She must have been wrong. "The theory isn't panning out any-way. I talked to Sabian's husband last night." He gave her a quick summary of the visit. "So I came up with zip."

"Not necessarily. Maybe we're just not seeing the pattern. What about the other two?"

"What do *you* think?" he countered.

"Nothing in the reports jumps out. But we should talk to them."

"I know," he sighed. "Riley thinks I'm going way out on a tangent when we have two big cases already in front of us."

"Remind him that we could have three if we don't figure out how this guy is picking his victims. Let's split them up. I'll take Johnson, you take Danilov."

"No!" The yelp startled her. "Investigating is my job. You don't need to be walking up to people in the parts of town you don't find in the real estate section, if you know what I mean."

"I do. But Thalia Johnson's mother works at the West Side Market, and I need something for dinner and some decent cheese. It may not be detailed in my job description, but forensic specialists *are* investigators. Let me try to explain away my failure to follow up on a piece of evidence by saying I'm *not* an investigator and believe me, I'll be disabused of that notion double-quick by Tony *and* the scientific community. Look, I'm not trying to steal your thunder. You can take credit."

"It's not that, for God's sake," he snapped. "It just wouldn't do much for my self-image to get somebody *else* killed."

"How many are you up to?" she joked, and in the long silence that followed she figured out it hadn't been a joke at all.

"Never mind," he said, and hung up.

After staring at the phone for a minute or two, she tried to push it out of her mind. After all, she'd been warned that he had a past. That didn't make it her problem or her responsibility. No reason to give it the slightest thought. Even if he was attractive. Even if he was attracted to her.

The last thing she needed in her life was someone else to turn her ability to love back on her like a fillet knife, and cut and cut until she bled out. Especially some rogue cop, married to his job and just looking for a little sex on the side. Oh, yeah, like she wanted to get into *that* situation.

Whatever. She went back to her fibers.

Working on a glass slide with a disposable scalpel, she cut off the end of the fiber, using a small metal roller to smash it into a flat strip. From there she transferred the strip to a round, transparent slide, or window, made of potassium bromide. She rolled the strip again until it finally decided to stop sticking to the roller and stick to the window instead, and put the window into the FTIR's beam of infrared light.

The computer monitor showed the spectrum of the fiber, obviously a Nylon 6,6, but she ran it through the library of spectra just to be sure. Then she printed the results, being sure to note the assigned number of this particular green fiber, which would now be stored mounted on a slide with the same number. The fiber now became a re-fined, precisely packaged, and analyzed piece of evidence, one that might prove to be the final weight that convicted a murderer or might prove to be nothing at all. It could have come from Lia's place of work—she'd have to remember to ask David to get her a sample from the construction office—it might be from Durling's apartment—ditto mental note—it might be from Lia's friend's house or a cab or a total stranger's carpet, one that had tumbled in the apartment building's washing machine just before Lia used it. If you weren't comfortable with uncertainty, she reminded herself, don't become a fiber expert.

Evelyn went on, repeating the process for a pink-red polyester fiber, a series of black cotton fibers, and a turquoise acrylic crimped fiber that most likely came from a fluffy sweater. She sighed again, and not with contentment. The coffee had cooled, her neck felt as old and stiff as a dinosaur skeleton, the xylene had invaded her head, and she no longer felt that fibers were fun.

CHAPTER

20

EVELYN LEFT WORK EARLY, nearly rear-ending a black Lincoln Continental stopped in the drive as she tried to exit the parking lot. Tinted windows kept her from seeing the driver, only the sleeve of his expensive suit resting in the window as he conversed with her own personal albatross, Jason. She tapped her horn, surprised to see a guilty look cross the kid's face rather than the glare she expected.

She drove Angel to her doctor, who put a Steri-Strip over a popped staple and pronounced her quite healthy. He also recommended that she take a few more days off from school and normal activities. This did not please Angel. After being cooped up for two days at home, she would not have been pleased by a lottery jackpot. Her emotions had fully recovered and returned to bitch mode.

No sooner had they arrived at home than Rick and Terrie entered. Rick went so far as to inquire as to his daughter's health and Angel allowed Terrie into the sanctuary of her room to help her dress. They were taking the poor girl out to dinner, Rick said.

At times like these Evelyn found it helpful to remember her long-ago martial arts training. Breathe in through the nose and out through the mouth. It might be the only thing she *did* remember from martial arts training, but it did the trick. She gave no indication of her true feelings when she inquired why Rick felt it wise for a teenager to go out on the town only three days after major surgery.

"She called me and said she's bored. I thought it might cheer her up."

"She already popped one stitch. She really needs to rest."

Rick shrugged. "We're just taking her out to dinner. She wants to go."

She's a child. It's not her job to safeguard her health, it's ours. How do you expect a sixteen-year-old to know how long a recuperation period is required for an appendectomy? "She's not even supposed to *have* dinner. She's supposed to be on clear liquids and some light carbohydrates."

Rick snorted. "She's not going to get better on *that*."

Evelyn bit her lip. Literally. She had the standard two choices: risk Angel's ire by putting her foot down, pushing Rick into a shouting match that she would most likely lose anyway, or sit back and let her child do something that might harm her.

There were many times when being a parent truly sucked.

She decided she could not stop them—the calendar dictated custody and the doctor hadn't *forbidden* regular food or activity. As long as Angel didn't attempt a gymnastic routine, it probably wouldn't kill her. But Evelyn couldn't shake the guilt of risking her daughter's health simply to take the easy way out.

Terrie and Angel trooped back through the kitchen. The activity had flushed Angel's face and gave her a temporary look of health. She toted a large backpack.

"Packing a suitcase for dinner?" Evelyn inquired.

"It's for the weekend. It's Dad's weekend." All three of them stared at Evelyn as if she had lost her mind.

She hadn't, but her temper threatened to explode and it would be best if she could be alone. "Fine. Have a nice time. Please don't do anything strenuous and get a lot of rest. In *bed,* rest."

"Okay," Angel said with a show of patience, exiting through the garage. "See you later."

"And keep drinking fluids!" Evelyn pleaded to the back of her daughter's head.

"Don't worry." Terrie smiled at Evelyn with what seemed, if Evelyn thought about it objectively, genuine sympathy. "She'll be fine."

Then the door closed and the house became silent.

"I'd almost prefer Nurse Neal," Evelyn said to herself.

Riley had gone home on the stroke of five, insisting that nothing more could be done on the case that day. They had interviewed and reinterviewed, it seemed, every single person who had ever met or even been in the presence of Destiny Pierson, and gotten nowhere. The older detective eagerly hurried home to a house that two ex-wives had abandoned. David figured he had a date.

David, on the other hand, felt no hurry to get home to an apartment that no one had had a chance to abandon. The high school girl who lived next door would take Harry out when she got home, so he didn't have to worry about the effect of working late on his dog's bladder. With no other clues to follow, he decided to check on the second of his three missing women. Blair Danilov had lived right on his way home. She had been an attractive, athletic girl with long, light brown hair who had disappeared Friday, August 31.

Blair's apartment building had been built with inexpensive style and had seen better days. The stained carpeting in the lobby smelled of last spring's mildew. The small doorman's desk apparently hadn't been used for a decade or so and a plastic tree listed in the corner. The elevator groaned and creaked. He took the stairs.

The door of apartment 373 opened to show a small woman in Birkenstocks with a woven hemp bracelet and cropped blond hair. Except for the hair, she looked enough like the file photo of Blair Danilov to be the sister, Bonnie, who had filed the report.

"Miss Danilov?"

She scowled at him, putting her whole body into it. "Have you found her?"

"I'm sorry?"

"Blair. Have you found her?"

"No." David felt no desire to prolong what had to be agony every time the phone rang or a stranger approached. He had learned from his experience with Roberto Sabian. "I'm sorry, there isn't any news. I'm just—"

"Then what are you doing here?" Arms crossed, weight balanced, she stood in the doorway and issued no invitations.

"I'm from the police department."

"Duh."

"How did you know that?" he asked curiously.

"Duh." She ran a hand through the spiky hair. "You're wearing a corduroy blazer. No one but cops and college professors would wear something so lame, and if there's one thing I can recognize faster than a cop, it's a college professor. What are you doing here if you haven't found Blair?"

David stifled a sigh, determined to make allowances for the woman's pain. "I'm going over some missing person cases, trying to find out if there is anything the victims had in common. Do you mind if I ask you a few questions?"

"I mind you jerks asking *stupid* questions, coming out here every so often just to poke my wounds open again and then going off and not doing a damn thing—yes, I mind. Go ahead, ask."

"May I come in?"

"No, you may not. I don't let strange men into my apartment."

"I have a badge."

"I don't care if you have a letter from the pope. Go ahead and ask if you want, and make it quick so I can eat dinner, run a few miles, and then lie in bed awake wondering what the hell happened to my little

sister." Her eyes were small and black and filled with despair, and hatred for anyone who couldn't relieve that despair. David felt too sorry
for her to get angry. He didn't have the energy anyway.

"Blair worked as a graphic artist for a greeting card company,
right?"

From the look on her face she worked to stifle another *duh*.

"Did she have a boyfriend?"

"Grant Porter. Otherwise known as Jerkface. He was grooming
her."

"*Grooming* her?"

"For marriage, I suppose. He told her how to wear her hair,
arrange her clothes, talk to her boss. Et cetera. I guess he wanted her
to be smarter, prettier, and make more money before he'd consent to
take her on."

"Did he get angry at her?"

"No, anger wouldn't be New Age. If you think he killed her,
you're way off. He couldn't kill a cockroach—obviously, if you've
seen his apartment. If you think she scooted out of town to get away
from him, I wish I could agree."

"Really?"

"It beats the alternative."

David waited.

"That she's dead," Bonnie said impatiently, defiantly mentioning
the unmentionable. "Blair either ran away from Jerkface or she's
dead. There's no other explanation. You're talking about the most stable, nine-to-five, hardworking, sweet, did-everything-for-everybody
person ever. If she worked late, she'd call me *and* Grant. There's no
way she'd just take off."

"Before she disappeared—"

"Let me make this short for you." Bonnie held up a hand and
shifted her weight from foot to foot. She made him think of an aerobics instructor with a glacier-size case of PMS. "She did not report
any stalkers, threats, or weird guys. She had no arguments with me,
Jerkface, or anybody at work. She was healthy as a horse, no seizures,

blackouts, or breakdowns. She didn't pawn anything or zero out her checking account. Her car remained in the garage until the leasing company repossessed it because I couldn't make the payments. She didn't take any trips. I've been through all this with the Missing Persons guys and it would save us all a lot of time if you'd just read their reports before reinventing the wheel. You're in the same department, aren't you?"

David began to feel like an idiot. To redeem himself, he threw out: "Has she ever worked for a Mario Ashworth?"

"Who?"

"He owns a construction company. He's done a lot of large buildings around town."

"Never heard of him."

"So Blair never met him? Maybe at a social occasion or something?"

"Never heard of him. And Blair hadn't been to a party since the last millennium. Jerkface didn't think she needed any company but his own, and she agreed, poor dope."

"You didn't agree with her choice of men?"

"Gee, does it show? *I* loved her." The woman pounded one fist into the opposite palm. "He just saw a sweet, gullible thing that might fit into his master plan."

There could be a vital clue here somewhere, but David had had all he could take of Bonnie Danilov's furious aura. "Where can I find Mr. Porter?"

"Across the hall."

He looked at her and she gestured impatiently. "He lives right there. That's how she met the idiot. But I warn you"—she added as David turned away—"he'll tell you she disappeared to get away from me."

The door slammed and left him alone with the stained carpet and a resolutely empty hallway. David sighed, deciding that he'd quit the force before he'd accept a transfer to Missing Persons. Which might be on the table if he didn't find Destiny Pierson's killer.

He knocked on 376. Then he knocked three more times, increasing the volume each time, until the door swung open to reveal a handsome young man in a white terry-cloth bathrobe, wet brown hair pointing in all directions.

"Sorry!" the guy said. "I just got out of the shower. How long have you been there?"

"Just a few minutes."

"Sorry."

"I'm from the Cleveland Police Department—"

His expression changed instantly, from handsomely friendly to handsomely concerned. "Did you find her?"

"No. I'm sorry but I have no news for you. I'm just double-checking some cases, trying to pick up a clue. Do you mind if I ask you a few questions?"

"Sure. Come on in." He stood back and waved David in. An attempt had been made to decorate the one-bedroom efficiency with understated style. Unfortunately, the end result matched the building: inexpensive to begin with and not wearing well. David sat down on a white leather couch that did not feel anything like real leather and studied Blair's boyfriend. The man otherwise known as Jerkface.

"Want anything to drink?" he asked.

"No, thanks. You're Grant Porter, right?"

"That's me." He lounged easily on the other side of a marble coffee table, not at all uncomfortable with his attire. After careful scrutiny he did not live up to first impressions. His eyes weren't large enough to counterbalance his nose and the shower had reddened old acne scars, but his chest and limbs seemed toned and fit. And he didn't mind answering the same questions over and over. He told David that he had known Blair for eleven months prior to her disappearance, that they were very happy (though he did not mention any marriage plans), and that she had been a sweet, stable girl. He went through the same chorus of noes that Bonnie had when asked about unusual occurrences before she disappeared. Except when it came to him, Porter and Bonnie were in complete agreement about Blair.

"Have you talked to Bonnie?" Grant asked.

"Yes."

His pretty face creased into a pout. "I can imagine what *she* said. She's a nasty little bitch that couldn't stand someone else having influence over her sister."

"What do you mean by influence?"

"Bonnie's the big sister to Blair's little sister. They were so used to those roles that Bonnie would tell Blair where to go, how to dress—luckily Blair has much better taste when it came to clothes," he added, slipping to present tense, then back again. "It's not that Blair did everything Bonnie said, it's just that egotistical Bonnie never noticed until I came along. It's not that Blair did everything *I* said—it's just that Bonnie never noticed that, either."

"What do you do for a living?"

"I'm an Executive Assistant." He pronounced the capitals. "For Hogan Financial Management."

"Wow," David said, pseudo-impressed. "You must handle accounts for some pretty wealthy people."

"Mostly businesses, but some individuals."

"Is Mario Ashworth a client of yours?"

Porter raised his eyebrows, a man in the know. "No, I don't *think* so."

"You know him?"

"I know *of* him. He's a gangster. I doubt he would let anyone glimpse his finances, and frankly, he isn't the sort of client that Hogan Financial Management would want."

"Have you ever met him?"

"No thank you."

Grant could preen his sophisticated image all he liked, but David had to be sure no connection existed, no matter how slight. "Had Blair ever met Mario Ashworth?"

Grant goggled as if David had suggested that Blair might be the next Dalai Lama. "*Blair?* No, of course not. Blair didn't get to meet anyone outside her cubicle. Graphic arts work is a legal sweatshop for artists. She liked it there, don't get me wrong. But she couldn't expect it to amount to much."

"She wasn't an executive assistant, in other words."

"That's right," Porter said with an unattractive lack of self-consciousness. "What's Ashworth got to do with it?"

"Nothing that I can see. I'm just shooting in the dark. Thank you for your time."

"Anything to find Blair," he sighed.

David returned to his car, suddenly eager for his dog's company. There were no power struggles in their apartment and Harry never tried to influence him. If Blair Danilov had disappeared of her own free will, it must have been to get away from *both* of them.

On the other hand, Blair might be lost to a watery grave, leaving her sister and her boyfriend with nothing but a memory with which to play tug-of-war.

CHAPTER
21

SATURDAY AT THE WEST Side Market resembled a circus of smells and noise, some good, some bad, like the greasy smell of raw sausage that forced you to think about what made up sausage—and of course you didn't know, which made it worse. The earthy smell of vegetables competed with the tang of cheese. On top of it all floated scents of the lake water, oil, and dead fish.

Evelyn hadn't exaggerated about needing to shop. The contents of her refrigerator, excluding items in the process of establishing their own ecosystem, could fit in one of the crisper drawers. Rick and Terrie should just petition for custody, she thought; it wouldn't take much to prove my lack of nurturing. But she didn't worry: 24/7 parenting would crimp their style.

She entered through the open pavilion. A rare winter sun warmed the backs of the workers as they busily unpacked crates or tended their stalls. They were black, Hispanic, first-generation immigrants, and children of immigrants from central and eastern Europe who had come over to work in the steel mills. The shoppers were the same mix, plus an occasional set of yuppies who had decided to gentrify the downtown area one loft at a time.

She found Artemis Johnson behind a large glass case of meat: sausages, salamis, pork chops, Cornish hens, and steak. Nothing for Angel here. She studied the woman for a few minutes before approaching. Fiftyish. Slender for her age, but sturdy. A pleasant, round face shiny with effort. Short nails on elegant fingers. The woman somehow made a bloodstained plastic apron look fashionable, a trick Evelyn had not been able to pull off with her lab coats.

Evelyn stood at the end of the counter so she could see behind it without standing on her toes. "Mrs. Johnson?"

The woman looked up from a tray of chicken Kiev. "Yes?"

Evelyn explained herself, trying to gloss over her occupation without success.

One hand went to the plastic apron, covering her heart. "ME's office? Have you found her body?"

"No. No, ma'am, I'm sorry but I don't have any new information about Thalia at all. I'm really just trying to find a common denominator among a number of cases. If they're related—I don't even know that."

"Seems like you don't know much," Mrs. Johnson said, but cautiously, displeased with Evelyn and the entire law enforcement community but unwilling to alienate them. The police might be her only hope of finding her daughter. Alive or dead.

"That's what I'm trying to fix. Do you mind if I ask you some questions about Thalia?"

"Who else are you investigating? They must be dead if you're involved, right?"

"Yes."

"Well?"

"I can't tell you that."

The woman's eyes narrowed. "That would be my cue to tell you that I can't tell you anything about Thalia, then."

"I'm sorry." She really should have let David handle this. Corpses didn't have to be convinced to give up their evidence. Not verbally, anyway.

"But." The woman absently arranged overstuffed sausages to fill every inch of space on an aluminum tray. "There's always a *but* in life, isn't there?"

Evelyn nodded, stepping out of the way of a tiny Mexican woman with a brown bag on one hip and a toddler on the other.

"But I'll do anything to find my baby," Mrs. Johnson said simply, without looking up from the sausages. "I'll tell the deepest, darkest secrets I have to the devil himself if he would tell me where she is. You have kids?"

"One. A daughter."

"Hang on to her."

A cold chill passed through Evelyn. "I'm trying to."

Mrs. Johnson looked up at her, as if she heard something in Evelyn's voice that Evelyn hadn't known was there. Fear, maybe. Desperation. "What do you know so far?"

"That Thalia disappeared on her way home from work, September first, two weeks before her scheduled wedding to Roger Dean."

Mrs. Johnson just nodded, squirming the last few meat links onto the tray before she slid it into the window, to rest on a bed of ice. The incessant beeping of a truck backing up pierced the air. The woman at the next stall had three children, including a pale blond girl who communicated her voluminous thoughts only in shrieks. Eardrum-shattering shrieks. Evelyn went on.

"Her coworkers at the law firm noticed her catching her bus about five. The bus driver is sure she got off at her regular stop, a couple of blocks from your house, about five-thirty, which at that time of the year would have been broad daylight."

Thalia's mother nodded again as her bloodstained fingers now placed steaks on a wooden board, with a slip of waxed paper in between each one.

"She never came home."

The woman's hands stilled for a moment, as if the fact remained unbelievable even three months later. Then she pulled out another piece of waxed paper.

"That's it."

"Ain't much, is it?" The mild tone belied the rebuke.

"Would she have stopped on the way home? A friend's or a business?"

A shake of the head. "Nothing there but houses. She might call hi to someone, but nowhere she would have stopped."

"Could someone have happened by and given her a ride?"

The woman frowned. "No one who would murder her. Thalia didn't make it that long in that kind of neighborhood by being stupid enough to go by strangers."

Evelyn hadn't wanted to use the word *murder* instead of the official term *missing*, but she didn't insult the woman's intelligence by protesting. "Her fiancé, Roger? He spent the day at work, at the Tower City Gap store."

"He don't get off till six-thirty," Mrs. Johnson said, and looked Evelyn in the eye to make sure she got this and got it good. "The cops eliminated him, and I do, too. He went crazy with worry after she disappeared. No one ever treated Thalia the way she deserved until Roger. He's a fine boy." She poked listlessly at the steaks, deep lines creating trails in her face. "He still calls me all the time, to check on me, he says, but I know he just wants to see if I've heard anything. He wouldn't even cancel the wedding. He never got his deposit back from the hall or the caterer, because he couldn't bear not to have things ready if she came back in time."

Evelyn believed her. No one inspected a man more closely than a prospective mother-in-law. "What about ex-boyfriends? Anyone upset about her wedding?"

For the first time a faint breeze of a smile crossed her face, and she abandoned her wares. "Plenty of them. My daughter—and," she added with unexpected humor, "I ain't saying this just because I'm her mama—was a prize. Beautiful, intelligent, sweet, had a good job. There were quite a few of her former young men who thought they'd just come swinging back in their own time and found out they were too late. I told her, the heck with them. They had their chance."

Evelyn waited as the smile faded into the present.

"But none that would have murdered her."

The word kept coming up—an obvious assumption perhaps, but she couldn't destroy the woman's hope with an assumption. For Mrs. Johnson to use it was one thing, but for her to hear it from a law enforcement authority might be something else entirely. Evelyn continued to avoid the term. "What about work?"

"What about it? She liked her job, everyone liked her. Her boss had just given her a raise. Well, he gave all the secretaries raises, but it came in real handy, right before the wedding."

"What kind of cases did her law firm handle?"

"Criminal defense."

Evelyn raised her eyebrows.

Thalia's mother nodded. "Yeah, we thought of that, too. The cops say they checked it out. I talked to her boss myself. The thing was, she worked in the office, doing research, writing things. She never even saw the scum that firm defends. Mr. Brayer assured me that no way would they even know her name. Thalia told me that herself—she never saw anyone but her coworkers."

Evelyn digested this. If some former client had been unhappy with his legal representation, why not attack the lawyer, instead of some obscure paralegal? Unless they had kidnapped Thalia in some strange plot to force her employers to provide some legal move. But that course of action required convoluted thinking for the average criminal, and the follow-up investigation did not suggest it. It still didn't mean that Thalia hadn't run into her attacker at work and he had followed her home. He could have taken the same bus, but then how did he make off with a five-four, hundred-and-twenty-pound girl on foot?

"I always wondered about one thing, though," Mrs. Johnson said, pulling Evelyn from her reverie.

"What?"

A look of discomfort hovered on the woman's face. "I didn't point this out—"

Evelyn waited.

"We stick by our own, you know what I mean? I wasn't going to help the *po*lice to be any more racist than they already are. But it always seemed to me—" She glanced at Evelyn with a despair that went beyond personal. "We don't live in Beachwood, you see? No way a white boy wouldn't be noticed on our block."

CHAPTER
22

"**WHAT ARE YOU DOING** here?" Mrs. Anderson asked when Evelyn punched in on Sunday morning.

"I already scrubbed my toilets and mopped my mother's kitchen," Evelyn told the thistly receptionist. "Went to church and read the paper. I had nothing else to do."

"So you come in to work? That's just pathetic, that's what that is. And I thought my social life stank. Yours would put a Himalayan monk to shame. Mother Teresa has more of a social life than you."

"Mother Teresa passed away."

"That's what I mean. What, you can't have a hobby? Like gardening or something?"

"Why waste time trying to convince something to grow when most things grow perfectly well by themselves? Besides, *you're* here."

"I'm reading a book and getting overtime for it. You go and have a great time working yourself to death. We'll put that on your tombstone: 'worked herself to death over people who were already dead anyway.' "

"It's not just the ones who are dead," Evelyn argued. "It's the ones that are still alive and would like to stay that way." She went upstairs, literally bumping into Ed in the stairwell as he ate Ritz crackers and read an article in the *Journal of Forensic Sciences* at the same time. The impact nearly knocked her down both flights.

"It's not ether," he said without so much as a hello. "It might be chloroform. I have a few more metabolites to check first. It turns to phosgene in the liver and kidneys. It shouldn't be hard to find if I can get past the damn formalin."

"Would it work?"

"Sure, hell, yeah, it would work." He coughed, his lungs making a sound like crinkling cellophane. "But like I said, the person would probably puke. Do they even sell it anymore?"

"Beavell Scientific has both pure ether and pure chloroform. You can get a hundred milliliters for about twenty bucks, according to their website."

"Mmm." Ed walked away. Evelyn entered the Trace lab.

"What are you doing here?" Marissa asked. "It's my weekend on call."

"I know. But I had nothing else to do and I want to take another look at the victim's clothing."

"Girl, don't you have any life at all? It's the weekend, for Pete's—"

"Don't you start," Evelyn snapped. "I already got bawled out by Mrs. Anderson."

They were interrupted by a knock at the door. Half hidden by the gold lettering, David Milaski hovered with both the appeal and the foreboding of a good mystery.

"I'm beginning to think that man likes you," Marissa said.

"Don't be silly."

"Then why are you blushing? There ain't nothing silly about falling for a cop. They work lousy hours for lousy pay and they cheat on their wives—that is, if they don't beat them."

Evelyn glared over her shoulder as she opened the door. "Good morning, Detective. This is Marissa, our serologist." The woman nodded.

"Hi." He looked around. "This is smaller than I expected."

"No kidding," Marissa told him. "Besides us, there's two PhDs who do most of the final DNA work. They stay in the back rooms and emerge for occasional sightings. We had a third person doing the trace stuff with Evelyn, but she quit last year and somehow the county never got around to filling her position. They prefer to run Evelyn's ass off instead. And mine. We live to be Tony's grunts."

"I take it you won't be nominating him for boss of the year."

Marissa shook her tubes of blood, responding to Evelyn's frown with an innocent gaze. "He's a dyed-in-the-wool moron who uses a microscope only to get splinters out of his fingers, but since he never steals anything or stands up to the ME, the only fireable offenses when you work in civil service, he'll probably be supervisor until he retires or we find him keeled over his desk with his coffee cup still clenched in his chubby little fingers."

"Let's change the subject," Evelyn suggested, "before Jason wanders in and I wind up at the unemployment office. Did you want something, Detective, or did you suddenly wish to survey employee satisfaction in Cuyahoga County offices?"

"Are you busy?"

"Not yet."

"Feel like visiting some of our local hardware stores?"

She smiled for the first time all day. "To look for chains?"

"Unless you need to pick up some nails or something."

"I'll get my coat."

She moved into the back, out of sight but not out of earshot, and left David with Marissa.

"Hi." He sounded a bit uncomfortable under her scrutiny. Most men were.

"Hi."

"I get the feeling you don't like me. That's mysterious, considering we've never met."

"We have a mutual friend."

"Oh, really?"

"Maria Hardin."

"It's a small world," David said coldly.

"Isn't it."

Evelyn returned with her coat, twirling the Egyptian mummy fob, wondering but refusing to ask. Maria Hardin, whoever that might be, had nothing to do with her. David's past had nothing to do with her. Riley could keep his covert little warnings to himself and so could Marissa. "I'm sorry, but given the choice between hardware stores and jewelry stores, it's no mystery what I'll choose."

David looked confused.

From a locked drawer she pulled out Lia Ripetti's emerald ring. Marissa's attitude turned a hundred and eighty degrees and she and Evelyn spent several minutes cooing over the jewel before David grew impatient.

"What is it with women and jewelry?"

"What is it with men and cars?" Evelyn countered.

"Point taken. Now what is the significance of this particular piece of jewelry?"

She explained, adding, "It's got the name Corelli engraved on the band. Corelli's is a jewelry store on East Ninth. Been there since 1949. Open seven days a week except holidays."

"How did you find that out?"

"Yellow Pages."

"You're kidding."

"Sometimes it really *is* that easy."

"So before we hit the hardware stores, we can ask the Corellis about Lia Ripetti."

"At least we can find out what this ring is worth," Evelyn said. "I'm curious about how a young bookkeeper like Lia could afford an emerald this big. Unless it's just green glass."

"Find out if they're having any sales while you're there," Marissa added.

They left via the front door, which stood, unfortunately, in full view of Mrs. Anderson. "Glad you took my advice, sweetie!" she called after them, in a voice that could have carried all the way to Severance Hall.

"Advice?"

"Never mind," Evelyn said, but smiled.

The Corelli jewelry store in downtown Cleveland had the same hushed atmosphere as most jewelry stores, but the cabinets were real cherrywood and an antique crystal chandelier hung from the ceiling. No customers cluttered the plush carpeting. Evelyn felt uncomfortable in expensive shops. She did not belong here; she could not afford any of these fine things and never would. But a short, beaming man greeted them as if they were his first customers in ten years and offered Evelyn a chair. Antonio Corelli ("Junior," he explained) did everything he could to make her feel like a blue-blooded society matron.

"What a lovely couple!" he exclaimed. "Engagement rings? I have some beautiful marquis cuts, just in from South Africa."

"Pardon?" David asked.

"No." Evelyn felt her face flush. "We're not engaged."

"And why not?"

"Well, er, because this isn't a social call," David stammered in the face of the man's birdlike intensity. "I'm from the police department. We'd like to ask you about a ring."

"A retirement ring? Something for a man or woman?"

"No," David tried again. "We're not here to *buy* a ring—"

"This." Evelyn held out the emerald. "We want to ask you about this."

Corelli Junior grew quite still as he examined the ring, but out of professionalism, not wariness. He looked up with the bright eyes of one who recognizes greatness. "Yes, this is mine. I designed it myself. See how the setting shows the most of the gem, and yet it is quite secure."

"So that's a real emerald?" Evelyn asked.

The man grew as close to affronted as he could. "Of course! It's a Colombian emerald of great quality. See the depth of color? I assure you its clarity is of the highest definition. It's—"

"It's beautiful. Really stunning," Evelyn assured him, which mollified him somewhat. "I only wish I could afford something so exquisite. I assume you recall who purchased the ring? We have to ask because it belonged to a young lady. A murdered young lady."

The man raised his eyebrows in an expression of shock. "Murdered?"

"Brutally," she added for good measure. "We're not sure how this woman could have afforded such a ring. Did someone give it to her?"

The eyebrows nearly disappeared into his hairline. "I'm terribly sorry for this poor young lady. But my customers are lovely people and—how do I say it?—privileged. I go to a great deal of trouble to make them happy. One of the ways I do that is by protecting their privacy," he concluded, giving the word an English pronunciation: *prihv*-a-see.

David could have gotten angry and growled phrases like *subpoena, search warrant,* and *drag you down to the station and sort this out there.* Instead, he pulled out Lia's picture.

"This is her." He placed the photo on the glass countertop. Lia Ripetti smiled up at the jeweler. "Young, bright, pretty. Now her body is still at the ME's office because the only person in the world who really cared about her doesn't have enough money to bury her." He let that sink in. Beside him, Evelyn didn't breathe.

Corelli couldn't take his eyes off the photo. "She *is* beautiful. Looks just like my Laurina. She's about that age. And smart, just like her mother."

"So," David said, "who gave this girl an emerald?"

Corelli switched his gaze to the ring, still nestled in his left palm, and sighed.

"I don't know how she got the ring," he told them, "but I made two of them, identical. I made them special for Mr. Ashworth."

"Mario Ashworth?"

"Yes. You know him?"

"We've met."

Corelli paused and pursed his lips as if he had something to say, as if he wanted to ask them not to tell Ashworth where they had gotten the information. Then with the barest of sighs he stood back, balanced his weight on both feet, and said nothing. Evelyn thought she could read the set of his jaw—a professional, the son of a self-made man, he would answer to no one. Not even one of his best customers.

Their sense of accomplishment melted away like a spring snow by the third massive, overbright, crowded home-improvement store. Chains were heavy, cold, and uncooperative. People who inhabited chain aisles were heavy, cold, and pushy. Chain-aisle salesmen were more interested in talking to burly auto mechanics who wanted to buy the half-inch links in order to install a chain hoist in their garage for removing engines than in helping a hapless couple who probably wouldn't know a decent chain if they tripped over it.

Then David would flash his badge and the chain-aisle boy would grow sullen or intensely curious and tell them nothing or ask them everything, respectively. They learned that chains came in decorator, twist, straight, and passing links, along with a smaller version called jack chain. The chain from the murders formed the twist design, which meant the chain would lie flat against a level surface.

With this slow process they assembled a collection of chains of the same approximate size and formation as the ones in the cement block. The backseat of David's car slowly filled up with brown paper bags covered with black marker, all of which made complaining noises when he took a corner too sharply.

"Don't worry," she told him when he glanced in the rearview mirror. "This is just part of our Other Duties As Assigned."

"If you don't mind my asking—"

"What's a girl like me doing in a place like this? Or, as I put it, what kind of sick human being wants to do this for a living?"

"You said it." He grinned. "I didn't."

A new noise joined the fray.

"My stomach," Evelyn confessed.

"Mine agrees. Let's get some lunch. Pizza Hut okay?"

"Pizza," she said solemnly, "is nature's perfect food." After they settled in the restaurant and ordered, she continued her story. "I just sort of fell into the job. Most people in this line of work do. I had planned to be a chemist like my father. It took me a while to finish school, what with getting married and all. Then one day my biology professor took our class on a field trip to the ME's office and I just fell in love. This dingy building, these bizarrely cheerful workers, and all these stories. You'd think the victims would all seem the same after a while, but that's not true. They were all individuals when they were alive and they're still individuals, with a story to tell. Anyway, it was a chance to work on mysteries, follow the clues, and yet I never have to wrestle a suspect to the ground or interview his cop-hating girlfriend."

"Yeah, that's always a pleasure."

"I never looked back."

"What does your family think of it?"

"Rick didn't care as long as I brought home a paycheck. Angel thinks it's gross. My mother is supportive and worried in equal amounts. My father thought it was great. He pretty much thought any-thing I did was great, though."

David snorted. "*That* must be nice. My dad thought anything I did was idiotic. Problem was, he was right." Evelyn opened her mouth to argue, but he rolled on. "I intended to go to college, major in business, anything just so I wouldn't wind up at the mill like my dad. But the day before graduation I went to pick up my girlfriend and found her making out with my best friend. Kind of a shock to the system when you're only eighteen."

"It's a shock to the system at any age."

"So of course I had to make it even worse." He grinned at her with a painfully self-deprecating smile. "I joined the Marines. I figured an idiot like me could at least be a warm body between our citizens and the violent world outside."

"Boot camp must have been hard on a kid of eighteen."

He dropped the grin. "It was a damn sight easier than seeing the disappointed look in my father's eyes every time I raised my head."

"He was hard on you?"

"No, he's—he's a kindhearted guy. Unfortunately that just made me feel worse. So you see how I know about second-guessing past decisions." He had made the same comment after Evelyn revealed her past relationship with Darryl Pierson. "I've spent my life to date doing just that."

"But why a cop?"

"Another warm body."

"Protecting us," she pointed out. His chin set more firmly and he looked away.

"Pizza's here."

To smooth over their mutual confessions, they talked about the case. She gave him a list of fiber samples to collect, including the carpet at Lia's office, her boyfriend's apartment, and her boyfriend's car. "And not just the interior of his car—his trunk."

"Okay." David nodded and scribbled illegible notes in a small notebook.

"Just cut off a thread or two. You don't have to cut a hole in their carpet."

"Would I do that?" he asked innocently.

"I don't want to know." She popped another piece of double-cheese-and-pepperoni into her mouth, using a knife and fork, a practice on which David said he frowned. He glanced at her quickly emptying plate.

"Nature's perfect food?"

"It has all four food groups—grains, meats, dairy products, and vegetables."

"Vegetables?"

"Tomato sauce."

"I see."

"I could eat it for breakfast, lunch, and dinner," Evelyn said.

"How do you keep that figure?"

"I eat steamed vegetables for breakfast, lunch, and dinner. Why do you think this is such a treat?" She snagged another piece of garlic bread, thinking that no matter what Mrs. Anderson thought, this was not a date. They were discussing the case, right? "There's no connection between Durling and Destiny Pierson?"

"Not that we can see. He's never in her part of town, and there are no obvious common denominators. For that matter, there's still no connection between Lia and Destiny Pierson. As near as we can tell, the two girls never met. They didn't go to the same school, church, or hairdresser. Lia Ripetti's never been in the Beat Club in her life. Destiny wouldn't be caught dead on Emory Road. Neither of them frequented the park where they were found. Neither of them seemed to be afraid and neither changed their habits or routines in the past few weeks. Destiny Pierson had been featured in *Cleveland Magazine* last May, but no one had ever heard of Lia Ripetti."

"Why do you think Mario Ashworth bought her an expensive ring?"

"Only one reason I can think of. Same reason he gave her a job. So maybe she threatened to tell the missus, and he's as likely to take orders from her as from your average third grader. So he gets her out of his life—for good."

"That would all make sense. Except . . . what possible reason would he have to kill Destiny?"

David thought. "There could be some dirty dealings between the mayor and Ashworth that we could never prove or guess at. There always are at that level, and I'm not being a paranoid conspiracy theorist here. I mean there *always* are. So the mayor double-crosses him and Ashworth kills his daughter."

"Not a chance."

As if choosing his words with care, he said, "Because you don't think your . . . old friend could be involved with someone like Ashworth?"

"Because if he knew Ashworth killed his daughter, he'd stop at nothing to get him back." Evelyn spoke with conviction, eyes glittering. *And he wouldn't ask me for information if he already had it.* "Even if it brought his career down."

David held her gaze for a moment, then shrugged. "I didn't really buy it, either. Not even Mario Ashworth would dare a high-profile killing like this; the one thing he isn't is stupid. Besides, from everything I've been told, the mob kills you, you get two bullets in the back of the skull. They don't do over-the-top dramatic stuff like this. I can't shake the feel that this is a nutcase, a serial. Someone who isn't killing for profit or over a business deal. He kills because he likes it." He shook his head, black hair falling over his eyes. "And while we're getting nowhere, he's somewhere out there picking his next victim."

Evelyn shuddered. "Let's hope not."

"Why should he stop? He's doing okay so far. The Metroparks can keep him supplied with rivers and bridges until next autumn."

"No one else has turned up."

"Unless we send a dive team through every body of water around here—how do we know? We found these two by accident. How many other corpses are slowly rotting through their chains?"

Evelyn shivered again and abandoned her garlic bread.

David reached over and put his hand over hers. "I'm sorry. I didn't mean to ruin your lunch."

"Very little could ruin pizza for me," she insisted, but he didn't seem fooled by the flippant tone of her voice. "It's . . . well, I'm used to seeing every kind of death there is. I don't think about it. I'll tell you a secret: When you work with dead people, you convince yourself that everyone died quickly. Shot—okay, maybe they bled out, but they were probably unconscious. Car accident—probably never knew what hit them. An unattended death at home—must have died in their sleep. If I really think about it, I know it can't always be true, so I just don't think about it. But this—this is different."

He nodded and left his hand where it lay. It felt warm and comforting over hers.

"I just keep wondering what it felt like, to see that cement on your feet and hear the water and know you were down to the last few minutes of life. It's not just drowning, it's *freezing* and drowning. The water had to be like being stabbed with icicles, and yet not cold enough to let you die instantly or to numb the pain when you couldn't hold your breath any longer."

He removed his hand. "Were they conscious? Can we be sure of that?"

"Anything else?" interrupted the rounded high-school-age waitress as she refilled Evelyn's Diet Coke.

"No, thanks. That's a good question, David. I think there would be more signs of a struggle if they were conscious, either before or after they went into the water. Both of them had some scrapes on their hands, but I think that's from when they were placed on the edge of the bridge. They had some bruises from the chains around their neck and their wrists. Destiny had minor scratches from clawing her way out of the river. But there were no head injuries sufficient to cause unconsciousness, and there were no bruises where you would expect them if the girls were overpowered—like on their upper arms, their necks, or their face."

"So he probably put a gun to their face and told them to behave."

"I would still expect more bruising around the wrists. You think he would have sat there the whole time the cement hardened?"

"Obviously he didn't, since Destiny loosened her legs enough to slip out once he pushed her over."

"But Lia Ripetti didn't."

"Maybe Lia just couldn't get out of the chains. I still don't know how Destiny did it."

"No." Evelyn shook her head. "I examined her legs while they were still in the cement. That girl was *stuck,* chains or no chains. How long would it take for it to harden?"

"I talked to a guy in Street Crimes who does cement work on the side. He said a couple of hours, with the quick-drying kind."

"So either she couldn't move while the cement dried, or she had been knocked out."

The waitress left the check, which David grabbed. "I'm using your professional services, I can at least provide lunch. Destiny could have been slipped some Rohypnol in the bar; that could have made her complacent enough to grab her off the street without a cry for help. But what about Lia?"

"Durling could have slipped her something—they ate together. That would mean he either killed her or is working with someone who killed her."

"An accomplice? That's not likely, is it?"

"The Hillside Strangler case," she reminded him. "But no, it's not likely."

"Could he smother them until they passed out?"

She thought. "Possibly. They would have petechial hemorrhaging—that's broken blood vessels in their eyes, but they would anyway from the drowning and, in Destiny's case, the strangling. So it wouldn't be conclusive under these circumstances. If he'd smothered them, they'd still fight for a while first, and I'd expect to see at least a few bruises on their face, maybe a cut on the inside of their lip."

"Couldn't he have something on a cloth or in his hand that would knock them out?"

"Like in old detective novels?" Evelyn grinned. "Yeah, ether or chloroform would work, though they'd leave burns on the face. I have Ed working on it."

"Who's Ed?"

"The best-kept secret of the Toxicology Department."

David paused. "I know it's selfish, but what really bothers me the most is that this guy might simply pick up and move to another city, and we'll never catch him. I'll never solve the case."

"Don't even think it." Evelyn shuddered.

"At least your career isn't riding on it. Besides, you're a scientist. You love puzzles, right?"

"Not puzzles," she corrected. "I like stories. And if I can't know the ending, I lose interest. And don't be so sure my career isn't affected by our conviction rate." Absently she tied her napkin in a knot. "This guy can't leave on us. He just can't."

David patted her hand again. "I think the waitress wants us to go. She's hovering."

Evelyn rubbed her abdomen. "I have a feeling I'm going to regret having three pieces instead of two."

"Well, if you get food poisoning, you can probably buy this place." He stood up and pulled on a leather jacket with languid movements that caught the attention of two young women at the opposite table. "Coming?"

Evelyn looked up at him, her skin abruptly pale. "David? Didn't you tell me her supervisor said that Lia Ripetti had come down with food poisoning?"

"Yeah. Only time she missed work."

"Bad enough to go to the hospital?"

"Yeah."

Evelyn felt an ill wind blow through her heart. "*Which* hospital?"

David pensively consulted his notebook, then looked at her with both fear and a frightening kind of thrill in his eyes. "Riverside."

CHAPTER

23

THE STAFFING COORDINATOR'S DESK at Riverside Hospital could have been declared a monument to nonconformity. Files that appeared to be in imminent danger of sliding to the floor at any moment had managed to gather dust. Sticky notes of every conceivable size and color clung precariously to a plaster figure emblazoned with *You don't have to be crazy to work here . . . but it helps.* The coordinator's stained smock sported cartoon cats and bore only half a hem. She took a long drag on her cigarette and blotted the stub in an ashtray, placed defiantly in front of a "No Smoking" sign.

"Don't know if I'm supposed to tell you this," she said in a voice suspiciously like Mrs. Anderson's. "I don't mind, understand, I just don't want to get reprimanded."

"We just want someone's work schedule." David gave her a sweet, earnest smile that didn't come close to fooling her. "Not their medical records."

"It's still records." She looked at Evelyn, who huddled in a folding chair with her sweater pulled tightly around her body. The hospital's interior had not warmed any since her last visit. "Well, what the hell. Who did you want to know about?"

Before he could answer, a teenage girl in a candy-striper uniform leaped through the doorway. "Letitia!" she said breathlessly. "When do I work next?"

"Thursday and Friday. Six to nine."

"Great, thanks." The girl disappeared in a puff of youthful energy. Evelyn looked at the staffing coordinator with new interest.

"How did you *do* that?"

"Real good memory. And a healthy concern for job security. Anyone who tried to take over for me would get lost in here, never to be seen again."

"James Neal," David told her. "He's a nurse. I think he said he's a floater. Did he work on October twenty-eighth or twenty-ninth?" Admissions had already told them the dates of Lia Ripetti's hospitalization.

That proved too much even for Letitia's memory. She pulled a heavy blue binder to the edge of her desk and balanced half of it on her knees while she flipped the pages over. The resulting wind denuded the plaster statue of half its remaining sticky notes.

"Let's see. He worked in ER on the twenty-eighth, eleven to three, and in OR three on the twenty-ninth."

Evelyn shivered.

Lia Ripetti came in to the emergency room on the night of October 28. They could not tell if James Neal took care of her without access to her medical records, but the ER consisted of only four exam areas. He had to see her even if he had not worked on her.

David asked the woman to check the night Destiny Pierson came in with her broken finger, and just as Neal had said, he had worked that night on her floor. Then she added, "He's on six right now, if you want to go talk to him. Pediatric unit. He's always a big hit up there." She gave them a curious look, obviously dying to know what was going on but too proud to ask. "He gets off at three."

"Maybe we'll do that," David said. They thanked the staffing co-ordinator and made their way to the elevator.

"It's nothing substantial, really." He spoke as if trying to keep a lid on his rising hope. "A whole lot of people pass through this hospital every day, it's not surprising two would have the same nurse. But it's the only thing we've found so far that the two girls definitely had in common."

"And Angel." Fear spread rapidly through Evelyn.

David turned to her, the ebullience wiped off his face. "What?"

"Angel has the same denominator. Neal took care of her, fussed over her, made her laugh." Her voice rose with every word. "God! It's how he's picking his victims! They come in here, he's got access to their address, phone number, next of kin, their damn cell phone number!"

"Where is Angel?"

At least he didn't try to reassure her, tell her everything would be all right or not to overreact. "She's at her father's."

"Then she's safe." He held her with one hand on each shoulder. "Neal wouldn't be able to find his house, would he?" The elevator doors opened and they were surrounded by four children with one harried mother.

Over their excited chatter Evelyn tried to think. Had Rick's address been included on the ER admitting form? She didn't think so. Phone number, maybe. "I guess not."

"Then don't worry. She'll be okay. Neal must see a lot of pretty teenagers every week, that doesn't mean he kills all of them."

The children's mother gave him a startled look and wildly pushed buttons until the elevator stopped, herding her brood out into the hallway. David and Evelyn got off at the ground floor, which smelled damply of wool overcoats and people.

"I need to get back to the office, David."

"I think you should be with us. If you do have any worries about Angel, let's let him see you. Let him figure out that your daughter is the one girl he should stay away from unless he's got a death wish." He stepped outside the automatic doors and pulled out the antenna on his cell phone to call Riley. Evelyn remained in the warm lobby. She couldn't shake the chill she felt seeping through her blood. It wasn't fair, she thought.

I spend my life trying to thwart the forces of evil. Shouldn't I be immune to them? Is that so much to ask?

She pulled out her cell phone. As usual the display was dead. She hadn't recharged the battery.

She dug a coin out of her purse and crossed to the pay phones. She dialed Rick's number without hesitation and wondered what the hell to say when he answered. Don't let Angel out of your sight because some psycho bastard might have the hots for her. Never mind why I say that, I'll explain later.

The answering machine, with Terrie's resolutely animated voice, told her that they were not in at the moment but would call back as soon as they could.

Evelyn could not formulate a coherent message and hung up. They couldn't call her back; she would just have to try again later. If Rick had a pager, he had never given her the number. He might have given it to Angel, but of course that did not help.

Get a grip, she told herself. As long as Neal stayed up on the sixth floor, he couldn't be out murdering Angel. And if she'd gone missing before Neal's shift began hours ago, Rick would have called by now. *Calm down. Everything's fine.*

Particularly if they took Neal into custody. Then Angel would be safe.

Riley showed up fifteen minutes later, at five minutes to three, and joined them in the lobby. "Sorry it took me a while. I was on the phone with our esteemed County Prosecutor Rupert, getting the 'arrest somebody before I start to look bad' speech. Let's follow Nurse Neal home. All cars from the employee parking lot go through one exit gate. We'll wait for him there."

"We don't know what he drives."

Riley smiled, his so-sharp-I'm-scary smile, and held up a DMV report. "Yes, we do."

Outside, Evelyn slumped in the backseat. She didn't want to be there at all, but had finally agreed with David. Let Neal see her. Let him figure out that he had become suspect number one and that she knew he had a connection to her daughter. It might put him off. On the other hand, it might turn him on.

"A blue Chevy Camaro, 1997, license number 435 GHU," Riley repeated for the fourth time.

"Say Neal is our guy, Evelyn," David said to her. "Why is he doing this?"

"I'm not a behavioral scientist," she protested gently.

"Stop qualifying, you're not in court. Just give me an opinion."

"Because he's nuts, that's why. And that's my scientific opinion."

"Why cement?"

"He appreciates the classics. And he likes to keep his secrets. Unlike most of us, who are dying to blab them"—David gave her a nervous look—"he really doesn't want the bodies to be found. But he had bad luck with Lia and then Destiny escaped."

"You think there are others?" he asked.

"You can bet on it."

"What's he likely to do when we question him?" Riley asked.

"How the hell should I know?"

"Apply the scientific method."

"Okay. He kills girls, young women, small, slender. He knocks them out with something and then ties them up with chains. Conclusion: He needs the other person to be at an intense disadvantage before he's comfortable with them. He is not a brave man. He will probably crumble if you, a big guy, give him a stern look."

"Good. I can look real stern. Hey, there's—no, that's a Corvette."

"However, he's been thorough with these murders and gone to a lot of effort to do them a particular way. He's not stupid and can pay attention to detail. He may not crumble. He may be just smart enough to keep his mouth shut."

"This is him," Riley said.

He followed the car just closely enough to keep it in sight. They already knew where Neal lived—Riley had gotten that from the DMV as well—but they couldn't be sure Neal would head home. They spoke little during the trip. Once Evelyn asked what they were going to ask Neal, and both detectives said they would wing it. This did not reassure her.

CHAPTER

24

JAMES NEAL LIVED IN a small brick bungalow in Lakewood with a neat lawn under a layer of snow; this unassuming piece of real estate most likely had a six-figure value purely because of its location. They parked behind his car in the narrow driveway and knocked on the door he had entered minutes before.

Still in his printed scrubs, the young nurse answered the door and looked merely puzzled to see them. "Hi."

Riley held up a badge. "Hi, Jimmy. Can we talk to you?"

Neal's kitchen consisted of grimy fake wood cabinets, a small table, and wallpaper patterned with twining ivy. It took Neal a moment or two to figure out the relationship of Angel's mother to the police.

"You work for the ME's office?"

"Right."

"That's cool," he said. "You want some coffee?"

Always trying to be her pal, always working for her trust. "No, thanks."

As easily as if he were entertaining friends, Neal popped up, did not notice how the two cops immediately felt for their sidearms, and plucked a Diet Coke from the ancient refrigerator. "You sure? I have some broccoli-caper muffins. They're really good."

"No thank you, Mr. Neal," Riley said so firmly that Jimmy took his seat without another word. "As you may have gathered, we're investigating the two recent deaths. You were at Destiny Pierson's funeral, right?"

"Yeah." Again he told them how he had cared for her at Riverside.

"You were friends with Destiny?"

"I wouldn't say friends exactly. I didn't know her that long." He looked around the kitchen, decorated in early American bachelor, with pseudowood Formica cabinets that hadn't seen a bottle of degreaser in several years. The whole place smelled of french fries and bleach. "She was just a nice girl."

"You meet a lot of nice girls at the hospital?" David asked.

"Yeah. Like Angel." He smiled at Evelyn, then seemed hurt when she gazed at him in horror.

"How about Ophelia Ripetti?"

Neal's face went blank. "Who?"

David pulled out the picture of Lia on the hotel balcony and slid it across the table. Her face smiled up at the nurse.

Neal didn't touch the picture, but gave it his attention for a second or two. Then he began to fiddle with the scalloped edge of the tablecloth, gathering each fluted section together like a seamstress measuring material, then dropping them and starting over. "I don't know her. Why are you asking me all these things? I'm sorry Destiny's dead, but it's got nothing to do with me."

"Did you see this girl in the hospital?"

"No."

"In the emergency room, maybe?"

"No."

"Funny, because you worked that night."

Neal looked up, the first sparks of real worry igniting in his eyes. "What night?"

"October twenty-eighth."

Neal snorted. "That was *weeks* ago. How am I supposed to remember?"

"You remembered Destiny," David pointed out. He didn't mention Angel, to Evelyn's relief. If she had to listen to Neal speak her daughter's name even one more time, she would leap across the table and strangle him with her bare hands. She laced her fingers together in her lap and took a deep breath.

"I don't remember this girl. Did she break something, too?"

"She had food poisoning."

Neal shook his head. "I don't remember her. I don't remember having anyone with food poisoning lately."

"She visited your ER," David insisted.

"Lots of people do," Neal said with reasonable exasperation. "That doesn't mean I work on each one. I don't remember seeing this girl that night, if I even worked that night."

"You worked. Miss Letitia says you're quite reliable."

Neal flushed as if he'd been insulted. "I *am* reliable. I do a good job. I don't know why you guys are trying to make trouble for me, but I had nothing to do with what happened to Destiny, and I've never even seen this other girl."

"Nobody said you did." Riley's tones were smooth and utterly rational. "But both our victims were at the hospital, so we have to check out any connection between them. And so far, Jimmy, the only connection is you."

Beads of perspiration began to squeeze out of Neal's face. He forgot the tablecloth, clasped his hands together on the table as if pleading, and sat very still. "I didn't do anything. I don't know what you're talking about. I want you to go now. I don't have to talk to you if I don't want to, and I can't call a lawyer to be here because I don't have one. So you'll have to go."

"Do you use chloroform at the hospital?" Evelyn asked. She might as well take a stab at him, they weren't getting anywhere anyway.

He knocked over his Diet Coke. Then he used the edge of the green tablecloth to mop it up, giving him several seconds in which to avoid eye contact.

"Sorry," Evelyn said automatically.

"It's okay. I got the tablecloth for free anyway," he added. "What did you say?"

"Chloroform."

His eyes widened despite the pause. "N-n-n-oo," he stammered. "No one uses chloroform anymore. It's carcinogenic."

"Not even in the laboratories?" she pressed.

"I don't know. All I know is, nurses don't have anything like that. Why would we?"

She didn't answer.

"Mr. Neal—" David began.

"No. You have to go now. We're through talking."

"What's the rush?" Riley asked, settling back in his chair as if he were prepared to stay there all night. "This is just a little informational chat."

"No." Neal got up and crossed to the door. He opened it and snow rode in on a gust of arctic air. "I don't know why the hell you're trying to connect me with Destiny Pierson, but I'm not going to help you do it."

Riley didn't move. "We were hoping we could talk awhile longer, maybe take a tour of the house."

"I want a lawyer," Neal said. "I want a lawyer, I want a lawyer, I want a lawyer. You can't question me after I say that, and if you did, anything I said would be inadmissible anyway."

The front two legs of Riley's chair settled to the ground with a shuddering thump. "You watch too much TV, kid. The admissible thing only applies if you're under arrest, and you ain't."

The three got up and filed out of Neal's house. He stood as far away from them as he could and still keep one hand on the open door, as if they were diseased.

"Now what?" Evelyn demanded, as soon as the Grand Marquis's car doors slammed shut.

"He's got one thing right from TV—we can't search his house without his permission or a search warrant. We have neither."

Riley started the car. "He's hiding something."

"But what?" Evelyn asked as they reluctantly drove away from the bungalow. "He genuinely seemed not to know Lia."

"I'm not so sure," David said. "Maybe he just realized his mistake in admitting his attraction to Destiny, so he thought he'd be more prudent when it came to Lia. Besides, we only have a picture. Maybe she looked different at first—had her hair arranged differently or something."

"So now what?" Evelyn asked again.

"Now we find out as much as we can about Jimmy Neal," Riley said. "See if he's got a past, that kind of thing."

"Meanwhile, he's running around loose."

David shook his head. "We don't have enough to pick him up, Evelyn. We'll get Lia's medical records, see if he's on any of them. If not, we can talk to the other ER nurses, see if they noticed any interaction between the two. It still wouldn't be enough for a warrant."

"Yes, it will," Evelyn said. "It's a high-profile case and he's the only thing remotely like a suspect so far. It will be enough for a warrant to search his house and car. If we don't find anything else, at least I can get some fiber samples."

David looked at her. "You mean if the *mayor* gets involved, it will be enough for a warrant."

She felt betrayed. "He won't have to. I'm sure your chief wants to see this solved, and the district attorney, and the county judges."

"I'm sure they do. But not as much as the mayor. You make one phone call, and James Neal will find himself in a holding cell, won't he?"

Riley caught the malice in the air. "Now, children, clue Uncle Bruce in to what you're talking about—"

Evelyn sat up, ignoring him. "There I go again, circumventing the criminal justice system to further the interests of Darryl Pierson," she spat out.

"I don't give a shit about the criminal justice system," David said, his voice low and angry. "I do give one about blowing any chance we have of making this case stick."

Only the barrier of the car seat kept her from hitting him. "He keeps talking about my daughter!" she burst out, her voice escaping from the dam. "He keeps mentioning her name! What am I supposed to do, sit back and wait for him to look up our home address in the hospital records? You have to get a warrant *now*! Lock him up *now*!"

David looked torn, as if he vacillated between agreeing with her and worrying that she would make this case completely unprosecutable. "There's no reason to think Angel's in danger."

"There's no reason to think she's not. There were only three, maybe four days between Lia and Destiny. It's been five days since Destiny. How much longer is he going to wait?"

Riley stopped at a red light. An inexorable snow fell and the sun slipped toward the horizon. Evelyn viewed the encroaching darkness with panic. "Let me use your cell phone," she said to David.

He handed it back. "Can't you ship her off to your great-aunt Agnes or something?"

She dialed, peering at the tiny buttons in the dimming light, and muttered: "I don't have a great-aunt." Rick's number, as before, rang uselessly before the answering machine picked up. She disconnected and gave the phone to David.

"I need to go back to the ME's office," she said. "Now."

Once there, she tried Rick one more time—still no answer, but this time she left a message—and then pulled out the Beavell Scientific catalog and found the ordering information number. Through the dark lab she heard someone moving around in the back. Probably Marissa, working oddly late. She turned on the desk lamp over her blotter and dialed the phone. Thank God for twenty-four-hour customer service.

"Good evening, this is Beavell Scientific, Marla speaking, can I help you?"

"Hi." Evelyn hesitated, for she couldn't lie even as well as the average five-year-old. "I'm calling from Riverside Hospital in Cleveland, Ohio, on behalf of James Neal."

"Uh-huh." Marla made it sound like a question.

"He needs to know when he can expect his latest order of chloroform. It was supposed to be here last week and he hasn't received it yet."

"Your account number?" Marla asked without any real interest.

Evelyn's mind froze shut with panic. "Um . . . I don't have it handy. I'm filling in for another person tonight and her office is a shambles." A metal clank sounded from the back room; the mystery worker had just opened the water bath.

The customer service representative sighed, no doubt cursing customers who didn't have the sense to get the proper information together before they wasted time on the phone. But Marla, willing to go the extra mile, asked: "What is the name of your business again?"

"Riverside Hospital." Evelyn tried to keep the relief out of her voice. *Tell me what I want to know,* she inwardly promised, *and if I ever have another girl I'll call her Marla.* She could afford it—the odds of a pregnancy were none to don't even think about it.

Muted clicks sounded over the wire as Marla dutifully pulled up the Riverside account on her computer. Evelyn tried to think ahead and frantically turned pages to the *C*s.

"What did he order?"

"Chloroform."

"Item number?"

Evelyn scanned the page. "Uh . . . the anhydrous kind. The 99.9 percent pure."

A pause, and another sigh. Then the woman said, "No."

"No?"

"Nuh-uh," Marla repeated absently.

"No, it's not on its way, or no he didn't order it?"

"Who are you again?" Marla was either suddenly suspicious or just curious.

"I'm his supervisor." Evelyn made an effort to sound firm. "We're getting a little behind here and I'm trying to get rid of some of the excuses for things like missing reagents."

Marla let air pass through her nose into the receiver, no doubt to express her opinion of supervisors who complained about employees being "a little behind." "No, that's not the kind he ordered. He ordered the HPLC quality, which has .75 percent ethanol as a preservative. But he received that order a month and a half ago. If he's placed another one, we don't have it."

"And it was sent to James Neal? At Riverside Hospital?" Evelyn pressed as her eyes darted around the room to burn off a sudden burst of adrenaline. A figure in a white lab coat emerged from the back hallway.

"Yeah. James Neal, emergency room. Shipped on September twenty-third."

"Do you know who signed for it?"

"No." Marla seemed annoyed that she would ask. "You'd have to contact billing for that. They'll be in at eight A.M."

"Do you show any previous orders?"

Marla seemed to be getting very suspicious indeed, or maybe just tired. "Why?"

"Just trying to get the stockroom in order."

Another sigh, more quiet clicking. "Yes," Marla said, in the "can I go now?" voice of a child. "We shipped a hundred milliliters on July first. Is there anything else I can help you with?"

"No. Thanks very much."

She hung up. The white lab coat spoke.

"You're working late." He moved into the weak circle of light distributed by her desk lamp.

"Hi, Jason." She still heard Marla's voice in her mind. "What are you doing here?"

"Just changing over a gel. What are you—"

The phone rang, and Evelyn gave the jump of the guilty. Had Marla tracked her down so quickly? Ready to accuse her of obtaining chemical information under false pretenses. "Hello?"

"Evelyn?"

"Terrie?"

"Yeah, hi," Terrie said. "I just wanted to know—do you know where Angel is?"

CHAPTER

25

THE ROADS WERE SLICK but she didn't notice. Some particularly sympathetic angel of God kept her tires from skidding all over I-71 as she drove home at an unsafe speed. Some other angel kept the highway patrol from ticketing her, or perhaps they were too sensible to pursue her in the freezing rain.

She replayed the conversation—although *conversation* seemed too genteel a word—in her mind, once more.

EVELYN: What do you mean, where is she? She's supposed to
    be with you.
TERRIE: She was until tonight.
EVELYN: What happened tonight?
TERRIE: Well, she and her dad had a little . . . argument and
    stalked off to their respective rooms. I tried to give them
    some quiet time, and—
EVELYN: Where the hell's my daughter?
TERRIE: She left.

EVELYN: She has no car. It's freezing out. Her stitches from *Tuesday night's surgery* are still delicate. What do you mean, she *left*?

TERRIE: I'm sure she's fine. Angel's very sensible. She—

EVELYN: How long has she been gone?

TERRIE: We're not sure.

EVELYN: Terrie, I swear to all the stars in the heavens, if you don't start making sense real soon, you're going to be our next customer here, you got it?

TERRIE: There's no reason to lose your temper. I'm sure Angel walked to her friend Melissa's house. It's only on the next block, and Melissa's mom says that Melissa went out about an hour ago without telling her where or why, which frankly I don't see why she puts up with—

EVELYN: What does Melissa drive?

After she wrote down the information so she could call the Strongsville Police Department and have them put out an APB on Angel—a lieutenant on the night shift there who was grateful for a speedy gunshot-residue result would be willing to do her a favor—Evelyn asked one last question before she freed herself from the telephone to make a panicked dash to her car: Why did they argue?

Terrie clearly didn't want to answer.

"Spit it out. I need to get out of here so I can go find my daughter. What did she and Rick argue about?"

"About me. I wanted to be honest with her. I think it's important that—"

"Spit it *out*."

"I told her that her father and I had a . . . relationship before your divorce. I feel it's vital that—"

Evelyn felt her heart disintegrate into a shower of sparks, and when she spoke her voice echoed from dark, frightening places. "You told a girl four days out of the hospital that her darling father boinked you when he was still married to her mother?"

"Well, I didn't say it like—"

"Are you *nuts?*"

"I thought that you might tell her, so—"

"Listen to me, you bitch. My daughter is wandering around in the snow in a weakened physical state while a depraved psycho might be ready to check her name off his list, tortured with the thought that her own father is a lying, cheating bastard, all because you wanted to *cover your ass?*"

It took Terrie a moment to catch up with all of that, and as usual, she honed in on her most pressing point: "He didn't lie. You knew he—wait, what was that about a psycho?"

Evelyn hung up.

The trip home had taken a few lifetimes. She hadn't even gotten up from her desk and Darryl called; too upset to care, she blurted out his name in front of Jason, then told him abruptly to call her at home later. So she had hurt Darryl's feelings and given Jason more gossip fodder, and she still had to stop for gas or she wouldn't make it home at all. At the station she'd phoned her own home—no answer. This day would be the stuff of nightmares for months to come.

She pulled into her driveway, where a short skid put her rhododendron bush out of its misery, and made one more effort to calm herself. She tried unsuccessfully to pull her mind away from the satisfying image of cooking Terrie over a spit and reluctantly admitted that perhaps the woman had just tried to do the right thing. No matter what, Evelyn respected sincerity. If it happened to come with a healthy dollop of self-righteousness and a smidgen of sheer stupidity, well, no one was perfect. Besides, Angel had argued with Rick, not Terrie. Evelyn pulled her car into the garage.

She stormed into her dark house and dumped her too-heavy purse on the kitchen table, snatching up the phone. She had already pressed the talk button before she realized she had no one to call. No one could help her.

She heard a faint rustle upstairs, like a light scrape of a foot along the carpet. Evelyn froze.

It's Angel!

What if it's not?

She flew up the steps and called her daughter's name. Even if the psycho killer lurked above, at least her daughter would be with him, maybe still alive, probably still alive. She could discern no sound over the pounding of her feet.

She reached the hallway, then Angel's bedroom. She flicked on the light.

Her daughter sat on her bed, arms crossed, giving her mother a look to make her think perhaps the psycho killer would have been the better option.

Evelyn's knees gave out and she slumped against the doorjamb. "Where have you been? Everyone's looking for you. Are you hurt? Where have you been?"

Angel was unimpressed with this show of emotion.

"Where have you been?"

Her jaw set, Angel spoke. "Why didn't you tell me?"

Evelyn took a few deep breaths, then picked up her daughter's phone and dialed Rick's number. When he answered, she said, "She's here. She's home. She's okay . . . I don't know, haven't asked yet, I called you first, which frankly is damn nice of me." She hung up. "You scared the crap out of everyone, you know."

Angel continued to glare, in the white-hot intense way that only adolescent girls who truly believe in evil can glower.

"I can't believe you didn't tell me," she repeated.

"I can't believe she *did.*"

"She said you'd probably tell me, and she wanted to explain first." A preemptive strike. "And did she?"

"What?"

"Explain."

Angel's face contorted in disgust. "Yeah, they were in love, da-dee-da, all this other bullshit."

"Language," Evelyn warned automatically.

"Why didn't you tell me?"

"Because I would only have been making you miserable in order to make myself look better in your eyes. I don't consider that responsible parenting."

Angel didn't see it that way. "I deserved to know!"

"No, you didn't."

Her daughter looked at her in amazement.

"Your father and I were a married couple," Evelyn went on. "We are allowed to have things between us that no one else knows about. That is not unfair. Now Terry and your father are a married couple. They deserve to have things between them that no one else knows about. That's the way it is."

"He's a liar! He lied to you and he lied to me," Angel shouted, unable to keep up the appearance of anger rather than misery. She burst into tears and flung herself facedown on the blue-and-white quilt, her shoulders quaking as they had at ten when she was told she could not have a pony. But she wasn't ten anymore.

Evelyn moved closer, perching on the edge of the mattress, trying to guess what her daughter felt. Angel wanted to hate her father and couldn't; she wanted to blame her mother and couldn't; and she probably couldn't even decide why the whole thing bothered her so.

"Everyone does things they're not proud of later. It doesn't have anything to do with you."

"It has everything to do with me," Angel insisted between sobs. "It's my parents."

"Our divorce doesn't mean we love you any less."

"Oh, for God's sake." This annoyed Angel enough to stop her tears. "Like *that* makes everything okay."

"It makes up for a lot, yes. You'll see that when you're older."

"Could you be a little more condescending?" Angel asked between sniffs. "I mean, if you really worked at it?"

She sounds more like me every day. "People can't always be what we want them to be," Evelyn went on, stroking the long hair scattered like a raven's broken wing. "You would like to have parents that weren't divorced. I would like my father not to have smoked all those years so he wouldn't have died of lung cancer. I'm sure Rick would have preferred that his mother not walk out on her family on his fifteenth birthday. We all wish things could be different."

"In other words, tough."

"In other words, learn to forgive people for not being what you want them to be."

"*How?*"

"I wish I knew."

A trace of a smile curved Angel's mouth before she could stop it. "That's great, Mom. Give me completely impossible advice."

"Some things I can't fix," Evelyn said simply.

Back to sullen. "I'm going to move out as soon as I'm eighteen. Melissa and me are going to get an apartment."

Not after you get a load of what rent costs these days. "Okay. But just tonight, no matter how mad you are, I need you to be here, okay?"

Angel turned on her side, looking up.

"No shinnying down the windpipe, no having Melissa or JoAnn or Cindy pick you up. Please. I've had all the panicking I can take for one day."

"Okay." Angel pretended to be reluctant, but Evelyn could see that her daughter had no plans to go anywhere. Angel had not recovered completely from her surgery and after a very emotional evening looked as if she wanted nothing more than her own bed and a long, dreamless night.

Evelyn got up and reached over the single window frame for a pair of nails.

"What about you?" Angel asked.

"What about me what?" Years ago she had drilled two small holes in the middle sash of the double-hung window. She slid a nail into each hole so that neither the upper nor the lower part of the window could move.

"Do you have any other men? *Did* you have any other men? And what are you doing that for?"

"Just locking the window. Work has me a little paranoid right now.

And failing at marriage kind of put me off men, preferably forever. Go to sleep, you need it."

That Angel didn't protest gave proof of her exhaustion. Evelyn waited until her daughter had gone through her nightly routine of washing and toning her face, brushing her hair fifty times, and forcibly throwing her laundry into the hamper. When the bedsprings creaked and all was quiet, Evelyn checked the locks on every door and window, then laid two long pieces of aluminum foil down the upstairs hallway. It could not be crossed or removed without making a sufficient amount of noise. She left her bedroom door open.

The phone rang.

Evelyn dived on it, cursing whoever dared to disturb her daughter's slumber. It had to be Terrie or Rick, calling for an update. It was neither.

"Evelyn?"

"Darryl?"

"I hope it isn't too late to call."

That depends on what you mean. "No, I'm still up. I'm sorry I couldn't talk before. I had a crisis on my hands, more or less. How are you? I mean, how are you holding up?"

"Barely," he said. "I just wanted to know what you've found out."

Silence.

"You're deciding what you can tell me without getting yourself in trouble."

"That's right. I also don't want to raise any false hopes. We're following some leads. We may have a connection between your daughter and this other girl, but it may turn out to be nothing."

She expected a flurry of questions, but none came. Finally the mayor of Cleveland said, "What is it?"

"I can't really say yet. I'm sorry, but I can't. I do want to ask you a few things, though. When Destiny broke her finger, did you go to the hospital?"

He gave a sigh that sounded oddly like relief. "No. I had an important council vote to attend, and Danielle stayed with her."

"Do you remember her saying anything about their time there?"

"Like what?"

"Anything at all."

Obediently Darryl recalled: "Dani said Destiny liked the osteopath and he assured her that Destiny would be unscarred, not crippled, and untraumatized. She also said that the food in the cafeteria appalled her and they had some obnoxious boy for a nurse."

It's not fair, Evelyn thought, *that just as I begin to relax for the first time in three hours I have to tense up all over again.* "Really?"

"I can tell that means something to you. Why?"

"Darryl, I don't know what to think. I'm completely exhausted, and as far as the case goes, we have all sorts of little facts that don't add up to any specific answer. All I can tell you is that we're working on it as hard as we can."

The silence lengthened, as if he were making a decision. And he did. "Tell me."

"Darryl, I—"

"Tell me. I don't give a damn about ethics or justice or the proper way of doing things. Just tell me."

"We're not sure of anything yet!"

"Then tell me what it is you're not sure of."

"No," she said stubbornly.

"I need this, Evelyn. This was my *daughter*. Can you imagine what it would be like if Angel—"

"What would you do with the information anyway, Darryl? There's nothing you can do! If you tried to interfere, he could use that as a basis for appeal or to have evidence thrown out. Is that what you want?"

"I want to know!"

The time for reason had passed. "No."

"Damn it, you used to love me! You told me every day how much you loved me!"

"And what did it get me?" she slammed out. "Dropped to the side like a used condom because you loved your ambition more!"

Silence. Then: "Fair play. Now you love your job more."

A soft click told her he had hung up.

Just as well, she thought, that they finally made the break that neither one of them had the courage for seventeen years earlier. It was too bad. A lot of things were too bad.

As she climbed into bed, she thought that she didn't really believe that Jimmy Neal or whoever their killer might be would come to kidnap her daughter. Strongsville was a good distance from downtown Cleveland and Warrensville Heights (but right off the freeway) and Jimmy had been genuinely scared by their visit that afternoon (but it might just put him over the edge). He had to encounter a lot of girls at the hospital (but how many were beautiful teenagers?), so why Angel? He would almost certainly believe that the police would now follow him if he left his house (unless he could lose them). Besides, Evelyn was home and Lia and Destiny had both been alone (though Destiny had been with a group of friends). No logical reason existed to worry over Angel.

All the same, when it came to her daughter she had no intention of being logical.

Evelyn slept through her alarm the next morning, not waking until Angel came in, turned it off, and shook her, saying, "Mom? Why is there foil in the hallway?"

CHAPTER

26

EVELYN'S MORNING COULD BE described as merely lousy if the Sahara could be described as just a patch of sand. She had no time for makeup or breakfast. It took five tries to wake her daughter since, after discovering the foil, Angel had gone back to sleep. Only the threat of having ice water dumped on her head convinced her to emerge so that Evelyn could drop her at Melissa's house. If Angel had briefly considered forgiving her mother for concealing her father's behavior, this hour before dawn changed her mind.

It took fully an hour and a half to get to work through the slush-filled freeways. Her favorite radio station had fired its morning program personnel overnight and replaced them with two goons who thought they were funny. The last thing Evelyn wanted to hear first thing in the morning was a man who never matured past the age of fourteen and thought he was funny. She would have preferred even her daughter's sullen silence.

The news did not improve matters. The media played Destiny Pierson's murder—Lia Ripetti did not command the same attention—

to the hilt and talk-show callers were positive the killer would prove to be a Ku Klux Klan member, the rival mayoral candidate from the last election, or a rogue cop protected by a conspiracy of his fellow officers. In other news, the council would vote today on the new ME's office contract. The mayor had already postponed the vote twice and council members were determined to pin him down, family tragedy or no family tragedy. Evelyn turned the radio off and wedged her car into a space at the edge of the lot.

Then Marissa called in sick and Jason took the last cup of coffee before he closeted himself in Tony's office. Through the glass window she watched their huddled conversation, resenting her lack of caffeine. But at least it kept both of them out of her way.

She walled herself up in a cubbyhole with the stereo comparison microscope and her bags of chains. It went more quickly than she expected, since most were easily eliminated by their size, thickness, and shape; some links were twisted, some were flattened at both ends, some were flattened and grooved to lie flat when extended. Two sets, one from Home Depot and the other from Home Warehouse, seemed to match the chains found on the victims. A company called SteelWorks manufactured the chain from Home Depot and George Industries made the chain from Home Warehouse, but that didn't necessarily mean they hadn't come from the same vat at the same factory. Manufacturers often sold the same items under different names. This allowed retail stores to have their own distinct brands and created the illusion of competition. X-ray diffraction, or EDX, could analyze the steel further. The FTIR wouldn't work—the beam would simply reflect off the shiny steel instead of penetrating. Unfortunately, they didn't have an EDX, and without further elemental analysis she would not be able to say for sure where the killer had bought his chains.

She set the purchased chains aside and returned to the evidence chains. The ones used on Destiny and Lia had been excavated from the concrete. Some of the end links had deep scratches on them, as if he had tried to cut the chain at that point, then gave up and cut a different link instead. If she found tools she could compare the marks.

The short chain used to strangle Destiny Pierson matched the others in every respect, so it was not likely that she had escaped one madman's icy grave just to run into another psychopath down the road.

Surrounded by chains, Evelyn suppressed a shudder. They were so hard, unchanged, impersonal. Heavy and cold. She couldn't imagine how it would feel as the links bit into the girls' skin, pulling them into the freezing water. Or maybe she didn't want to.

"Didn't have breakfast, did you?" Riley asked David as he watched the younger detective pilfer a third banana-nut bagel from a bag next to the scarred coffeepot. This earned David a dark look from the unit secretary.

"I haven't had breakfast in two weeks." He slumped into his seat and glanced around the unit. An untidy convention of desks that should have been sold at auction twenty years earlier crowded a view of the parking garage. David's chair had a broken axis and lacked one wheel, but today he didn't care. "I also need some energy. I couldn't sleep, so I began the day at an obscenely early hour."

"Really? Why?"

"I had to do something while I waited for you," he said slyly. "So I looked at Lia Ripetti's medical chart."

Riley eyed him over a chipped coffee cup that bore an embossed gold shield labeled *Metro-Dade Police Training Facility*. "You'd have to have a court order to get those."

"I got it. Judge Fallon is a health nut. Gets up and jogs around the John Carroll U. track at five every morning. I caught him on the fourth lap. I think I pulled a muscle, but he signed the warrant."

"And did Riverside turn over the file?"

"I bought the senior records clerk a cup of coffee. That and the court order softened her considerably."

Riley sniffed in suspicion, as if surprised that someone with a reputation that smelled as bad as David's would show such gumption. "You've been busy."

"You're telling me." He basked in a moment of self-satisfaction. "Did you know the freakin' birds start singing at four A.M.? Four! I thought for sure they'd all be in Florida or something, but no. Pitch-dark outside and they—"

"So?" Riley demanded.

"So, what?"

"Did Jimmy Neal work on Lia Ripetti?"

"I'll assume you mean in the medical sense. Yes. He did her pre-liminary history, took her vitals, and, I presume, held her head while she puked her guts out. His signature is on five of her eleven forms. He very definitely met Lia Ripetti."

Riley's brown eyes took on an unhealthy gleam. "Well, well."

"I think Evelyn might be right. We do have enough to pick him up."

With deceptive calm, Riley said, "Incidentally, you leave her the hell alone. She's worth ten of you. Just because you're jealous over some ex-boyfriend of hers—"

"I'm not jealous."

"—doesn't mean you can pick on her. She knows what she's do-ing. She just worries about her kid."

Two cops across the aisle busied themselves with their desktops. The secretary wrapped up a phone call to be able to listen. Everything he said, David knew, would be taken down and used against him.

"I know she's worried," he snapped. "I know she's the Homicide Unit's best friend and I'm some screwup—"

"That's putting it mildly."

"That's the whole reason I can't have this case fall apart." David hated the desperation he heard in his own voice. "I need it."

Riley just stared at him for a long moment. The secretary started to type.

"Okay," he said. "Let's go."

"To see Jimmy Neal?"

"To talk to County Prosecutor Rupert."

"Why? Jimmy Neal could be sliding out of town as we speak."

"He had all night if he wanted to slide. We need Rupert's support if we're going to move on Neal, not that I'd ask Rupert for so much as a cigarette or take it if he offered one, which the cheap SOB would never do." He gave David a surly grin. "You said you didn't want to hit a foul here."

David sighed.

They took the walkway from the police headquarters to the Justice Center. As they walked, David added that he had called Lia's boyfriend, Durling, about the ring Evelyn found in her pocket.

"You really have been busy."

"According to him, Lia's always had it—meaning she's had it longer than six months, which is how long they've been dating. It belonged to her mother."

"That's a sweeter story than the truth."

"You think she and Ashworth broke up, that's why she's dating Durling?"

"Who knows? Maybe her and Ashworth aren't star-crossed lovers, he's just a handy source of income for a working girl. Or he doesn't make it an optional part of her duties—she wants to keep her job, she puts out."

"Obviously Durling doesn't know, so that just leaves Ashworth, and he's got no reason to tell us anything. Besides which, if Neal killed her, it's all a moot point."

"I'll bet the point will never be moot to Mrs. Ashworth," Riley pointed out.

The prosecutor's offices were on the ninth floor. Their lobby—they *had* a lobby—had a wide receptionist's desk and overstuffed chairs, but David felt maliciously glad that the magazines were a year out of date and the carpet had a stain.

The prosecutor's office, large and airy, boasted a corner view of Cleveland from nine stories up and unstained carpeting, but a curious lack of adornment. The walls were bare, and not out of respect for the wallpaper. The shelves held a haphazard row of legal volumes and the desk hid beneath files and folders. Three filing cabinets, one with a dent in it, and three chairs of worn leather completed the room. David couldn't decide if he found this appealing or simply odd.

What the room lacked in decor, it made up for in personnel. Prosecutor Rupert had an entourage, in the form of a slim, dark-haired man with a permanently harried expression, a pasty-faced assistant, and a giggly blond girl, obviously a college student intern whose parents, David hoped, were keeping a very close eye on her work activities. Impressionable young things and the weaselly Rupert could not be a healthy mix.

"Detectives!" Rupert greeted them as if he assumed they were bringing good news. Where he would have gotten that impression, David couldn't guess. He explained about James Neal and watched as the intern's eyes lit up with visions of Court TV. Rupert wasn't quite as impressed.

"It's not enough for an arrest." For once he made a non–camera face. "It's enough to bring him down to the station as a potential material witness. But it's not enough for an arrest."

"But—"

He held up an imperial hand, which only inflamed David more. "All you've managed to establish is that he met both victims. You haven't tied him to the location or the murder weapon—I mean the cement and the chains."

"He's lying about something," Riley said. "Just ask the right questions and it's obvious."

"I can't list a hunch on the arrest warrant. Even if you arrested him, you wouldn't want him to come up for trial while you're still scrambling to figure out exactly what, if anything, he's lying about." Rupert didn't mention how stupid he'd look if they arrested one person, only to find out that they were wrong, or worse yet, that they were right but lacked the evidence to convict. Rupert wanted his ducks in a row before he took a shot. "Good luck, gentlemen. I'm sure you're on the right track."

Riley sighed in defeat. David said nothing.

"Just keep on it," the prosecutor advised in a portentous tone. "This case can make or break a lot of people."

"Gee." Riley led their way out of the lobby toward the elevators. "What do you think he meant by that?"

"I think he meant 'solve this in a hurry or I'll have your badges,' but he didn't want to sound like a total asshole in front of his groupies."

"At least we have permission to lean on Neal."

"Will he back us up if Neal complains?" David asked.

"If he's sure Neal's the guy and he sees a high-profile conviction in the future, sure. If not, he never heard of us."

"How comforting."

"Remember the rule," Riley said. "If you need love and support, join the fire department."

Between the fourth and third floors, David's pager went off. When they cleared the parking garage he called the number, and Evelyn told him what she had learned about Neal's chloroform order from Beavell Scientific.

"I wish I'd known this last night."

"I had more immediate problems to deal with last night," she said icily.

"What's the matter? Is Angel all right?"

He could hear the ice melt over the phone. "She's okay. She gave me a little scare but everything's cool now. I farmed her out to a friend so I could breathe easy today. Thanks."

"For what?"

"For asking."

He told Riley about the chloroform.

"Why?" Riley asked. "What would you have done if you knew last night?"

"Camped outside Mr. Neal's house, that's what I would have done."

"Can Evie prove he used chloroform on our victims?"

"Not yet."

"Then cheer up, it still wouldn't be enough for an arrest warrant. We're loading the bases, but we're not quite ready to swing." With one hand on the wheel he lit a cigarette with the other, traveling the ice-covered streets as if it were the middle of July. "How do we know Nurse Neal isn't at work, comforting the afflicted?"

"Because I called. Letitia says he isn't scheduled until tomorrow night. Another item I wish I'd asked earlier. If he wanted to leave town, he'd have two days' head start before anyone missed him."

He needn't have worried. James Neal was at home, but not alone. After they knocked on the kitchen door, banged on the kitchen door, and pounded on the kitchen door, James Neal opened the door and practically threw himself into their arms.

"Help me!" he cried. "He's in there!"

Cursing, David ran past the young man and entered the neat living room just in time to see the front door swing shut. He burst through it only to be stopped short—the guy had taken a second to lock the screen door, and David nearly decapitated himself trying to slam through the frame. He rattled the latch in frustration for a split second before taking out the whole door with a high kick, eyes trained on a solitary figure moving across Neal's postage stamp of a front yard.

A black man in a long black coat and a black hat, he moved way too fast for someone that big. It shouldn't have been possible, but he got in a car parked on the opposite side of the street and drove away in a squeal of rubber before David reached the middle of the yard. He saw only a black Continental, last year's model, sporting a license plate beginning with BY. David cursed, heaved a deep breath after the unexpected aerobics, cursed again, and got his radio out of the car. He called in an APB for the immediate area on his description, or what little of a description he had. The man had not turned around once.

He stomped into the kitchen, where Riley looked down at Nurse Jimmy Neal, his face a bright though fading shade of fuchsia.

"Jeez, can you shut the door?" were the first coherent words out of Neal's mouth. "It's freezing in here."

David obliged, but not gently. The door shut with window-rattling force; then he took only two steps to get in Neal's face. "What's going on?"

Neal looked at him, literally crying. Enormous tears escaped from his eyes, his chin trembled, his nose ran. He wiped it with the sleeve of a faded CSU sweatshirt. The unmistakable smell of urine wafted up from stained pants.

"Who was that guy?" David asked.

"I don't know," Neal whispered, his face riven by terror. "I don't know. He came in here just before you guys got here, and he said—"

"What did he say?"

"I don't know."

"C'mon, Neal!" Riley shouted, and leaned in further until he and David were fixated on the boy like a pair of jackals over a wounded antelope. "Tell us what's going on here!"

"It didn't make any sense!" he protested. "That's what I mean. He just walked into my house and said he wanted to ask me something and I'd better tell him the truth."

"So what did he ask?"

"He said people who didn't tell him the truth regretted it. Such a simple thing to say—I remember thinking that those words were almost polite. It was the *way* he said it, as if all the tortures of hell would await anyone who refused him, as if nothing I could possibly meet in the rest of my life could be as frightening as this man." Neal sobbed. "And he didn't have to say any of that, because I already knew it. I knew it as soon as I looked at him."

"So what did he ask, Neal?"

"Nothing," Neal said. Riley put a hand on his shoulder. He did not mean to comfort and did not. Neal trembled so violently that his very bones rattled, but he persisted. "Nothing. You guys pounded on the door and he ran out."

Riley and David looked at each other. "So after all this buildup about not lying to him, he never got to ask his big question?"

"Yeah."

"Who was he?"

"I don't know."

"We got our own ways of dealing with guys who don't tell us the truth, Neal."

"I don't *know*. I never saw him before in my life." He looked up at David. "Please, you gotta believe me."

"I don't."

"Look, I want to change clothes. I . . . wet myself. You gotta understand, this is the scariest thing that's ever happened to me. And he didn't even raise his voice."

David's mind moved so fast it hurt. If he hadn't known better, he would have sworn that Jimmy Neal's confusion rivaled his own. "In a minute, Neal. For now, you tell me again the situation here. This guy you don't know just happened to choose this morning to pay you a visit, to ask you an important question that he never gets a chance to ask. And you have no idea who he is or what he may have wanted?"

Neal nodded with pathetic eagerness.

"Who might think you know anything worth telling?" Riley asked.

"Your drug connection? Are you moving stuff out of the hospital?"

"No!" Neal insisted, and on this he didn't seem confused at all.

"Someone's husband? Father? You taking advantage of all those pretty girls lying helpless in hospital beds?"

"No!"

"Maybe making them a little more cooperative with, say, some chloroform?"

Neal's eyes widened at this, worried at either the mention of chloroform or the suggestion he had molested patients, which would surely get him suspended until further investigation. How many parents, David wondered, had complained about his coming on to their daughters?

"No! I've never done anything wrong at work! I am good at my job, a hell of a lot better than those bitches in their white polyester. I don't know who this guy is," he finished, his voice calming. He took a deep, forced breath, and his eyes dried. His words grew firmer. "And I don't know what he wanted."

Riley sighed. "I'll tell you what we want, Neal. We want you to come down to the station and talk to us."

The nurse looked at them both for a long minute, and David knew, the way anyone who's ever interrogated a suspect knew, that Neal had made up his mind to tell them something. "Okay. But I'm going to change clothes first."

"I'm not real thrilled about you getting chummy with my upholstery, either," Riley said. "So go ahead. We'll be right here."

He checked the house quickly to make sure there weren't any other doors, then allowed Neal to go upstairs and get a change of clothing. David called in for a DMV report on the black Continental's partial plate. They would run a list of possibles, then narrow it to the Cleveland area. Maybe he could come up with something that way.

David believed Neal's story, which on the face of it wouldn't convince a ten-year-old. But Neal radiated genuine terror, and besides, David had a pretty good idea why a black guy in an expensive car would suddenly be interested in one James Neal.

David rocked on his feet, allowing himself a rush of satisfaction. Neal would fess up, plead out, case closed. The other Homicide cops would have to admit he had a few brain cells that weren't between his legs. Most important, no other young women would be sliding into the Cuyahoga.

The mayor would be grateful to him. Evelyn would be grateful to him, at least until she lost her job for leaking information to the mayor's office. The idea erased his satisfaction. He didn't want that to happen, but realistically couldn't stop it. Heavy fallout would occur when they traced the car to someone on the mayor's staff, and David wouldn't be able to protect her. Damn the woman. They could have been friends. They could have been a lot more than friends.

Neal returned promptly to the first floor, entered a small bathroom, and locked the door. They listened to the rustling sounds of someone's changing clothes and then heard the faucet running.

And running.

By the time Riley kicked the door down, David had raced outside and around the house to see the open window and the deep shoeprints in the slushy mud underneath it. They continued through the snow and led off to the street, where they faded out on the now-dry asphalt. Neal had escaped.

"Damn!" David shouted. His voice echoed uselessly down the street.

CHAPTER

27

"DID YOU CANVASS THE neighborhood?" Evelyn asked as she stood in James Neal's kitchen, too edgy to sit. Neal's flight had given Rupert enough for a search warrant, and she came to collect fibers from his house and car. Tony had left his office to attend, more out of curiosity than for any interest in making a professional contribution.

"Immediately. We called for backup and got more guys, searched thoroughly. A uniform finally found his trail cutting through the backyard of a house across the street, but lost it again in the woods. The trees blocked the snow and there were no tracks," Riley told her.

"Has he got a girlfriend?" Evelyn asked. "Friends? Someone who would hide him?"

"He's got two brothers," Riley answered. "Both moved out of state, but we're still checking them. If he's really on the run he wants out of the state. He's got a few girls he goes out with, a bunch of boyfriends, and four or five cousins."

"How'd you find all that out?" Tony asked.

"The fair Letitia. We grabbed his address book and patrol is contacting them, but nothing so far and who's to say they'll tell us the truth? We can't search the house of everyone he knows."

Evelyn looked at David, who looked as if he'd won the lottery and then lost the ticket. She couldn't help but feel sorry for him; he had tried so hard. On the other hand, a suspect in multiple murders who knew her daughter's name and address now walked free.

"So he's on the loose."

David slammed the door of the cabinet he'd been absently nosing through.

"Nobody got what they wanted here today, Evie," Riley said, in a tone that sounded suspiciously as if he were coming to David's defense.

"It's all right." Her words lacked conviction. "I've packed Angel off to her friend Melissa's house with strict instructions and our Blockbuster card. I've hidden our address books over at my mother's. Angel thinks I've completely overreacted and that she isn't in danger of anything worse than getting a C in math, but she's not in the mood to be around either of her parents right at the moment anyway."

"There's something else, Evelyn," David said, his voice trapped between misery and anger as he slumped into a kitchen chair. "Neal had a visitor here when we arrived." He explained about the strange man.

"I don't want to ask this," he went on simply, "but let's face it. Why do you suppose a big black guy would suddenly be interrogating Jimmy Neal?"

She gave all three men a blank look. "I don't know. Because he's been dealing drugs out of the hospital?"

"Too well-dressed," David said. "Why would an upstanding-looking black man suddenly be scaring the shit out of Jimmy Neal?"

Tony's head did the tennis-match swivel, fascinated. Riley looked ill.

Evelyn began to feel even worse than she already felt, without knowing why. There were too many sickening factors to the situation to even tell which one held the pole position. "I don't know. What are you asking me for?"

"Come on!" David shouted, and jumped to his feet so fast he knocked his chair backward. "Don't be stupid. Who else would take such an interest, who would have the information and the muscle to make Neal pay for killing his daughter?"

"Darryl? You think Darryl sent this guy over? How would Darryl know about Neal, anyway?"

"Because you told him."

This can't be happening, she thought. *This can't be happening.* Finally she spluttered: "I didn't tell Darryl. Besides, Rupert knew, too. You told him."

"We had just left Rupert. Besides, Rupert isn't his ex-girlfriend."

"He's more in bed with him than I'll ever be, and I'll thank you to stop throwing my past in my face. It has nothing to do with . . . Besides, why would Darryl go after Neal if he thought we were going to arrest him anyway?"

Riley interrupted. "Evelyn—"

"Don't be so naïve." David looked around as if he wanted to pace but couldn't find enough room. "Pierson doesn't care about a trial. He just wants revenge."

"I didn't tell Darryl anything about James Neal. Do you want me to repeat that? I didn't tell—"

"You talked to him last night," Tony said in a puff of cigarette smoke.

The other three turned to him.

"Well, yes, I did." Evelyn lost some of her forcefulness. "But how . . . oh, Jason." She gave Tony a look usually reserved for the gunk left at the bottom of a garbage disposal. "Your little spy."

"Did you tell him about the investigation?" Riley asked tonelessly.

"I—I did ask him about Riverside Hospital," she admitted. "I just asked what Danielle's impressions of the place had been. He mentioned an obnoxious male nurse. But I didn't ask any more or give him any idea of our interest in the nurse. That was it." She looked at them one by one, and said what she never thought she'd say, the trite phrase repeated in every B movie. "You have to believe me." Her desperation didn't feel trite to her. She couldn't lose her daughter. But she also couldn't lose her job.

She didn't deserve this. Did she? *Had* Darryl figured it out from her question? He always said she'd make a lousy actress, that she couldn't help communicating her innermost feelings. *Was* it her fault?

No. Not even the mayor could have tracked James Neal down that quickly, with nothing but her vague question to go on. They were wrong.

The silence seemed as loud and irritating as nails on a blackboard. She began to stalk out when Riley spoke. "It can't be helped at this point anyway. What's done is done. The ball is out of the field."

She turned. "I didn't tell him. Don't you believe me?"

The old cop looked at her for a long moment. "Yes, I believe you, Evie," and she wanted to hit him for being so completely unconvincing. She couldn't look at David. Tony remained scarily silent.

"Fine." She retrieved her kit from the county station wagon.

Three hours later they had covered the house from top to bottom and found very little. Evelyn had photographed, cataloged, and examined everything she could find from the loft over the garage space to Neal's collection of *Playboys*, but there were no chains, no cement, and no chloroform. She had collected a number of tools, particularly ones strong enough to cut chain. Neal may have gotten rid of the cement and the chains, but he would not have thrown away the tools used to cut them. She could still compare the tool marks. David appeared in the doorway as she gathered swatches of the bedroom carpeting. She ignored him. She would be civil and professional, but in her mind he had been labeled persona non grata forever.

"Find anything?" he asked.

Civility and professionalism evaporated like spring fog. "Get bent."

He seemed unsurprised. "I should be saying that to you, frankly.

This is my first big investigation and it's about to be declared a disaster area."

She concentrated mightily on labeling the manila envelope.

"It's not that I blame you. I don't want to see this come back on you, but once they trace that Continental to Darryl's staff . . . We all do favors for friends. I have, too. I know how it goes."

She placed the carpet fiber inside and sealed the flap with tape.

"I mean, I *really* know how it goes," he whispered, his voice strangled with bitterness.

She looked at him, but he stared at the floor; only the tremor of his shoulders gave witness to the hidden tension. A transparent struggle took place to hold back something that had been held back for far too long, and when it broke, the words surged forth on a wave of self-loathing.

"It started with a birthday party," he began. "Just a birthday party, that's all. I worked in Vice with a guy named Jack Imler. He threw his wife a party for her fortieth birthday.

"At the time we were investigating a ring of massage parlors, busting the girls—standard Vice stuff. I could practically do it in my sleep and I'd only been there a year. But we had a tip on a child porn racket, stuff coming in from Detroit. Jack and me, we were kind of excited. Stuff like that is high profile, gets you all sorts of kudos from the higher-ups. Gets you noticed."

Evelyn waited.

"So," he went on, "I'm standing in his kitchen eating a piece of Carol's friggin' birthday cake and talking to their neighbor. A neighbor, an investment banker by trade. This guy showed up at this stupid little party in a three-piece suit."

Evelyn waited, frowning. His words took her toward the first few pangs of sympathy and she didn't like it. It would be so much easier to despise him. Her anger needed someplace to go.

"I'm in Vice, so I've got a beard and long hair and generally look like I invented the grunge look. So deep down I want to impress this guy, let him know policing is more than eating doughnuts, and maybe a little more exciting than investment banking. So I told him about this child porn thing, something that just me and Jack were working on. I didn't mention any names, I didn't give any specifics. Except Detroit, I mentioned that." He paused. "That was enough."

He looked away from her, at the wall, the ceiling, anything inanimate. "The problem was, the child porn ring happened to be one of this guy's investments. He laundered all the money it made, and he got excited about my job, all right. So excited that he shot Jack Imler the next day as Jack came home from the grocery store. He died carrying a box of Frosted Flakes. He died because Mr. Investment Banker didn't know where I lived. He died instead of me."

Okay, sympathy. She couldn't help it. She gazed at him, sharing his horror. "I'm so sorry." The words sounded hopelessly, stupidly inadequate.

"Oh, that's not the icing on the birthday cake," David went on. "He was a better banker than a murderer, so I caught up with him in about two hours, solved the murder, closed down the ring, and arrested Mr. Investment Banker. He denied it to the last, so he couldn't reveal how he found out about Jack. He didn't make it three months in jail before getting a shiv in the back. I got promoted to Homicide. Happy endings all around, except for Jack and Carol, of course."

"You couldn't have known," Evelyn said weakly.

"I know I couldn't. That's exactly why I should have kept my own damn mouth shut." He paced around the small room as if he wanted to crawl out of his own skin. "I'm telling you this because I want you know that I mean it when I say I know how it is. So if you told Darryl Pierson about James Neal, just tell me so. I'll understand," he insisted through gritted teeth.

"I'm sorry for you, David." She got to her feet. "I really am. But I didn't tell Darryl. If he knew about Neal, I have no idea how he found out. I swear it. That's all I can tell you."

He tried, it seemed. But then logic took over and the angles of his face hardened into granite planes. "You don't know how much I want to believe you. You don't know how much I want you, period."

She had the sinking feeling of loss, of some vitally important piece of her life slipping through her fingers like a cold draft. "But you don't. Believe me, that is."

"No," he told her coldly. "I don't."

She brushed past him with fury and regret and made her way downstairs. "I'm going back to the lab," she said to Riley as he smoked a cigarette at Neal's kitchen sink. Tony had long since departed. "I'm going to get started on these samples."

He tried to be kind, which only infuriated her further. "Don't worry about it, Evie. It's the final score, not the point spread."

"Fuck you, too." She opened the door, grateful that her mother wasn't in earshot. Her mother wouldn't believe Evelyn even *knew* those words.

Riley's cell phone rang, and the sound reminded Evelyn to call Angel and make sure she remained inside Melissa's home instead of hitting the teen clubs in order to pointedly disobey her mother. As she hesitated, hand on the knob, Riley's unhealthy complexion began to pale further at the news he received.

Muttering several soft curses, he closed the phone and looked at Evelyn. "Don't go anywhere," he said. "They just found James Neal's body."

CHAPTER

28

JAMES NEAL HAD BEEN unceremoniously dumped by the side of a park road, five hundred feet from a picnic area, several miles from the nearest body of water. He had been found by a fit young man determined enough to jog in six inches of snow. Every once in a while the trees towering above would slide a pound of wet snow off their limbs to hurtle downward like a missile.

Evelyn climbed out of the car, mind and body numb. Her body had not warmed up since the hour she spent over James Neal's unheated garage, and her mind busily slammed doors to keep out the fact that she now found herself in a great deal of trouble. That it was not her fault did not change anything.

Neal lay between the tree line and the bike path. His death had not been pretty or quick. His arms were convulsed in crooked bends and his pants were ripped at one knee. He had been strangled, but unlike in Destiny's case, the killer did not leave the murder weapon for them.

Evelyn's eyes filled with tears, though for Neal or herself or simply from the cold she couldn't say. "Tough way to die."

"Yeah," Riley said. "But he was pretty tough on Destiny Pierson and Lia Ripetti."

Neal wore a sweater but no coat, since he had not had time to grab one when he fled his own home. Evelyn bent closer to his neck and tried not to look at the eyes, bulging with both knowledge and terror. "The killer probably used a chain. You can see the marks of the links."

"The same kind of chain? Can you tell?" David asked.

It pained her to have him so close, yet with a world of misunderstanding between them, but she forced herself to be professional. "Not for sure. The pathologists can tell us if it's the same general size and shape."

"He used a chain on the women, so someone used a chain on him?" David asked of no one in particular.

"Revenge murders usually leave some kind of calling card," Riley told him. "Using a chain could be symbolic."

The snow continued to fall, silently but inexorably, and would eventually cover James Neal and all his sins if they didn't interfere.

If Neal killed them both, Evelyn thought, *and Darryl had Neal killed, then I'm in deep trouble, but at least Angel is safe.*

"When his clothing dries, I want hairs and fibers." David paced a few steps, then turned, speaking to her and Riley in a deliberately toneless voice. "Neal might have been a brutal multiple killer, but that doesn't mean the mayor can just have him killed and dumped. Not on my beat."

"Yeah," Riley said with dark humor. "If he had any common courtesy, he would have made the body disappear. Doing it this way puts us in a real bind."

"He didn't do it." Evelyn spoke without hope. "He's not like that."

Both men stared at her.

At the ME's office, Evelyn immediately set to work with the fibers from Neal's house and car. At the moment she had less interest in who killed Neal than in making sure Neal killed Destiny Pierson and Lia

Ripetti. He had known both of them and ordered the chloroform—but she wanted to prove it, to know for sure.

A flash of color caught her attention.

She refocused on a thick green fiber that looked familiar. She shuffled through the reference slides she had made of just about every piece of carpeting and upholstery in James Neal's house, and reminded herself that she really should leave, just in case Angel deigned to come home.

The green fiber collected from Destiny Pierson's shirt looked exactly the same as the green fibers from James Neal's tablecloth. She'd have to run it through the FTIR to make sure they were the same substance. She removed the fiber from the taping and cut it in half, mounting half with a drop of PermaMount. Sixty seconds with the polarizing microscope and she saw the pale pinks and greens that indicated a synthetic with a high refractive index. Polyester. The tablecloth fibers gave the same result.

But the tablecloth still lay on Neal's table. Did he eat his dinners off a cloth he had used to wrap Destiny's body?

"Ewww," she said aloud.

But then Destiny had not yet been dead when he transported her from wherever he had placed the cement on her feet to the river. And maybe it appealed to whatever sick-as-hell impulses drove someone like him.

She pulled out the tapings from Neal's clothing, which she had not yet had time to examine. In no time at all she found another green fiber; in fact, there were five of them on the front of his shirt alone. This told her nothing at all. He owned the tablecloth. Perhaps he had a habit of folding his laundry on his kitchen table or even laundered the items together. Perhaps Destiny had been at his house, joined him for dinner, leaned on the table? Destiny and Neal? Not likely.

What had he said about the tablecloth? "I got it for free." How did one get a tablecloth for free? Had he won it? Stole it? Lifted it from work? And where in a hospital would they use full-size tablecloths? She had been to Riverside's cafeteria. It wasn't that fancy.

She couldn't imagine what a tablecloth had to do with anything, yet the fibers existed, small but solid. Any physical link between Neal and one of the dead girls deserved more study. Neal had to be the killer. The possibility that he had *not* done it was too confusing to contemplate.

She found Neal's name in the White Pages and dialed his house, which of course still crawled with cops. She explained herself to the rookie who answered the phone. His young voice sounded even younger when presented with a chance to do something other than mill about. "Oh, yes, ma'am. What can I do for you?"

"This is going to sound odd, Officer, but I need you to look at the kitchen table."

"Oh-kaay." From his tone this must have ranked pretty high on a list of the oddest requests he'd ever received.

"Is there a green tablecloth on it?"

"Yes."

"I need you to look along the edge of it, see if there's a tag or something."

"Oh-kaay. Hang on." Apparently he couldn't reach the table from the phone. "Yeah, there's a tag."

"And," she asked, "what does it say?"

"It's kind of faded. But I think it says *Monitor,* then it says *Marquis Royale, 64 by 48.*"

"And that's it?"

"I think so."

"Look again. There should be an RN number, a five-digit number."

He set the phone down and she waited, rattling her fingernails on the counter.

"It says 38619. Oh, it also says *polyester.* Does that help?"

"I'm not sure yet," she told him.

She could contact the FBI library for information on Monitor, but that might take a few days. Instead, she called the Textile Publication Company, which published a directory of RN numbers. At least all this activity kept her mind off her disintegrating career and her arguments with David. After she assured the operator that she worked at a government forensic laboratory and therefore could be issued the information without purchasing their $600 directory, she learned that Monitor was a division of MasterFabric, a textile corporation out of St. Paul, Minnesota.

Armed with phone numbers for both corporations and a lack of concern about the county's long-distance bill, she called Monitor, and after wading through a voice-mail jungle actually managed to converse with Velma, a real live human being who had a real live knowledge of her job and company. In a soft southern accent (Monitor manufactured its products in northern Alabama) she happily claimed the Marquis Royale line of tablecloths as their own. In fact, it made up 10 percent of their linen sales in the higher-end market.

"What stores would carry it up here?"

"We don't sell retail, ma'am," Velma corrected, as if Evelyn had made a substantial but forgivable faux pas. "Our products are for the restaurant and housekeeping industries. They're sold directly to businesses."

"What kind of businesses?"

"Restaurants," Velma repeated patiently. "Hotels, banquet centers, caterers. They purchase through our catalog, though a lot of sales are made at trade shows."

"Can you tell me what businesses in the Cleveland area bought these tablecloths?"

A pause ensued. "That would be Billing, ma'am. They'd have to run all the order numbers against inventory. When did they place this order?"

"I have no idea. Some time in the past couple of years."

Velma choked on another disapproving pause. "You'll have to talk to Billing about that request, ma'am. But I'm sure it would take a while."

Velma transferred her to a man in Billing who did not have his coworker's social skills. He whistled at every third word she uttered and made it clear that Evelyn asked for something on the level of a full-scale model of the Taj Mahal made entirely out of cheese and Popsicle sticks and delivered by Friday. He seemed to think that they *might* be able to have a list by the end of the month. Evelyn gritted her teeth, but did not know the official phrases to make him work more quickly. It would make no difference to James Neal.

"THAT WASN'T VERY SUBTLE."

"That's because I didn't do it," Mario Ashworth said, and Darryl wondered how many times in his life he'd repeated that phrase.

"What?"

"I didn't kill him. We were following him, yeah. My guy found out the cops were looking at him, that they figured he took out Lia and your daughter."

"How did you—"

"Do you really want to know that, Darryl?"

Did he? "No, I don't. But why didn't you tell me first? Why didn't you just make him disappear, never be found? Like this—my sources tell me that the cops are positive I had the guy killed."

"Why would they think that? You can't be connected to Neal."

"Evelyn."

"Oh."

"They think she told me about Neal and I had him killed."

"Did she?"

"I never heard of the guy until I turned on the TV this morning. Something like this could follow me for the rest of my career, Mar. God, listen to me. I can't believe I'm talking about my *position* when my daughter's dead."

"You've got to keep going, Dare. Besides, your popularity will probably go up. People will think you did just what they wish they could. But I didn't do it. I didn't have that man killed. I knew they suspected him and my guy went to lean on him, but was interrupted before he got the chance. We don't know what happened to him after that."

Darryl Pierson cursed quietly to himself, but he didn't doubt it. If Mario had killed James Neal on Darryl's behalf, he would say so.

"Yeah," Mario said. "I know. If I didn't kill him and you didn't, then who did?"

"No matter what, will the city believe *I* did?" Darryl wondered aloud, and hung up.

Ashworth sounded quite friendly for a gangster, she thought, but perhaps he employed better manners with an attractive and gullible forensic scientist than with Homicide cops. "What can I do for you?" he asked.

"I'm sorry to bother you at home," Evelyn said. "I just have one very quick question and it might sound odd. I tried to call your branch office, the one Lia Ripetti worked in—"

"What is it?" he interrupted, friendly but still efficient. "I'll be happy to help you."

"Ashworth Construction hosted a grand opening ceremony at which Lia Ripetti got food poisoning. Do you remember that?"

In the silence she wondered if he was examining the question from all angles for hidden dangers. Apparently he found none and answered, "I remember the grand opening ceremony. I don't remember Lia being there, but I know a lot of people got sick afterward."

"What catering company did you use?"

He laughed, probably because the question seemed both irrelevant and absurd. "Sorry, you just caught me unawares." She could hear brushing sounds as if he had moved some items on his desk. "Hold on just a moment, won't you? Don't hang up."

He did not provide music for those on hold. Evelyn spent the time looking at the tapings from Lia Ripetti's clothing. No green fibers, but then there were hardly any fibers at all. She had been in the water much longer than Destiny Pierson.

Ashworth came back on the line. "We used Kopecki Catering. I remember the name now. I didn't hire them, but I remember it because a lot of my guys were bugging me to sue them afterward. Construction workers can be whiners sometimes."

"Thank you." Christine Sabian had worked at a catering company. She couldn't remember the name of it, but Kopecki sounded strangely familiar.

"That's it? That's all you wanted to know?"

"That's it. Thank you very much."

"You're an interesting woman, Miss James."

"Mrs." She had learned during two years of singleness to smell an approaching date request a mile off. "I have to go now, my boss is signaling me. Thank you for your time."

She hadn't lied. Tony loomed in front of her like a cloud full of rainwater on the day of the company picnic. Behind him, Jason flashed her a frighteningly triumphant grin before he flitted off.

"What are you doing?" Tony asked.

"Looking at the fibers from the Neal house."

"Finding anything?"

"Just one thing. It's a little bizarre, but if I can nail it down then I'll *know* that James Neal killed those two girls."

"Stop trying."

"What?" She peered at him.

"You're in trouble," he said, and for once seemed genuinely pained by the idea. He sat on a high benchwork stool, holding the counter as the wheeled base tried to scoot away from his bulk. "With the suspect dead, Rupert saw his big Court TV trial go down the tubes. It would have been televised just in time for reelection. He's talked to the ME. The ME says you're suspended pending an investigation."

"What?"

"I tried to talk him out of it, Evelyn." He probably had, though not with as much vehemence as he implied. Tony had to be torn between malicious delight in her misery and the unhappy knowledge that he might lose his best employee. He avoided her eyes and wiped at a stain on his ample chest, from which the overstretched Izod shirt would not recover.

"But—"

"But what? The guy's dead. The case is blown. Yeah, we can wrap up Pierson and Ripetti, but no one's going to be happy about how we did it."

Evelyn fought the sick, sinking feeling that washed over her. She couldn't lose her job. *She could not lose her job.* "Why don't they just ask Darryl?"

"What, Rupert's going to call up the mayor and say, by the way, did you hire someone to murder your daughter's killer? Rupert isn't *that* crazed. He needs the mayor on his side for a lot of years yet."

"Then how is he going to accuse me of causing Neal's death without involving Darryl?"

"Exactly, Evelyn." Tony spoke in a low gravelly voice that passed for kind. It scared her. If Tony was trying to be *nice* to her, then the situation must be worse than she could possibly have imagined. "He just hasn't thought that far ahead yet. Once it sinks in, he'll quiet down and just forget about you, let it go."

"I don't think so. Rupert isn't the type to forgive and forget. He'll work out a way to blame it on me."

"Maybe he'll say you hired the guy without the mayor's knowledge because you're still in love with him," Tony said helpfully. "The mayor, I mean."

She glared at him until he left, but once alone she let her face sink into her arms and sighed in utter despair. If a professional killed Neal, they wouldn't catch him. That left no one in the headlights but her to bear the brunt of the prosecutor's disappointment. If she lost her job under these circumstances, she could be sure she'd never work again in the field. How could she pay Angel's college tuition? Or her mother's medical insurance? How could she go back to rote hospital work, typing blood and prepping Pap smears for hours on end?

What the hell was she going to do?

One thing at a time. She called Melissa's house and asked her daughter to please meet her at home. Neal was dead and her mother needed her. Angel had never been impressed with the potential lethality of her former nurse. She remained, however, quite angry about the nondisclosure of her father's past and hung up without answering.

Evelyn put her eyes to her comparison microscope, hiding for a moment between the bright snakes of color that danced before her eyes. Maybe this would turn out to be a bad dream, an overwork-induced hallucination.

Yeah, and maybe I'll go home to a fifteen-room mansion and a houseboy in Speedos. And a maid. And a cook.

Catering . . . she looked around for the Yellow Pages. What the hell, Angel wouldn't be home for a while and she wasn't on the county clock anymore. And she wanted to know that the multiple killer of young women was without a doubt lying on a slab downstairs and would never encounter her daughter again.

Letitia had just packed two cans of Sprite and a romance novel into a leather purse the size of a wheeled carry-on when David darkened her door. She looked up.

"I'm leaving."

"I need some more help on Neal."

"I told you everything," she pointed out, her gaze a direct line of mistrust and disappointment. "And now he's dead. So why should I tell you any more?"

"I didn't intend for him to die, believe it or not, even though we think he murdered those two women."

"Jimmy didn't kill nobody! Jimmy couldn't step on a cockroach."

"Then why did he run away from us?"

"I don't know," she admitted. "I really don't know. I just know he wouldn't have killed nobody."

"I think he did. But I still want to find out who killed him. We're going through all his friends and relatives, but no one is talking. It's taking too long. We can only spare so many men to canvass at a time, so I need to know who he talked to. Who did he hang out with the most?"

"What do I look like, his social secretary? I just work here."

"I know, I know. Just give me anything you can. Who did he mention the most?"

She softened in the face of David's sincerity and grew pensive. "He did used to yak every time he came in here, and since he worked flotation he came in here a lot. Never could shut the kid up," she added regretfully. "Poor guy. He palled around with the other male nurses. There are only three of them in the whole hospital, always said they were going to form a support group. Ed Tinkins and Leroy Johnson. Aside from them, he had a cousin who came here once or twice, looking for him, picked up his check when Jimmy stayed home sick once. His name's Max." Anticipating his next request, she shuffled through the tidal wave of paper on her desk. "Ed is off, but Leroy's working in Pediatrics. Third floor east."

"Thanks."

"Yeah, yeah."

Obviously no one had posted "Hospital—Quiet, Please" signs in Pediatrics. The cries of unhappy children, each with its own pitch and roll, wormed into David's ears as he approached the nurses' station. An angel of mercy with a purple streak in her hair looked up at him.

"Is Leroy Johnson around?"

Suspicious did not begin to describe her attitude. She peered at

David as if he were an IRS agent, there to arrest Leroy for a misplaced decimal point. "Why?"

"It's personal."

She mulled that over. It took a while.

"Personal how?" she asked.

It occurred to David that he had been up with the birds at four A.M. and was in no, repeat *no,* mood to be questioned by some punk-rock candy striper. He pulled his badge and leaned closer to her. "None of your fucking business, that's how. Where is he?"

It did nothing for his mood that she remained unintimidated. However, she did mutter, "Down the hall in 303. Somewhere around there."

He discovered Leroy Johnson, dressed in a set of bright blue scrubs, adjusting the IV of a school-age girl so thin she might be sucked in if anyone around her took a deep breath. What she lacked in physical presence she made up for in sheer will.

"What is that?" she asked as Johnson prepared to insert a large needle into her IV.

"Vitamins."

"I don't need vitamins."

"Girl, you need vitamins so bad, I could empty a case of Flint-stones into you and it wouldn't make a dent."

David spoke. "Leroy Johnson?"

Both the nurse and the patient looked at him without concern.

"I'm Detective Milaski, Homicide."

The girl's head swiveled back to Johnson. "You kill somebody?"

"Not yet," he warned. "But there's always a first time."

"I just need to ask you a few questions."

"I'm a little busy here, ace," Johnson said, but without malice—in fact with such easy grace that David felt like smiling for the first time that day.

"Now what's *that*?" the girl demanded.

"Potassium. It will firm up your muscles."

"Uh-uh, don't want it. They gave me that stuff when I broke my arm." Thoughtfully including David, she added to him: "It was *so* gross. The bone stuck out and I bled all over the car. Daddy had to have the carpet steam-cleaned." She turned back to Johnson. "They gave me that stuff and my arm just *throbbed*, all the way up to my shoulder, for hours. I *cried*, it hurt so bad."

"I can't imagine you crying," Johnson said to her.

"I did and I will. You stick that stuff in me and I'll have you sued for a violation of patient's rights."

Johnson couldn't stifle a grin. He returned the syringe to the med cart. "Well, I ain't going to be sticking no potassium where potassium ain't wanted to be. This is Lissa, Detective. She's going to be a lawyer."

"No I ain't. 'First thing we do, let's kill all the lawyers.' Daddy says that all the time. Who have you killed?"

"I haven't killed anyone," Johnson insisted. "Unless you, if you don't quiet down and get some rest. I will remove the offending potassium."

She giggled.

The two men moved into the hall, which had miraculously calmed. David looked around in surprise.

"It's dinnertime," Johnson explained. "Put something in their mouths, it's the only time they're quiet. Probably why childhood obesity is on the rise. What do you want, Detective? Jimmy didn't kill those girls."

Johnson's voice resonated as if from a great height, so round and comforting that you appreciated everything he said no matter what the actual words were. He could have talked Lissa into the potassium if he had really wanted to, and she would have giggled through her pain. He balanced his weight easily on both heels, looking David in the eye, and David already believed him.

He tried anyway. "What makes you so sure he didn't?"

"Jimmy couldn't kill anything. Jimmy could hardly start an IV because he hated pricking these little kids. I don't know who killed those girls, but it wasn't Jimmy. Are you going to find out who killed him? I mean, if you don't already know?"

"What do you mean by that?"

For the first time Johnson looked away. "There's talk goin' round."

"What kind of talk?"

"You guys think Jimmy killed the mayor's daughter. Now Jimmy's dead. Maybe the mayor couldn't wait for the court system."

"We have no reason to believe that," David lied. "But speaking of Destiny Pierson, did you meet her when she came to the ER?"

"Didn't have the pleasure. I heard plenty about her from Jimmy, though."

"Did he ever mention Lia Ripetti? Ophelia?"

"No."

"Never?"

"I'd remember a name like that."

"Did Jimmy ever order medical supplies that weren't for the hospital?"

"What, like drugs?"

"No, not drugs. Like solvents?"

A frown marred his smooth features. "No. Not that I know of. Jimmy only worked this unit once in a while. I mostly saw him on breaks."

"Who else did he hang with, besides you?"

"I wouldn't say he *hung* with me," Johnson said—not disloyalty, but a statement of fact. "We didn't see each other outside of work—got our own lives after quitting time, you know?" He thought for a moment, his face in grave repose while he mentally reviewed past events. "I guess his cousin Max. He mentioned him every so often. He's got a mess of cousins, I don't remember all their names. But Max kept him fed."

"Fed?" David asked, not sure he had heard correctly. A young nurse pushed a cart with wheels that sounded like a train wreck down the hall. She passed them, leaving a wake of disinfectant mixed with Opium.

"He'd get free food from Max all the time. He works for Kopecki Catering, they always got food left over after shindigs. You should see the fancy stuff he'd bring for lunch. Oysters Rockefeller and shit." Leroy chuckled gently and sadly over his late friend, then gave David a sharp look. "You okay? You look like someone just walked over your grave."

"Not mine," David said. "Jimmy's."

He pulled out of the hospital parking garage at an unsafe speed as he spoke with Dispatch on a cell phone. They provided him with an address for Christine Sabian's former workplace, Kopecki Catering, as well as a message from DMV.

"This just gets weirder and weirder."

"Come again, 417?" the dispatcher asked.

"Never mind."

SHE DIALED THE PHONE, then typed in a quick search on MSN Yellow Pages as it rang on the other end.

"Mayor Pierson's residence."

"Can I speak to Will, please?"

"May I tell him who's calling?"

She gave her name and listened to a violin concerto—the man had *hold* music on his home phone—as the computer produced a dismaying 426 entries for caterers in the Cleveland area and made her hungry as well. There had been no time for lunch. Will picked up the line.

"Miss James?"

"Yes, I—"

"I'm afraid the mayor does not wish to take your call."

Evelyn paused, momentarily stumped. Either Darryl was still mad or he had begun to distance himself, planning to let her career go down in flames while he floated above the murder of James Neal.

Someday, when she had time, she could learn to hate him for that.

For the moment she said frostily: "I don't wish to speak to the mayor. I just have a question and I hope you will have an answer. What catering company did you hire for that campaign fund-raiser last week?"

Silence fell as the mayor's assistant digested what had to seem a bizarre question. But he had made a career of fulfilling any request, no matter how unexplainable, so he excused himself and turned her back over to the violin concerto and the list of caterers. She abandoned the idea of checking each one for Marquis Royale tablecloths. A redundant name—a marquis was already a royal.

When he returned, Will told her: "A place called Kopecki's. We hadn't used them before, but the mayor likes to spread business around."

"I'll be sure to remember that on election day."

Evelyn left the building, passing Jason on his way in from a break.

"Going home?" He smirked.

Perhaps she was being paranoid, but he seemed entirely too delighted with the idea that she might be leaving for good. "No, I'm tying up some loose ends on the Ripetti and Pierson cases."

His face fell at the thought that her job might not yet be up for grabs. "Where are you going?"

"Just checking out a catering company—Kopecki's."

"Got a lead?"

"Maybe I'm just getting a jump on Thanksgiving." Petty, perhaps, but it gave her ego the only boost of a low day.

She pulled out of the lot as the last tendrils of dusk dissolved into a night worthy of Poe. She hated this part of winter—leaving home in the dark and arriving home in the dark. Her eight-year-old car made wet sounds as it stirred up the remaining slush in the gutters. The cloud-stuffed sky threatened rain or snow or some horrible combination of both, and she cranked the heater knob to the end of the red zone.

. . .

David had rung only once before Marcus opened the door, a mountain of black skin and expensive fabric. He waited for David to speak as the darkening sky surrounded them.

"Good evening, Mr. Marcus."

"Just Marcus will do, Detective. I'm afraid Mr. Ashworth cannot see you at the moment."

"That's too bad, because we have a matter to discuss, and I'm sure he would rather address it personally." He held out the emerald ring.

Marcus gazed at it, taking his time while David suppressed a shudder. The icy wind passed through his coat in freezing waves.

"Come in," Marcus said at last.

David waited in an undersize, rather empty room. No knick-knacks or personal touches to distract one from the lush carpets and rich paintings of nautical scenes, probably on purpose. Untrustworthy people were put in this room, with nothing small enough for them to pilfer. Wise in its way, of course, but David wondered if all rich people were paranoid or only the criminal ones. He studied a portrait of the mister and missus.

Ashworth arrived in record time, dressed in somewhat scruffy-looking sweatpants as if David had interrupted his workout. He had obviously received a quick briefing from Marcus and appeared relaxed in the knowledge of exactly what David thought he knew.

"I believe you have something which belongs to me." He held out his hand.

"This?" David displayed the ring between thumb and forefinger. "No, this belongs to Lia Ripetti."

"Who is a dead orphan. I'd like the ring back," he added in good humor. "It cost quite a bit."

"That would create problems for you, surely," David pointed out. "Wouldn't Mrs. Ashworth wonder why she suddenly had two identical rings?" He nodded at the portrait. A woman with Ivy's coloring sat on a satin divan, one hand crossed primly over the other, the second emerald winking from her finger.

Ashworth followed his gaze. "I see your point. My own fault— I've always been lazy about jewelry. It all looks the same to me."

"Besides, Lia Ripetti wasn't completely alone. She had a boy-friend. Did she dump you for him?" He didn't mind irritating Ash-worth, but that was not his intention. He wanted to know if Ashworth felt strongly enough about Lia to avenge her death.

"Lia didn't dump me." Ashworth fell into an overstuffed leather armchair as if he were tired. Marcus, the silent sentinel, blocked the only exit. "She did, however, end our relationship."

"When?"

"Last year. Right before Christmas, I believe. Long before she met this Durling."

"Why?"

"Lia figured—rightly—that I had used her, and expensive gifts weren't enough of a consolation. Lia wasn't stupid, and she had pride. I always liked that about her," he added, almost to himself.

"So you just went your separate ways?"

"Quite amicably."

"And she kept working for your company?"

"Why not? I'm hardly ever at that office. It's not like we'd run into each other all the time."

"She didn't keep her job by threatening to tell your wife?"

"Lia never threatened anything. She didn't want anyone to know any more than I did, because, frankly, she felt foolish about it. Like I said, she had pride. Even if tempted during some spiteful moment, she possessed enough intelligence to realize I make a better friend than enemy."

"So you could keep her in line," David stated. He had remained standing, pacing along the edge of a Karastan rug. It kept his blood moving.

"You're not getting it. I didn't need to keep anyone in line. Lia and I were adults and had an adult relationship. Lia was a very sensible girl, and once she made a decision, that was it. She didn't go in for shows of hysterical emotion—unlike"—he sighed—"so many women."

"And yet, when you identified her dead body, you described her as someone you may have met once at some function or other."

"What do you expect me to say? Oh, yes, she's the girl I cheated with for a few months last year."

"Do you even *care* that she's dead?"

Ashworth thought for a moment, as if he found this an interesting question. David waited.

"Not a whole lot. I could get misty-eyed and tell you I'm deeply wounded, but the fact is Lia was simply an old girlfriend. I hadn't even seen her for months. I'm sorry for the girl, of course, but I can't pretend I formed any real attachment."

"You gave her an expensive ring."

Ashworth smiled, a smirk he probably intended to be dashing but came off as slimy. "One has to pay the piper if one wishes to dance, Detective. I can afford it."

"So a cheap fling is yesterday's news."

"I didn't say that. The ring was easily bought. Lia wasn't. I'm saying I cared at the time, but time passes."

"Then why did your man Marcus here terrorize Jimmy Neal this morning?"

"Excuse me?"

David flipped out his notebook and consulted a page. "Do you, Mr. Ashworth, own a black Lincoln Continental, license plate BYT 459?"

"Yes."

"And did you, Mr. Marcus, drive it earlier today?"

"No."

"Are you sure?"

"Quite."

David didn't expect Marcus to tell him anything useful—he wouldn't have expected Marcus to talk unless prodded with hot irons—but he had to make the effort to sort out the jumble of thoughts in his mind. Neal had a connection to Christine Sabian through his cousin Max. But Marcus had terrorized Neal—maybe over Lia Ripetti? If Darryl Pierson had *not* had Neal killed, Evelyn would be off the hook. The loose ends in this case had turned out to be vital mysteries in their own right. "That's odd, because I could have sworn you drove away in it after I chased you out of Jimmy Neal's house this morning."

"And who is Jimmy Neal?"

"It's kind of a compliment, really. Neal said he'd never met a scarier person. And I thought, who do I know who matches that description?"

"I don't take that as a compliment," Marcus rumbled.

"And I've just received a message from the DMV that the license plate I saw driving away from me this morning—which is, coincidentally, BYT 459—is registered to this household."

Nothing from Marcus.

"You move remarkably fast for a man of your stature," David went on, reasoning that *stature* sounded better than *bulk*.

Marcus *did* take that as a compliment. His upper lip twitched just a bit, barely discernible. But even he couldn't resist a brag that stopped short of an admission: "I played tight end at Brown."

"I'm not surprised. Not a bit surprised. Jimmy swore he didn't tell you anything. Didn't get the chance before we showed up."

The twitch disappeared. "I didn't speak with Mr. Neal."

"Did you kill him?"

"Nor did I kill him."

"You may find this hard to believe, Mr.—I'm sorry, Marcus—but I really want to believe you." And he did. Jimmy Neal had been understandably terrified of this imposing giant of a man. And Neal had been on the run, watching every shadow, perhaps sheltered by his relatives. How would Marcus get close enough to kill him? If he appeared on the horizon, Neal would have run for his life. Naturally, an experienced man like Marcus could have worked around that, but the whole idea made David more eager to talk to Cousin Max—someone Neal *wouldn't* have run from. He switched his gaze to Ashworth. "But

I'm still left with the question of why you would send your top goon to take out Neal if you weren't upset about Lia's death."

More silence. If anything, Ashworth seemed more relaxed. Marcus, who had stood unmoving through their conversation, seemed to lower his shoulders, and his reptilian gaze faltered. And David knew he had gone wrong somewhere.

Marcus had been at Neal's that morning. But it wasn't because of Lia Ripetti.

KOPECKI CATERING COULD BE considered on her way home
only if she took the scenic route down I-77. She discovered too late
that I-77 traffic had no advantage over I-71 traffic, but eventually she
found the right exit and crept along the crowded side streets until she
found Papel Road and turned left. She could have called Kopecki's instead of going there, but she felt a need for physical activity and she
wasn't even sure what she was going to ask. *Do you know a James
Neal? Do you have green tablecloths? Is anyone here a serial killer?*

Small industries lined the road, their tree-lined parking lots
mostly empty as employees headed home to holiday preparations. In
three days it would be time to eat turkey and she still had no idea what
to do about it. The way things were going, Angel would probably eat
at Melissa's rather than endure either of her parents. At least Rick had
a logical reason for keeping his secret from Angel. Evelyn did not, except for altruism, a concept entirely incomprehensible to a teenager.

She went past the address and had to turn around. A chain-link
fence surrounded the lot but lacked a gate. Apparently the manage-

ment did not fear attack by gun-wielding criminals demanding the recipe for crab dip. She hid her heavy purse behind the front seat, locked the car, and approached the building. The smell of food, some stale and some fresh, greeted her.

The unlocked front door led to a lobby, only half lit and decorated with posters of food that did nothing to alleviate her hunger pangs. A rounded area for the receptionist stood vacant. It was past quitting time.

"Hello?" Evelyn called.

No response.

She peeked down hallways extending from both sides of the lobby. Lights glowed farther on down the hallway to her left. She didn't want to startle any employees still on the premises—people got shot that way—but the door had been open and her stomach convinced her that employees who worked with food all day were probably good-tempered.

She continued down the lit hallway and scattered occasional hellos through the air. The few doors that were open showed small offices and desks that could have belonged to lawyers or advertisers or accountants. She wondered where they made the food, decided to follow her nose, and bumped into a small, wiry woman.

"Shit!" she cried, loud enough to shatter glass. "You scared the crap out of me!"

"I'm sorry," Evelyn began. "I'm from the ME's office, and I have a rather odd question—"

The woman couldn't have cared less if Evelyn had dropped in from outer space. "Back there." She waved her hand behind her, as if motioning a plane into the jetway. She brushed past Evelyn and left. Quitting time was quitting time.

Evelyn crept cautiously forward. The hallway ended in a larger room, evidently used for supplies, and from a door at the other end she heard murmured voices and clinking, metallic sounds. A mixture of aromas filled the air, from chili powder to baking bread, and her stomach growled again. They must be preparing for some evening party.

On her way around the shelves, she noticed that the boxes were filled with napkins, porcelain cups, and menu folders. She slowed down to look for tablecloths.

They were stacked against the north wall. Each set of shelves held a different color—dusty rose, burgundy, hunter green, and navy. She reached for a green one.

"Can I help you?"

She whirled, her car keys slipping from her startled hand. A young man stood by the door, shadowed by the sporadic lighting in the room. He slouched to one side, as if he were more uncertain of his authority than she was.

"Yes! I'm sorry, I think I passed your secretary in the hall and she pointed me in this direction. I'm from the ME's office, and I have an odd question about your tablecloths."

He stepped into the light. Melting brown eyes hovered over an indistinct nose. His body seemed too tall for itself and his shoulders drooped to compensate. He looked as timid and sweet as a new puppy.

And familiar. They had met at Destiny's funeral, been introduced by Jimmy Neal.

DAVID PULLED OUT OF Ashworth's driveway, trying to pair up the questions and answers so that they made sense. Marcus had to have killed Neal. Marcus, as Ashworth's right-hand man, had made a career of getting close enough to kill guys who should have known better. How he found Neal, David couldn't guess, but Marcus had his ways and plenty of money backing him up.

The problem was *why*. Ashworth made it clear he considered Lia a throwaway ex-girlfriend, so why kill Neal for killing Lia? Unless he wanted to make a political point—people who mess with Ashworth, even Ashworth's half-forgotten ex-girlfriend, would pay the price.

Or maybe she wasn't a throwaway to *Marcus*.

It still didn't feel right. He would bet his paycheck that Ashworth couldn't care less about Lia Ripetti and Marcus had just been doing his job. Only Darryl Pierson had a motive to kill Neal, but he had to have better sense than to hire Cleveland's most mobbed-up criminal to do it.

Didn't he?

Grief made for bad decisions, and Darryl Pierson was consumed with grief. But still David couldn't see the logical connections. Ashworth wasn't for hire and what could Pierson have that he could want?

Aside from the city council decision on the new ME's office.

Did Pierson grieve enough to take a hell of a risk, to put his daughter before his career? The theory had holes, but David could live with that. What he might not want to live with was proving it. If he even tried, he'd find himself mysteriously transferred to the Parking Division. It would also seal Evelyn's coffin. On the other hand, if he hinted his theories to the mayor he might wind up chief of Homicide one day, and finally know that talent and hard work meant nothing. He wasn't sure which was worse.

And where did Neal's cousin and the catering company fit in?

His right foot depressed the gas pedal, urging the car forward as he dialed his cell phone in complete violation of motor vehicle safety recommendations. Five o'clock. Too early to call his father—that would not be the routine—but he did anyway. Perhaps the distraction would keep him from speeding up until he wrapped the Grand Marquis around a phone pole.

"Dad?"

"Hi, son. What are you up to?"

"Still working on that case."

"The one with all your missing girls?"

"It's strange, Dad. Some of these women, I don't know if this guy killed them or they just ran away. Their families don't know if they're gone forever or if they'll walk in the door someday, just out of the blue."

His father chuckled. "That's how your mother and I felt when you joined the Marines."

David was silent for a moment. "Dad? Did Mom think I was a screwup?"

"Your mother? No, of course not. Hell, she thought you'd be president, but then all mothers do. Why do you ask that?"

"Well, not going to college, joining the service . . . not getting married . . . being a cop and getting shifted from department to department . . . you know."

"Son." His father spoke so firmly that David shut out the image of the thin man in the wheelchair and bathed himself in that strong, flowing voice of a man who knew nearly everything and didn't lie. "You're a good man. You have morals that don't shift with the wind— we taught you that. You work hard, you try to help people, and you taught yourself that. Your mother was proud of you. We were both proud of you every minute of your life." Another low chuckle. "But you don't need me to tell you that."

"Yes," David said. "Yes, I did. Thanks. I've got to go now, Dad, okay? I'll call you tomorrow."

He hung up and wiped his eyes. Then he drove for a while, taking deep breaths.

He tried Evelyn's home without knowing what he'd say to her, and got her answering machine. He tried again and got the ME's switchboard, which transferred him to Trace Evidence.

"Yo."

"Jason?" The toady.

"Yeah?"

"Evelyn around?"

"No."

"Did she go home?"

"I guess."

Thanks a lot, kid. "Has she found anything new on this Pierson murder? Did she mention any new leads?"

Too long a pause. "I have no idea."

David rang off, trying to ignore the quiver of worry that ran up the back of his neck, and went on to Part Two as he took the I-77 ramp from 480 West. Did Neal kill Lia and Destiny or did he not? Circumstantial evidence pointed to him, but nothing direct and no chance for a confession. If he could at least wrap up the two women with a bow, prove without a doubt that Neal killed them, maybe the brass would see it was in their best interests to let Neal's murder slip their collective mind. It would save Evelyn. It would also let Pierson get away with murder. The idea made him feel dirty.

He hoped Cousin Max could answer some questions. There was no reason to protect a dead man. Where else would Neal, fearing for his life, have gone but to his family, his cousin?

And then Neal wound up dead.

A terrible suspicion burrowed into David's heart.

Perhaps Ashworth *and* Evelyn, even Pierson, were telling the truth. There were no chains or cement found at Neal's house. Could Max be his partner? Jimmy picked them out and Max helped grab them? Or did Max do the picking? Christine Sabian had worked at Kopecki's. And she had never been to Riverside Hospital so far as David knew.

He pulled into the unlit parking lot and pulled into a space next to a blue Ford Escort. Didn't Evelyn drive an Escort when she wasn't in the county station wagon? He glanced inside, but the neat interior gave no clue to the owner, and Escorts were ubiquitous.

The front of the building was dark, so he walked around to the back, where there were at least five cars in a side lot and wonderful smells wafting heavenward.

The first person he saw was a teenage boy at a stove, giving a kettle of boiling ravioli a desultory stir. He gave David a hopeful look, as if he welcomed any break in the monotony. Beyond him three women and two men, all dressed in soiled white and hairnets, cooked with more enthusiasm than the boy.

"Hi," David said. "Where's Max?"

The kid jerked his head in answer. "Over there."

"Over where?"

The boy glanced over the rest of the kitchen. "I don't know. I saw him here a minute ago."

One of the men caught sight of David. "The offices are closed, sir. If you want to place an order, you'll have to come back tomorrow."

His tone was less polite than his words. He efficiently tore large leaves of lettuce into bite-size pieces.

"Can't we just cut that?" a middle-aged woman asked wearily.

"*No.*"

"I'm looking for Max," David said.

"He's—" the man began, then looked around. "He was here a minute ago."

"He went to get the dried parsley," another woman put in.

"And where would that be?" David asked.

"Right through that door." The man did not pause in his lettuce-tearing. "But you can't come in here."

David held up his badge. "Yes, I can."

He moved quickly past the cooks, feeling the various degrees of heat from the stove, steamer, and oven, and pushed open the swinging door. No one moved to stop him; indeed, no one even seemed particularly concerned. They had their own deadline to meet and a cheese soufflé waited for no man.

The next room was dark. David drew his Glock 9-millimeter and patted the wall until he found the light switch. Rows of shelves sprang into view, silent and unmoving.

He moved through it slowly and checked every dim corner. Nothing. He went on, cautiously turning on the light in each office, looking for any sign of movement and listening for any sound other than the faint metallic clunks coming from the kitchen. He explored the dark lobby as well as the opposing hallway. Various rooms held made-up tables, obviously displays to show how Kopecki Catering could provide a unique place setting for any occasion from baptisms to the big 4-0 birthday parties.

He found no sign of Max or anyone else and retraced his steps, self-consciously holstering his weapon. Perhaps he had over-reacted.

On his way through the supply room his foot kicked against something that clinked. He looked down at a key ring partially lodged under the lowest shelf; it held six keys and a heavy fob in the shape of an Egyptian mummy case.

Shit!

He burst into the kitchen, noted no more or less staff than had been there before, and marched up to the lettuce man. "I need to know Max's address and what kind of car he drives."

CHAPTER

33

EVELYN AWOKE TO SEARING cold and waves of nausea. She wanted to throw up but her teeth were too busy chattering. Everything hurt and her hands were numb.

Then she opened her eyes.

Dark, but plenty of motion. Her sluggish brain concluded someone had dumped her in a car trunk—a decidedly unheated car trunk—and tied her hands behind her. A rough blanket or rug lay beneath her and the driver did not care about her well-being or he wouldn't be taking the corners so sharply. She chose not to think about the fact that her confined space was most likely dirty, oily, and crawling with bugs.

She flexed her numb fingers and tried to rub her hands together. She did the same thing to her legs, only to discover that they were tied as well. And she still wanted to throw up.

How did she . . . Oh, yes. Jimmy Neal's cousin. The one who attended Destiny's funeral with him. The one who baked broccoli-caper muffins. He had recognized her first and knocked her to the ground before she could speak, much less call for help. She didn't remember anything after she hit the floor.

No, she did—a vague, dreamlike memory of a rustling sound, a sharp pain in her head, and then a cold plastic cone placed over her nose and mouth, like a party hat out of place or a surgical mask.

A filter mask, she realized. That's how he did it. A plastic form kept the cotton filter an inch off the skin so the chloroform didn't burn. He didn't even need to get them from Cousin Jimmy—a filter mask could be bought for a buck at the dollar store. She had a few herself for home projects.

She rubbed her face against the dirty fabric, dislodging the mask until it came to rest somewhere on her forehead, tangled in her hair. Not that it mattered—apparently the chemical had evaporated enough for her to regain consciousness. But how did he put it together so quickly? Did he drive around with a mask and a vial of chloroform in his trunk, just in case he happened to run into a likely victim?

Victim?

Was she now a *victim*?

She couldn't say why the idea came as a shock. His intentions were patently obvious. But the idea of being in the same category with all the dead women she had seen, encountered, worked with . . . the ones who were raped, stabbed, strangled, beaten, and set on fire . . .

She struggled with her bonds in sheer panic, the feeling returning to her hands only as pain when the twine bit into her flesh. The other victims—*victims*—didn't have ligature marks on their wrists or bruises on their heads, but she had caught him unawares.

Where had she left her cell phone? If she could call—no, the phone was in her purse, and her purse was in her car, and her car was, she assumed, back in Kopecki's parking lot, where it would sit for a day or two or three before the employees got curious about it. Perhaps sooner if they noticed the keys she dropped in the storage room.

This is why I don't carry a gun. If I ever needed it, it would be uselessly resting at the bottom of my purse.

She felt for the trunk latch. If she could get it open, she could jump out . . . except that the steady high speed at which they were moving meant they were on a freeway. Nowhere else in the Cleveland area could he drive for so long without hitting a stop sign or a light. She would simply toss her bound body into oncoming traffic. Not a good idea.

She rolled over instead, turning her back to the rear of the car, and tried to hook the twine over the latch. She felt around for a sharper protrusion and found none. It killed her hands but she rubbed the twine back and forth on the latch.

The car began to slow down. She rubbed harder.

Another car drove by them, the radio bass giving off headache-producing thumps. She heard a burst of conversation, as if people were out on the sidewalk. No light penetrated the trunk. The car stopped, then went on again. The twine had not even weakened. What had he used, nylon?

The other street noises quieted, and she could hear nothing but the sound of the tires on a wet road, the panicked beating of her own pulse, and the relentless scrape of the twine against the trunk latch.

Abruptly the car stopped and the driver's door opened. She gave up on the twine and started to wriggle round again so that she could face him when he opened the trunk. But his feet crunched away from the car. She heard a faint sound, and then his feet came back and the car rocked gently as he settled into the driver's seat again.

The car moved forward not more than twenty feet, and he stopped and killed the engine. Then she understood. They had pulled into a garage.

He had a plan. He had everything arranged. She would not live through the night.

In her early twenties, just for something to do, she had taken martial arts training and had forgotten nearly all of it, except for breathing and one other thing: Use your legs. Pound for pound, a woman's leg muscles are just as strong as a man's.

She waited for him to open the trunk lid. He had not turned on the light, she could see his silhouette against the windows in the closed overhead door. Before he raised the lid all the way she kicked out with both feet, bracing her back against the spare tire. This awkward position required slamming her thigh against the trunk edge, but it knocked Max backward.

She threw the upper half of her body against the trunk opening; she could not stand up inside the trunk with her ankles tied together and without her hands for balance. She had no choice but to literally fall out of the car, and landed with a painful jolt to her left shoulder on the cement floor.

Max sprang up before she could. She attempted to stand on the bound feet and he simply hooked his toes behind them and pulled. Evelyn fell over instantly, with no way to break the fall. Her head hit the cement floor and bounced, and her vision faded to bursts of white stars against a black background.

She wasn't unconscious, exactly. She felt—vaguely, as if it were happening to someone else—Max dragged her over to a small rug and rolled her up in it, and she hoped that she wouldn't suffocate. Then he hefted her over one shoulder—so that her back arched painfully over the top of his shoulder—and moved out of the garage and into, she assumed, the house. She felt brisk air make its way into the open end of the rug roll, yet it did nothing to revive her.

Max made his way carefully down some steps; she could feel them descend. He let her slip to the floor, but gently, as if he didn't want to damage her further. When he removed the rug she could see an unfinished basement. The light was too bright on her eyes, but she could not blink. *How odd,* she thought.

Then she passed out.

34

EVERYTHING HURT BUT HER feet. Her feet felt pretty good, even cozy. Her neck stung and her head felt like she had one of those three-day, no-aspirin-in-the-world-could-touch-it sinus headaches. Time to have a cup of tea and go to bed.

Then she opened her eyes and realized that tea would not be provided.

Her legs, from just below the knee downward, were lost in a five-gallon bucket of heavy gray warm cement.

As Destiny had done, she immediately began to wriggle. That set the chains to clinking against each other.

"Stop that," Max said.

She lifted her head slowly, straining the stiffened neck muscles. Lancets of pain stabbed her spine.

Max leaned against a bare wooden workbench, but not casually. His arms crossed over his chest as if holding his body together, hunched under his boyish but turbulent face. He had a bruise on his chin where her foot had caught him and a red mark the size of a baseball on his neck. He spoke calmly enough but with an underlying sense of urgency.

"I'm glad you're here, Evelyn. I like you. I just wish it didn't have to be like this."

"You mean," she whispered, her voice as broken as she felt, "you wish you didn't have to kill me?"

He gave her an irritated look, as if bemused that she could be so far off. "No. I have to kill you, that's the whole *point*. I just wish I could do it properly. I hate rushing. I mean, I have time, I just *feel* like I don't. You know how it is when you have too much to do all at once? After all," he added, "no one's going to look for you here."

She swallowed, trying to moisturize her throat, but it felt like a dirt road after a drought. "Actually, they will. I told two people at the ME's office where I was going before I left."

"And where were you going? Kopecki's? That doesn't help. You were totally surprised to see me, so you didn't know I worked there. Neither will they. Why *did* you go there?"

"Tablecloths."

He laughed. "What?"

She shook her head. *Find me, David. Please find me.* But why would he? What would possibly direct him to Kopecki's?

"Sorry," he said. "I didn't mean to get you down. Go ahead and talk if you want. Do you want something to eat? I've got salmon chutney I've been experimenting with, though I can't get the cilantro adjusted right. We have quite a while to go before that hardens."

And when it did, he'd drop her in the Cuyahoga. The freezing waters would close over her head and there would be no more breath. Her body would not be found. Angel would never know where she had gone. Her mother . . . "Thanks for the offer. You must be quite a cook."

"I'm a *great* cook."

She nodded at the cement. "Does this take a long time to dry?"

"Oh, yeah, hours and hours. But it's heavy, and frankly, that's all that's required of it. Once it sets a little bit and it gets completely dark outside, we'll be good to go."

His cool tone nauseated her more than the chloroform. A man in his element. His basement, his cocoon, and a woman he could never possess under his complete control. "Where'd you get the bucket, by the way? Do you have a pool? We thought maybe you had a pool." She was babbling, yes, but why not?

"City pool. It's only three streets over. A good, solid pool—and I ought to know, I poured the concrete myself, when I worked with my great-uncle at the utilities department. He used to tell me about cement shoes from *his* father's younger days. They really used to do that, you know, it's not just some kind of urban myth. He told me you have to have the cement come up past the calves. Just the feet isn't good enough. I added the chains myself, though."

"The cops know. We met you at the funeral. I did know you worked at Kopecki's. I just didn't exactly remember what you looked like. So they will get your address from your boss—"

"Well," he interrupted, completely unconcerned by these ideas, "that's another long story."

David drove along the city streets at an unsafe speed, refusing to slow even after near collisions with a bicyclist and a protruding garbage can. A practical voice in his head pointed out that while he was driving his own car, any accidents would go on his own insurance. If it were the city's car, that would be a different story.

He sped up.

Why would she go to Kopecki's? Had he told her that Christine Sabian worked there? He couldn't remember.

The portable radio crackled with information, none of it comforting. Max Chisholm's gold Lumina had not been spotted. Riley was en route to meet him at Max's house. Two uniformed officers were checking out Jimmy's house, just in case. It could still have been a two-man operation. Max picked some victims, Jimmy picked others. Jimmy got the chloroform, Max brought the cement.

He sped up again.

A patrol car came up behind him and flashed the blue and red lights. He waited until they reported his vehicle description to dispatch, then used their call number to talk to them. They turned off the lights but stayed with the parade—assisting in a Homicide arrest sounded more attractive than passing out speeding tickets.

The more, the merrier, David thought. For once he didn't want to go it alone. The more backup he had with this nut, the better.

He didn't think about what the guy might be doing to Evelyn right at that moment. He steered his thoughts away from her, pretending that it was not Evelyn involved in this drama but some sort of stand-in. He did not have time to ponder what he might have to do to this guy if he hurt her.

If he killed her.

If he wrapped her beautiful body in cement and dropped it into the ice-cold river, so that she drowned, screaming and struggling in the silent water.

If Darryl Pierson had Jimmy killed for killing Destiny, David thought, *I'm not going to do a damn thing about it. I might even ask the mayor for the name of a good hit man. No, wait, I already have one.*

He pulled onto Pullman Avenue, just off West Twenty-fifth. Brick houses were comfortably lit along the empty street. Music emanated at an easy level from one, as if the occupants had gotten an early start on Thanksgiving. He had one block to go.

He'd known Evelyn for only a week or two, really. She was just another cop—well, not a cop, but similar. It would be a pity if she died in the line of duty, but others had, right? It wasn't personal.

Right.

It was *very* personal.

He sped up.

.   .   .

She kept moving her legs. It had worked for Destiny, it would work for her. But how had the girl gotten out of the chains? Max had removed her parka, leaving only a white turtleneck sweater and jeans. The chains snaked around her neck, under her armpits, across her waist. They went between her wrists, too, but Max had left the twine there for good measure. Houdini couldn't have escaped from this.

The empty basement offered no help. The few tools on the workbench were too far out of reach. The chloroform mask lay on the planking, abandoned, underneath a 1994 calendar and a dusty photograph of a young woman with long dark hair and a stunning smile. Max had gone upstairs for a snack, he said, pounding up the staircase somewhere behind her. Now she heard his footsteps on the kitchen floor. He sat up there eating his salmon chutney, killing time before it was killing time.

She wiggled her legs. The cement felt like warm putty, heavy but not uncomfortable. Nothing stirred in the rest of the house, or outside it as far as she could hear. She could scream, but that would just get her another snoutful of chloroform and she'd be dead long before she woke up. For a moment it seemed like an attractive prospect. Why be awake for her own murder if she didn't have to be?

The idea made her want to throw up even more.

She debated the slight chance that someone might be looking for her. She hadn't told anyone her plans—except for Jason, who had probably gone out on a date and would not give her another thought for days—and she hadn't called David or Riley. No one had made the connection to Max as far as she knew. No reason why they should; only she knew about the tablecloth. No one would be checking out Kopecki's in the near future. Angel might call the ME's office looking for her, *if* she had come home at all, *if* she even cared where her mother had gotten to, and *if* she didn't just assume Evelyn had worked late and go to bed. Even if anyone missed her, the last place they would think to look would be Jimmy Neal's cousin Max's basement. Now she knew why cops always told Dispatch where they were headed, but she wasn't a cop and didn't have a dispatcher and because of that she was going to die.

Not only die, but *disappear*, and that she really couldn't stand. That Angel and her mother might be doomed to the same kind of hell that tortured Thalia Johnson's family . . .

This couldn't happen.

She wiggled her legs. If she had been able to stand, she could have pulled the chains out of the concrete, but Max had thought of that. Straps held her butt firmly to the chair, and the chair seemed to be bolted to the floor. Chains even kept the bucket against the rungs so she couldn't push it away. He had improved on his ancestor's model, had thought of everything. He had left her no way out.

There had to be time. The women's deaths had seemed bizarre from the beginning because that elaborate setup of cement and chains had to take time. How long did it take to harden again?

But then, when the plans fell through, he had resorted to simply strangling Destiny Pierson. And with Jimmy, he hadn't even mixed the cement. Perhaps he had decided not to bother with the more ornate form of murder, especially for a rush job.

Max Chisholm's house, a forlorn two-story firetrap, huddled in the shadows of its healthier neighbors. Duct tape held one window together and the second step leading to the porch had snapped through. David pulled into the driveway behind a patrol car, its occupants waiting for him to lead the way, and his heart sank like a marble in water. Something was wrong. The place felt abandoned. No lights, no car. He vaulted out of his vehicle before the engine died, eighteen-inch Maglite in hand.

He checked the garage first, aiming the light through the glass windows. Boxes, cobwebs, and a rat or two topped a few decades' worth of garbage, all of which looked as if it hadn't been touched since the last millennium. He headed for the house.

Riley joined him halfway across the snow-filled grass. "What's up?"

"It's Jimmy's cousin Max," David told him. "That's who our killer is. He has Evelyn."

Riley began to spout questions, which David did not answer or even hear. He pounded on the back door to the house with enough force to knock its hinges askew, waited exactly one second for a response, then raised his leg and kicked the door just beneath the knob. It flew open and bounced against the inner wall.

"Do we have a warrant?" Riley asked, more from habit than any real concern, but David was already inside and searching.

Followed closely by the uniformed patrolmen, they turned on every light and searched every room and closet, moving more quickly than safety SOPs would tolerate but to no avail. They found no one.

David stood in the kitchen and fought the rising swells of panic. Riley thundered through the upstairs rooms and a uniformed officer searched the basement, just to double-check, but David felt sure they wouldn't find any clues to Evelyn's whereabouts. Aside from some dusty mail, stale food, and last week's *TV Guide* on the coffee table, the place seemed uninhabited.

He had not anticipated this.

Max was neither at work, at home, nor at Jimmy's. So where the hell was he? And what was he doing to Evelyn right at this very moment as David stood motionless, without the slightest idea of what to do next?

She was going to die.

She was going to die because he, David, had screwed up. He should have investigated Kopecki's as part of the Christine Sabian disappearance. He should have put surveillance on Jimmy's relatives. He should have made Marcus tell him what he knew.

Evelyn would die while he waded in a morass of self-recrimination.

He pulled his portable radio from his belt and told the police operators to call the Metropark Rangers and get every man they had on the road, particularly those near bodies of water, and that they should check anyone out and about on this cold, dark night. Then he went out to his car and plucked the case file from the front seat. He had the reports of interviews with Jimmy's family members, which would be Max's family members as well.

He dialed the first phone number he came to and listened to the ringing on the other end of the line, eyeing the room. The curtains were atrocious but clean. Washed dishes gathered dust in a wooden rack on the counter. A wall calendar with a picture of an Alaskan glacier featured the correct month, the only notation a *1:00 pm* scrawled on the fourth Thursday. Evidently Max planned to take a break from killing people for a traditional Thanksgiving dinner. Under the calendar hung a framed photo, in which a very pretty young woman stood in front of an older house, her arms thrown up as if celebrating a victory. A much older woman scowled on the porch. Behind her, a child hovered in the entranceway, the screen door dissecting his image into a pixilated ghost.

No one answered the phone. David went on to the second report, propping the cell phone against his shoulder as he opened each drawer. Towels, silverware, Tupperware containers. Even the butcher knives looked harmless. The phone rang again and again. He cursed again as he figured it out—all Max's relatives were probably at a local funeral home, attending or at least planning Jimmy's wake.

But he didn't know what else to do. He tried a third number, that of Jimmy's uncle, also named Chisholm. As it rang, David opened another drawer and found a stack of self-stick notes and a battered address book. As if heaven had rewarded him for his perseverance, someone picked up just as he opened the book to the *C* section.

"Hello?"

David identified himself, saying he needed to ask Max Chisholm a few questions. He willed his voice to be calm, steady. Just routine.

"My nephew? He's not here."

"Can you tell me where I might find him?" The list of Chisholms filled a page of the address book, but with out-of-town addresses.

"No." The man sounded weary. "He dropped off a casserole earlier, but now he's probably at work."

"I just went to Kopecki's and he wasn't there. He's not at home, either."

"Then I don't know where he is," the man said impatiently. "We've had a death in the family, in case you cops had forgotten."

"I know, and I'm sorry. But if you want to clear Jimmy's name, we need information and we need it quickly." The only other local Chisholm was a Sarah in Lakewood.

The phone lines only amplified a derisive snort. "I may have been born at night, mister, but it wasn't last night. You guys are making my nephew into another Son of Sam. I'm just trying to help my sister bury her son and there's reporters on the lawn turning it into the movie of the week. Ain't they violating my civil rights?"

David hadn't thought of that. Jimmy's relatives were in the middle of a three-ring circus. It sounded like there were lights and action and lots of people. It sounded like the last place in the world Max would go with someone he wanted to kill.

"You have a right to order them off your property, Mr. Chisholm. But about Max—are his parents there with you?"

After a wary pause, he spoke. "Max doesn't have any parents, never really did. *My* mother had to raise him. What's this sudden interest in Max, anyway?"

A faint tickle moved along the back of David's neck, lighter than the touch of a butterfly's wing. He had found something important. "Your mother, Sarah? Does she live on"—he checked the address book again—"Warren Road? In Lakewood?"

"Lived. She's dead, too."

David's hope plunged to a forlorn death.

"She left the house to Max after twenty years of telling him he should have been drowned at birth. I keep telling him to sell it and oh by the way maybe split the money with me and Cindy since my mother left all her money to poor struggling Donna and never fixed the damn will after poor struggling Donna got herself blown to bits at Hanna's Diner. Her finest performance, if you ask me."

But David had hung up.

CHAPTER

35

IT NEVER OCCURRED TO Evelyn to wonder where she was. Frankly she didn't care. She had been sitting there for at least forty-five minutes, but she had no idea how much time had passed while she had been out cold. Max had finished his snack and they remained undisturbed, but this did not seem to reassure him. He grew more agitated instead of less, and padded back and forth in stocking feet over the basement floor. The top of the bucket showed pockmarks from his firmness tests. Evelyn could hear no sounds from outside, and all she could smell was fear.

She cleared her throat. "What time is it?"

"Who cares?"

"I do."

With a show of patience he looked at his watch. "Six-forty."

She had left the ME's office only two hours earlier. Even if Angel had gone home, she would not be particularly surprised by her mother's failure to show. She had grown accustomed to Evelyn's work ethic. Only the cat would miss her.

No one would be coming to her rescue. She could try to talk Max out of killing her, but that seemed unlikely. What about Lia and Destiny? Had they talked? Had they begged for their lives? Sobbed? Cajoled?

Whatever they had done, it hadn't worked.

She had to keep him talking until the weather turned and the rivers froze solid. Then he could toss her onto the ice and if the fall didn't kill her, the exposure would, but at least she would be able to breathe. "Who's the woman in the picture?"

He glanced at the photo, picked it up. "My mother."

"She was pretty." Instinctively she used the past tense.

"She could have shown Narcissus a thing or two about self-esteem." He set the picture down carefully, caressing the top of the frame as he did. "In other words, she was a self-loving bitch. But she taught me that you have to make your own dreams. The world won't do shit for you."

"I'm sure she loved you," she said, not at all sure this was true.

"Yeah, good try, Evelyn. Get the monster crying in his beer over dear old mum."

"Mothers always love their children," she persisted. "It's instinctive. Even when they don't show it." *Even when they're yelling at you to clean your room and do your homework. Even when they want to throttle you with their bare hands. Does Angel know that? Did I make it clear?*

Max startled her by coming closer, planting his hands on her thighs, his face four inches away. Salmon-scented breath warmed her face. "Let me tell you about my mother. My mother was an actress. Never mind that she couldn't act for shit and got what bit parts she did only after an enthusiastic turn with the casting agent. She told people she was an actress, so she was. See what I mean? You have to make your own dreams."

Evelyn put Angel out of her mind and listened. She listened with every pore of her being. There had to be a key here somewhere.

"I was the product of one of those enthusiastic turns, but motherhood didn't slow her down. She had Aunt Cindy and dear old *Grandmama* to do all the icky stuff like change diapers and see that I went to school. And so my life went. For fifteen years. One day she said, 'Let's go to the beach.' It was early June and way too cold to swim, practically too cold to be outside without a coat. I didn't care. My mother was actually going to spend an hour or two of her day with *me*. I couldn't believe my luck."

He straightened up, and Evelyn breathed out in a sigh. But he didn't move away. He circled her, trailing one hand along her shoulders as he spoke.

"We went to Edgewater Beach. I stood at the water. It was cold enough to numb my feet, but my mother had taken me swimming, and I was by golly going to *swim*. I turned around to show her, but she was busy chatting up one of those beefy types she went for. Her skin looked all crinkled up with goose pimples, but she never stopped smiling. And I saw."

"Saw what?" Evelyn breathed.

"That I was still too damn naïve to make it in show business." His fingers draped the curve of her neck, loosely, as he stood behind her. "She took me there to provide an innocent reason to take her clothes off in front of this guy. It had never been about me, not for a nanosecond. It was about her." He leaned down toward her ear. "I was just a prop."

"What happened?"

"I went there to swim. So I swam. After a while the cold doesn't hurt so much."

Evelyn shuddered.

"A really dedicated lifeguard came in and got me. I woke up as he was doing CPR, which was neither necessary nor expertly done. He cracked a rib, but hey, at least he tried."

"What did your mother do?"

He laughed. "What do you think? Grabbed the opportunity. Just like when I saw you at Kopecki's—see what I mean about learning from her? She grabbed the opportunity. It was one of her better performances, almost on a par with the aluminum siding commercial." The hand on her neck trembled against her skin, energized by the memory. "The next week the Hanna blew up and my mother finally achieved immortality."

"I was there."

"There?" He came around to look at her face. "You mean, like you worked there? With the coroner's office?"

She nodded, unsure how he'd take that news.

"Did you see my mother?"

"I—I'm sure I did."

He smiled gently. "Wasn't she beautiful?"

Evelyn didn't dare to breathe, didn't even blink, froze more still than cement.

"You're beautiful, too, you know." He traced one cheek with his finger.

She tried not to pull away.

But he noticed. He straightened up. "I'd love to sit around and tell you all about myself, but I'm afraid it's time to go."

She swallowed a rising tide of bile and spoke out: "I'm curious to see how you do this. Between this bucket and my body, I must weigh, what, two hundred pounds?"

"Depends," he joked as he opened a small storage closet. "Have you been dieting?"

"How are you going to do it without Jimmy to help you?"

That arrested his motion. "Jimmy?"

"Your partner?" she reminded him.

"You still think *Jimmy* had anything to do with this?"

Shit. Poor Jimmy Neal. "You mean he didn't?"

"Of course not. That's absurd. Jimmy wouldn't . . . Jimmy could never—"

"Kill innocent people?"

If he felt remorse, he did a masterful job of hiding it. "No-body's innocent, Evelyn. Someone in your line of work ought to know that." He pulled a two-wheeled dolly out of the closet and shut the door. It was a battered piece of equipment, red paint nearly worn off, an innocuous thing that could be found in any household. To Evelyn it might as well have been an iron maiden.

"Then why did you kill him?"

At last Max seemed genuinely regretful over someone's death. "He screwed up. He had ordered the chloroform for me. I told him I used it to kill rats—a stupid explanation, but Jimmy wasn't a real deep thinker. He didn't have a dream, a focus. He thought his nickname should be Slick, working at that hospital, everybody's buddy, always with a story to tell, but he was pretty simple, really. When you guys started questioning him, he finally figured out it had to be me."

"And he confronted you?" she asked, incredulous.

"Why would Jimmy be afraid of me? We grew up together. If it wasn't for Aunt Cindy, I would probably have starved to death before my mother or grandmother noticed. Jimmy and I were like brothers."

"And you killed him."

"He panicked. He wanted me to confess." He snorted, as if he couldn't help but laugh at such a foolish thing. "Like I would do that."

"But no cement bucket for him," Evelyn said as he positioned the dolly next to her chair.

"I was in a hurry."

David careened onto Warren Road in a cloud of rubber smoke. Two patrol cars followed, with lights but no sirens. Next to him, Riley cursed and clutched his lit cigarette as if it were a talisman that could ward off a fatal, body-wrecking car crash. It snapped in two, but at least snatching the lit end from between his thighs took his mind off the very real possibility of arriving at the ME's office as an MVA—motor vehicle accident.

"Take it easy, will you?" he protested halfheartedly.

"She's probably already dead." David tried to ease the pain in his heart by facing the worst scenario. It didn't help.

"No, she's not," Riley said, as if he knew it wouldn't do them any good to despair, while secretly agreeing. Last-minute saves came only on TV. In real life, people died. Evelyn was most likely dead, and neither of them could stand the thought. David's mind kept bouncing off the image as if it were coated with Teflon.

"She wouldn't ruin my record like that," Riley went on, as if barely listening to himself, resorting to cop humor to keep them going. "How is this case going to look? We scare an innocent kid straight into the arms of the real murderer, and then we lose one of the county's most valuable employees. They'll be doing an autopsy on *us*. We'll be writing parking tickets at the stadium for the rest of our lives, if we're lucky."

"Like I give a shit," David snarled.

"Oh? Suddenly Mr. Ambition doesn't give a shit?"

He got no answer and apparently didn't expect one. He talked only to direct their attention to something, anything, other than the picture of Evelyn laid out on one of her own autopsy tables.

The roads were fairly clear. Dinnertime and the crappy weather kept people indoors, but there were still plenty of cars for David to weave through. Large stone houses with neat faces lined the street.

"We never did determine," David said, his voice eerily conversational, "if he raped them first."

"Stop it," Riley growled.

They were silent the rest of the way.

The late Mrs. Chisholm's residence loomed behind its hedges, a brooding mountain of dark stone with a front porch wide enough for a picnic table and a detached garage in back. The light snowfall, which could not make up its mind whether to stay or melt, gave it a slightly unkempt look. There were no lights visible.

David pulled into the driveway, stopping so short that one of the patrol cars tapped his bumper. The headlights illuminated the snow in front of him and he could see them. Tire tracks. Fresh ones.

They were out of the car in an instant and approaching, taking care even in their haste not to step on the tire marks. David headed for the garage and Riley turned to the house.

David used the flashlight to glance into the garage with a strange feeling of déjà vu. But this one was not filled with junk; in fact, it held nothing at all. Darker streaks on the floor, however, could only have come from wet tires.

He had been there. And he had left.

"Damn!" David cried to himself.

"What the hell is this?" Riley muttered. David turned.

Between the house and the garage there were two sets of prints—one going, one coming—and two solid ruts. David bent closer. It seemed to be wheel tracks, but from what? A wheelchair?

"I'm going in," he told Riley, who didn't even mention a warrant as David kicked the door. Sturdier than Max's, however, the door didn't budge. In frustration Riley tried the knob, and it turned.

They spread through the rooms; Riley went upstairs, David went down, the uniforms stayed on the ground floor and took in the many framed photos of beautiful Donna Chisholm.

A light switch threw the basement into garish relief and David felt utter hopelessness invade his soul as he took in the view: Chains. Bags of cement. A chair with duct tape clinging to the seat. Evelyn had been prepared.

They were too late.

Riley pounded down the stairs to join him, and together they stared in mute horror.

"Where the hell is he?" David spoke as if anger could stem the futility. *"Where the hell is he?"*

"We'll find them," Riley said with an utter lack of conviction.

"There's miles and miles of Metropark system," David grated out. He wanted to move, run, throw himself at someone, yet he had no target, no direction, and his body flinched at the forced control. "He could be anywhere. We don't even know which way he went."

Riley's jaw clenched. "You ain't giving up, kid, and I know I ain't. This is the bottom of the ninth, and the bases are loaded."

"Meaning?"

"Think."

David thought. "Where's the nearest bridge?"

AT LEAST SHE WASN'T in the trunk. Trussed with chains in the backseat, duct tape over her mouth, Evelyn tried to move the bucket on the floor and tip it to one side. She assumed he had put her there because the cement had not fully dried and would spill out if turned over, so she tried to do exactly that. At the same time, she rubbed the duct tape against a heavy chain that ran over her shoulder. He had securely belted her into the seat, hidden behind pull-down shades that attached to the windows with suction cups. She could see out through the pinholes, but people outside couldn't see in—had there been any people around on a frigid weeknight.

"Sit still," Max commanded as he drove.

"Go to hell," she said, but it came out as "Mmm." She got a corner of the duct tape off, pressed the free end against one of the chains, and peeled further. It didn't feel good. *I won't need to wax my facial hairs this month,* she thought, and giggled hysterically.

"What was that?" Max asked.

She rubbed the opposite cheek against a shoulder until the piece came off entirely. "Why did you do this to Lia?" she asked, happy to see him give a little jolt of shock at the sound of her voice. It covered the sound of the seat belt *slipping* out of its buckle.

In the rearview mirror his face held no sign of recognition. "Who?"

"Lia Ripetti."

"Oh. *Ophelia*. The one who got food poisoning from our potato salad. That wasn't my fault, by the way," he added as he turned a corner, glancing in the mirror to make sure she got that part straight. "I did the lettuce salads that night."

"How did you get into her apartment?"

"The way most people do. I knocked on the door."

"And she let you in?"

"I told her I had a coupon from Kopecki's." He seemed proud of his subterfuge. "As a gesture of goodwill, so on and so forth. I figured she'd let me in. She was sweet, didn't look right past me like most people do at dinners. She talked to me." His expression dreamed of the past as if he saw a young woman with long dark hair instead of the wet city street.

"And then?"

His eyes snapped back to reality. "And then she walked away with that mobster she worked for. Sweet Ophelia. I just love that name, don't you?"

"Is that why you killed her? Her name?" Evelyn asked. She had to bite her lip to keep from asking about Angel. If he met the girls through catering events and their connection to Jimmy Neal had been coincidence, then most likely he didn't know Angel existed. She had no reason to bring her daughter to his attention, or he might get around to her after Evelyn was dead and gone and unable to protect her child.

He considered the name theory. "I don't know," he said at last. "Maybe. It gave her a certain classy quality, you know? She had beautiful eyes. Like they had seen their share of tragedy, but could still appreciate a sunrise or a perfect rose."

"And Destiny Pierson? Did you offer her a coupon, too?"

"That was something." He spoke as if it were a good fishing story that she just had to hear. "Right off the street, all her friends babbling and running along like a pack of jackals, and I plucked her out without a sound. I couldn't believe it worked, frankly. I had to have been three blocks away before they even missed her."

"But *why?*"

"She was so *on*—as in onstage. She just had that presence, you know? Smart. Snotty, but in a way that made you laugh."

"But she got away from you," Evelyn pointed out.

The memory didn't disturb him. "I said she was smart. But don't get your hopes up. I've made some improvements in my design."

Great, she thought. *A psycho killer who learns from his mistakes.* She gazed hungrily at the outside world, at the neon sign of a closed beauty salon, at teenage couples leaving a movie theater. Too far away to hear her if she screamed or hit the window with her head, they might as well have been on a different planet. "Blair Danilov?"

"Who's that?"

"Another of your victims, I'm guessing."

He drove along like a well-trained chauffeur, staying well below the speed limit and using his turn signals, staying away from other cars and populated sidewalks. He appeared to give her question careful consideration. "What did she look like?"

"Medium blond hair, blue eyes. Five-six. Slender." If she could just get out of the car. The knee she had injured falling out of the trunk sent shooting pains through her thigh, but still she turned her body slowly, quietly, so that the hands bound behind her were nearer the door handle. If she could get it open and tumble out . . . if the fall didn't kill her, the oncoming traffic might, but it would be worth it. Except that she couldn't tumble, not with a bucket of concrete on her feet. If she threw her upper body out, she'd be dragged alongside until Max stopped the car and finished her off. She'd have to throw the bucket, which had to weigh close to eighty pounds, out first. They hadn't covered this in martial arts training.

"Doesn't ring any bells."

"A graphic artist. Did greeting cards."

"Never heard of her."

She could feel the armrest, the cracked vinyl . . . her fingertips found the handle.

"Sit still, Evelyn. Don't make me come back there. Isn't that what Daddy always says? If I have to stop this car and come back there—"

"Disappeared August thirty-first."

Max caught her eye in the rearview mirror. "I haven't killed *everyone,* you know. I'm sure Blair whoever—"

"Danilov." She pulled the handle. Nothing happened.

"—Danilov is a very nice girl, but I don't know her. And you can't open that door from back there, you know. Only Fords unlock when you pull the handle. This is a Chevy."

She settled back in her seat. The knob had been unscrewed from the door lock, leaving it a vertical piece of stainless steel with threads, lurking uncooperatively in the door frame. She'd never reach it with her hands even if Max let her try. Perhaps with her toe, if she could get her legs out of the bucket. The cement had the consistency of very thick peanut butter. She was no longer strapped to the chair.

She pulled. The chains from her body looped around the bucket handle, which rested against her shins, and something must have secured the loops because the chains would not slide off. She couldn't see much in the dark backseat, but somehow the chain system kept her legs in place. Max had been right. He had made improvements.

"Thalia Johnson?" Her brain still went through the motions while her body occupied itself.

He didn't respond at first. She had to hurry, for the storefronts had given way to a residential neighborhood; at any moment she could find herself at a park entrance and that would be that. Even if she escaped the car, there would be no one around to help. No one would be strolling through a dark city park in the freezing cold of a November weeknight.

"Black girl," he said. "About to get married."

"Yes."

"Yes."

Evelyn closed her eyes, said a silent prayer for Mrs. Johnson, still waiting for her daughter to return. "How did you get her? Did you convince her to get in the car with you or—"

"I just gave her a ride. She recognized me, of course. I told her I lived nearby and had a question about her menu. Brides panic when you say that. They are obsessed with perfection for the only time in their lives."

"And no one noticed you, driving along in an all-black neighborhood?"

He turned the corner gently, driving past a sign that read: *Cleveland Metroparks—Mastick Road Entrance*. "I guess not. You really shouldn't be such a racist. What do you think they would have done, stormed my car? I just drove along and offered her a ride home. She was too sweet to refuse. She had good taste in food, too. She loved my idea for zucchini puffs."

"Why did you kill her if you liked her so much?"

He studied her again via the rearview mirror. His dark eyes reflected the passing streetlights and little else. "People are always coming and going. They come into my world and then they leave again. Sometimes I want them to stay."

"So you weighted her down and threw her in the river?"

"Now I'm the only one who knows where she is. She exists only in my world."

"It's about power."

He corrected her firmly. "It's about love."

"Excuse me if I find that hard to believe."

"Killing is a very intimate thing. Look how much time you and I have already spent together. Would I do all that for someone I didn't care about?"

"Sure. Nothing shows your affection like a bucket full of cement."

.   .   .

David refused to let Riley drive, even while he spoke on both a cell phone and a police radio to the police dive team and the Metropark Rangers, respectively. Riley had the Homicide chief on a phone in one hand and held on to the dash with the other.

"Bring every diver you can call in and bring a spare tank. If she goes in the water, it won't be a simple matter of throwing a life jacket. Understand?"

The radio crackled and the dive-team captain's voice crackled as well. "I understand perfectly."

"How long can she be underwater?" David stammered, cringing at the stupidity of the question, but he couldn't put his racing thoughts into coherent words, or perhaps he didn't want to.

After a pause, the captain said kindly, "As long as she can hold her breath."

"And after that?"

The second pause sounded even more disbelieving than the first. "Three, maybe four minutes before brain damage."

David could feel his pride deserting him at a great gallop, and didn't care. "What I'm really asking is, if she goes in the water, is there any hope?"

"There's always hope."

David resisted the overwhelming desire to throw the radio out the window. He switched to the cell phone instead, momentarily leaving the wheel free until Riley's gasp brought it to his attention.

"Lieutenant?" he asked, prompting a response from the ranger leader on the other end.

"Yes, sir, what can I do for you?"

"Where is this bridge, now?"

"Mmmm . . . you're on Lakeshore now, right?"

"Yes!"

"Get off at Riverside Drive. You see, this bridge I mean is the closest to your location physically, you understand"—he paused until David wanted to scream and instead cut off a tractor-trailer in a burst of self-destructiveness—"but it's fairly busy. You get a lot of traffic across it, even though it's only five hundred feet long, but it's near the hospital, see—"

"What are you getting at?" David shouted, and cringed at the sound of his own voice. He'd be squealing like a little girl in another minute. Either that or he'd find this lieutenant and kill him.

"If your boy knows the parks, he might not pick this one. Hell, all told, there's forty-two bridges he could choose from in the whole system. But let's concentrate on the upper west side."

David waited for him to go on, then prompted: "So what do you think would be a better place, more isolated, for his purposes?"

"Well, you're right there at the beginning of the Scenic Park Trailhead—dunno. Isaac, what do you think?" he asked to someone on his side of the phone.

I can't stand it, David thought. *I can't take this.*

"Yeah"—he could hear the lieutenant's voice continuing—"but what about the—oh, the *Valley* Parkway? You sure?"

Just as David was ready to explode, the lieutenant spoke again. "Well, hey, Detective, Isaac here has an idea. A couple miles down from the bridge we're talking about is a footbridge off the Valley Parkway. It'd be more private for your guy, like, and there's a parking area there."

"Perfect."

"But at the end of the trailhead there's a covered bridge. That's a deep part of the river and there ain't much traffic there. I think at night that covered bridge makes people nervous. Too dark. But then your guy might want that."

"And that is where?"

"About another four miles down the road. It's just past—shoot, Isaac, where is that—"

"Lieutenant," David said through politely clenched teeth, "may I speak to Isaac?"

The trees, only the barest outlines against the night sky, crowded around as if they, too, were trying to hide her from the outside world.

She gazed at them in terror as the car wound slowly around a bend in the road. Lost in a dark world, she had entered their valley; they were the only authority and claimed Max as one of theirs. He belonged here.

She began to panic. She could feel the waves of hysteria surge up from her panting lungs, through her heart, and up to her throat, and she prepared to scream.

Instead, she bent over and vomited, coughing up a thin bile onto the floor behind the driver's seat. She spit the last of it out and wiped her mouth on the seat before sitting up.

"It's all right, Evelyn," Max said even as the noxious fumes wafted through the car. "The chloroform makes people sick. Lia threw up in my basement. Took me a while to get that smell out."

"I'm glad," Evelyn hissed. "Let them find my DNA on the floor after they search your car. You'll have a tough time explaining that."

"I'll wash it out."

"Won't help."

"I'll use bleach."

"It'll still be there," she lied. "What about Christine Sabian?"

He took his time to respond. "What about her?"

"Did you like her, too?"

He glanced in the rearview mirror again. "Everyone liked Christine."

His shimmering eyes made her skin crawl, but she prodded him to go on. "What was she like?"

"Everyone wanted to learn from her. So did I. She showed me how to make ham pinwheels and foolproof hollandaise sauce. I could never get it right until I met her. She was going to help me on my way."

"Way to where?" *Keep talking.* Just keep talking, though she no longer cared. The ghost of Christine Sabian could not help her. No one could help her.

"Hollywood." He smiled. "Max Chisholm, chef to the stars. All you need is a little self-promotion. I mean, the Food Network is on 24-7, how hard can it be to land a spot?"

She blinked at him. Even without the streetlights she could see his face darken.

"You think that's a dumb idea?"

"No! No, I don't. You're right—cooking shows are so popular these days. People want new, unique things to eat." He nodded, but his eyes continued to shimmer. Evelyn asked, "Christine helped you? Then why did you hurt her?"

He didn't answer.

"She was nice to you."

No response.

"But then she went home to her real family, didn't she?"

He stopped at a red light, stepping too hard on the brakes. The car slid a foot before coming to a rest.

"Like Lia Ripetti and Destiny Pierson. Christine walked away."

Then he spoke softly. "Not anymore."

The car accelerated, under control once more.

"Your victims—the women you pick—they look like your mother, did you ever notice that? Young, pretty, long dark hair."

"Is that psychology, Evelyn? Behavioral profiling? Impressive."

"I'm too old and my hair is short. I don't fit."

"Neither did Jimmy," he pointed out with chilling finality. And then, long before she was ready, he pulled the car off the road and put out the lights.

CHAPTER

ONE GLANCE AT THE Scenic Park Trailhead bridge, and David dismissed it. Too well lit, too public. He'd have to be nuts to try it here, and this guy seemed too cool to be nuts. He kept driving, with Isaac spouting directions in one ear and Riley spouting APB reports in the other.

"How many cops we got in this damn city, and they can't find one stinking Chevy Lumina?" he grumbled to David. "They'll let that grounder go right between their legs. What's next?"

"The footbridge. Tell the dive team we're moving on. And please tell me that dive *team* means they have more than one diver."

Riley consulted. "Two. They got Jerry out of bed."

"Send one to the footbridge and one to the covered bridge."

Riley relayed these instructions, then asked as if despite himself: "What if it's neither of these places?"

"Then she's dead."

. . .

The tiny lot had spaces for no more than four cars. A single street lamp threw a flickering orange light over the car and the snow. The river flowed as a black nothingness, visible only as a rushing sound. Max reached back into her seat, unlocked her door, and then got out and rummaged around in the trunk. He pulled out the two-wheeled dolly. They had not passed another vehicle in the past five miles. They were alone in the world, and she was about to die.

Max came around the side of the car.

Evelyn smashed her temple down on the bare screw in the door, locking it.

"Shit," David said. "Shitshit*shit*!"

The footbridge appeared like something out of a Robert Frost poem, sweet and old-fashioned. And empty.

"Let's go on," Riley suggested. They stared through the windshield as a man in a wet suit approached them.

"Nobody here," he told them, to David's despair.

"She may be there. She could be under the water and the guy's already gone. Could you—"

"No."

David's blood turned from ice to fire. "Look, you—"

"There's no footprints," the diver explained. "And the snow isn't falling *that* hard. Nobody's been on that bridge tonight."

David swallowed. "Let's move on, then."

"Bet you wish you had electric locks on this model," Evelyn said to him, even as she felt the trickle of blood down her face.

"Very funny, Evelyn." He returned to the driver's seat and unlocked the door again. He also unlocked the passenger door, then walked around the car.

She tried to hit the stripped knob with her elbow, but her arm wouldn't reach that far. She had no choice but to use her head again, piercing the skin once more and buying her exactly another second and a half of life, because Max merely opened the passenger door, reached back, held the screw up, and pulled the back door open from the outside.

His right hand still held the screw, and she leaned forward and bit his wrist.

He yelled, but not very loud. He pulled and she bit deeper, her teeth piercing his flesh. She could feel the salty tang of his blood in her mouth, and the bones of his wrist under her teeth. She couldn't hurt him, but she temporarily immobilized him. He was stuck with one arm through the passenger door and the rest of his body outside. As long as she didn't let go, he couldn't move.

He reached his other arm through the open rear door and grabbed her hair, pulling the red curls tight. The pain only made her jaw clench tighter. He let out a groan. She tried to pull back, immobilizing him against the door frame.

But he had heard enough tips for women on how to fight off an attacker—resort to the classics. He stuck an index finger in her right eye.

The pain was intense. The world went white and starry and she let go of his hand, falling back in the seat. She turned her face away from him and rested her eyes against the seat cushion, trying to calm the raging bolts of lightning that flashed across her vision. It took a second or two before she could hear anything, and another sixty before she could see. The right eye ached but it functioned. When her vision cleared she saw Max tying a rag around his wounded wrist.

"That wasn't very dignified, Evelyn." His patience had reached its limit.

So had hers.

"The hell with dignity. If you think I'm going down without a fight, then you sadly misjudged this victim. I have a daughter."

"Do you?" he asked, looking up.

Damn, damn, damn.

She just told him the last thing she wanted him to know. Now what had she set in motion?

She turned her head and vomited on the floor of the car once again, then spit until she could no longer taste his blood.

He waited with what seemed like patience, but wasn't. He simply enjoyed her weakness. "Are you *ready*?" he asked at last.

"Yes," she lied.

He reached in, grasped the handle of the bucket, and dragged it outside, with her shins in painful tow. With the bucket on the gravel, he tipped it and slid the lip of the dolly underneath.

"Come on," he said to Evelyn, still lying on the backseat.

"All right." She sprung her body up in an arc, thrusting all her weight at him like a wrecking ball. Her face hit his chest, and the dolly tipped back on him. They tumbled to the ground.

The covered bridge looked just as the Ranger lieutenant had described it. Dark. Scary. And unfortunately empty.

"Stop here," Riley told David. "Are there any tracks?"

David burst out of the car before it finished sliding to a halt and nearly forced a rear-end collision with the police diver, who was following in a Bronco. This particularly isolated bend in the road showed him nothing but the white banks, the less white road, and a black gash in the earth that held the sound of rushing water. Over the water hovered the hulking structure, enclosing the road as if swallowing it.

His flashlight threw a set of tire tracks into sharp relief. They ran along the right side of the road, moving in the same direction as him. He heard the snow crunching under Riley's feet as his partner joined him. The silent night sat around them. He followed the tracks into the mouth of the bridge. The temperature had dropped another ten degrees in the past hour, a famous Cleveland trick.

"This could have been anyone," Riley muttered. "Parks aren't *that* deserted, even in winter."

"I know." David kept his head down like a bloodhound, watching the tracks, and stiffened when a distinct shoeprint suddenly blew into the circle of light on the ground. They stopped and let the light follow.

The shoeprints ran next to the tire tracks, from the other end of the bridge to just past the middle. Then they turned and went back.

David scanned the length of the bridge with the flashlight. Nothing but snow and tracks and rotting timbers. Only the water moved, filling the structure with an echo of thunder.

In the dark space beyond the reach of the flashlight stood a man.

"Freeze!" David shouted, reaching for his gun.

"Police!" Riley shouted, pulling his gun.

"Don't shoot!" the man shouted, and stepped into the light. He wore some kind of uniform and he sure as hell wasn't Max Chisholm.

"Who are you?" David asked.

"I'm Isaac," he said. "Who're you?"

Max landed on the sharp gravel with the dolly and Evelyn on top of him, and it did nothing for his mood. He wriggled out from under her immediately, so that one side of her head hit the gravel and the other wedged itself under the dolly handle. It did nothing for her mood, either.

"Fucking *stop* it!" he shouted, and kicked her in the kidney hard enough to bring tears.

She tried to protest but didn't have the breath. Taking advantage of the lull and frenzied with anger, he jerked her body upright. None of the cement had spilled—it had hardened enough to stay in the bucket. Before she could catch her breath he wedged her onto the dolly.

Only ten feet separated the car from the sidewalk, but Max found it difficult to roll the heavy object over gravel. She caught a glimpse of stars as she rested for a moment while he struggled with the wheels. She had no opportunity to pitch herself to the ground again; he had one arm around her chest, holding her upward, and she could feel iron muscles through the light coat he wore. He was a hell of a lot stronger than he looked. He was also a hell of a lot crazier than he looked.

This is it, she thought. *I'm going to die, trussed up like some bad Hannibal Lecter imitation. I'll never see my daughter again.*

I need help. I need David.

She turned her head slightly. The last fifteen feet of snow-covered sidewalk before the bridge represented her last chance.

She screamed. The sound echoed through the trees, sending a rush of owls into the night sky. A fox barked in sympathy, then the woods fell silent.

Max chuckled in between his labored panting. "Good one, Evelyn. Do you really think there's anyone out here in this weather? We're miles from the nearest house."

"Crazy joggers," she suggested.

"Are never around when you need them. And anyone driving through has the windows rolled up tight."

"Unless they're smoking," she said, proud of herself for thinking of it.

"Let's see." He stopped at the edge of the sidewalk. They both faced the road, whose dark and deserted length robbed any hope she might have had. The frigid air bit her face. "Do you see any cars?" Max whispered in her ear, intimate as a lover. "I don't see any cars. I don't hear any cars, either. Oh, well, no rescue for you. Let's go."

"Wait."

"Waiting is the one thing I can't do."

"But I hear something."

"I can tell you what that is." He pulled the dolly onto the sidewalk with a sickening lurch. "That's your heart beating. Sounds loud, doesn't it?"

"There's a car coming."

"Don't you wish."

"Why are you doing this, Max? Why?"

"Because I like you, Evelyn," he panted, making slow progress, pulling the dolly with one hand and holding her still with the other. "I really like you. Besides, if I don't, you'll tell them I killed everyone and I'll go to jail for the rest of my life. What do you expect me to do? And don't tell me you won't tell—that only insults my intelligence."

"I have no intention of keeping any secret of yours."

"Thank you."

A picturesque trestle of wooden beams hemmed in the bridge, with a railing of rounded timbers. He simply stood her up against the railing and bent down to pick up the bucket. Once he hefted it over the side, nothing could stop her body from following.

She bent at the waist and slumped to the ground. Her right knee popped and protested and the impact sent a jarring thud through her skull to her brain.

Max swore, gathered her sweater at the throat and hauled her to her feet like a bag of laundry. She stayed limp so he had to support her entire weight, intending to make him work for every inch. But with adrenaline-induced strength he held her easily with one hand.

His face, only inches from hers, filled her field of vision. "You're only ticking me off, Evelyn . . . and that's not helping your case any."

"Go to hell."

"No," he said. "*You* go."

Before she could react, he hit her. His closed fist smashed into her jaw like a bullet, snapping her head back and knocking her mind clear. She floated at the edge of consciousness for a brief second, and in that time he pushed her back, grasped the handle of the bucket, and hauled it up to the rail. Her body lay perfectly balanced between life and death. All he had to do was let go.

CHAPTER

38

"NOW WHAT?" DAVID ASKED with an intensity that seemed to startle the young Ranger. "Where now?"

"The next bridge would be Hilliard Road."

"Okay."

"But that's a major road—four lanes, well lit, lots of cars."

David closed his eyes against the wave of hopelessness that stole through his body. He had failed. He had failed Evelyn and she was going to die because of it—if by some miracle she hadn't already.

"Then there's Christine Meadow, but that's—"

David grabbed the kid by the shoulder, startling him further. "What was that?"

"There's a bridge there that's kind of off by itself. The road eventually dead-ends so there's not much traffic."

"And it's called Christine—"

"Yeah, they named it after some little girl that—"

"Let's go." David gave Riley such a sharp jerk that the man dropped his cigarette. He didn't protest.

. . .

She had stopped struggling. She had stopped moving altogether, as gravity had become her deadly enemy. The snow fell on her face, appearing from the night sky like magic. Beside her, his breath came in heavy gasps.

She scarcely dared breathe, only whispered, "Why Christine?"

It began with Christine, she thought. *She's his weak spot.*

For a moment the falling snow made the only sound. Then he spoke almost conversationally. "Someone named Eaton Stannard Barret once wrote: 'Let no one who loves be called altogether unhappy; even love unreturned has its rainbow.' "

"And?"

"He lied," Max said simply, and pushed her over.

"Why this place?" Riley asked as David slid rather than drove through the falling snow. The car hummed with silence except for an occasional crackle of the police radio; the windows were closed against the cold and it sounded as if they were talking in a vacuum. Isaac drove in front of them in a Ford Bronco festooned with the ranger logo. With every turn he demonstrated the benefits of four-wheel drive. One of the police divers drove behind them. "What did that name mean?"

"The missing girls," David explained. "Christine Sabian disappeared first. He worked with her at Kopecki's. I saw him at Destiny's funeral. If I'd gone deeper into Jimmy Neal's life I could have put it together. If I had a few brain cells that worked, Jimmy would still be alive. And Evelyn . . ." He didn't finish. He couldn't finish.

"Sure you should have made the connection—if you were psychic. We can only hit the balls that come our way, kid."

"Don't comfort me," David told him. "You make it sound like she's already dead."

. . .

At first Evelyn saw nothing but white underneath her, and thought her wish had come true. The river had frozen. But it was the white froth of rough water, churning and capping, and she plunged into it without hindrance.

The water tore at her body like a thousand freezing knives. The shock of it made her gasp and she took in a mouthful before her lungs instinctively closed. After that the staggering cold paralyzed her body and kept her from trying to breathe.

The pressure surprised her. The current pushed her like a bulldozer, slamming her body with a force that faded the deeper she got. As the pressure of the depth increased, her sinuses protested in pain.

And then she hit bottom.

She knew she had only a few minutes to live.

Isaac, David decided, wasted himself on the Rangers. He belonged in SWAT or the friggin' FBI. When the convoy came upon Max's car backing carefully out of the tiny lot, Isaac immediately blocked its exit, pulled his weapon, and ordered Max out of the car and on the ground before David crunched to a halt.

Max sprinted for the tree line.

David shot after him, slipping once on the wet snow before looking up to see Isaac flanking Max like a tiger, both nearly camouflaged against the dark trunks of the pines. Isaac gave one great burst of speed and crashed against the long legs of their killer.

David hauled Max to his feet with one hand, just as Max had hauled Evelyn only minutes before. The Homicide cop persona had fled, self-control forgotten.

"Where is she?" He shook the man. "Is she in the water?"

His face only vaguely visible in the dim light of the moon, Max stared at him as if David were speaking an unfamiliar but not very interesting language.

"Did you throw her in, you son of a bitch?"

Nothing. If Max were concerned about having been caught, he hid it well.

David dragged him toward the bridge. "Show me."

Riley and the police diver met them. "She's in the water, Jerry," David said, his voice remarkably matter-of-fact when he felt as if his heart had just been cut from his body. "You'll have to go in."

"Damn."

"Where did she go over?" David shouted at Max, still dragging him along like a rag doll, the man following without protest, and without answering.

"Let me make this clear," Riley tried, falling into step beside them. "You're looking at the electric chair. Help us save her and we'll take the death penalty off the slate. You got one chance right now."

Max gave the Homicide detective the same look he had given David, and they could hear nothing over the ever-moving water.

"If she dies, you fry," David told him. "That is a promise. I will pull the switch myself."

Max turned to him and smiled.

The smack echoed to the treetops as Riley hit Max, knocking him flat on the asphalt. Without stopping to rub his hand, Riley turned to the diver and he and David screamed in unison: *"Go!"*

Evelyn had never been able to hold her breath very long. She had never been much of a swimmer. No point to it anyway—the freezing water racked her with agony every split second, so she might as well just take a breath and end it . . . but she couldn't make herself do that any more than she could sprout gills.

Her feet, as she had hoped, pulled out of the cement block with only a minor struggle, but the chains held her in place. She strained against them with pointless energy born of panic. The chains bit into her flesh, but the pain leaked away as the water numbed her skin.

A light appeared—she saw it gleam through her tightly clamped eyelids and opened them. The water of the Cuyahoga flowed dark green and murky, but she could see floating bits of sand, algae, and fish against the glow. It did nothing to comfort her since she was about to drown. Her mind had passed beyond thought.

Then something enveloped her, a tenacious being that forced an object into her mouth and pinched her nose. It seemed for a moment that the situation had progressed from worst to worser still, and then she felt a bubble against her tongue.

Oxygen.

She sucked in a mouthful of air as best she could. She brought in some water, choked, coughed, but kept her teeth clenched on the regulator and tried again. Whoever held her nose released it and she tried to breathe out through her nostrils.

Oxygen.

She could make it. Maybe she could make it. She was taking in as much water as oxygen but who cared? Her deadline had expired and still she lived. Maybe she could hang in for a few seconds more.

This angel in a wet suit helped her, though not gently. He pushed something between her legs—the oxygen tank, she realized. She held on to it with her knees; it slipped as her muscles convulsed with pain and cold, but she hung on. Her whole being focused on breathing the air in and forcing it out. In, out. The light went away.

Come back. *Oh, God, please come back.*

To be left in the black tomb was unbearable; only the physical work of breathing kept her sane. The flesh of her face had lost all sensation. She could not feel her lips and had no idea if they were secure around the regulator—probably not, because she pulled in water with each breath and her lungs were filling up, freezing from the inside out.

Max, the most comfortable of everyone at the scene, rested in the warm patrol car with his hands handcuffed behind him. He sat docilely, ignoring the incredulous stares of the two young police officers in the front seat.

David clung to the railing with both hands, and they were all that kept him from jumping over the side. His skin froze to the wet wood, but he didn't know it. He felt like a side of beef, suspended, immobile, iced through and through, until the diver surfaced. He shouted something over the waves.

"What?"

"She's in chains. I need a bolt cutter."

"Oh, God," David moaned. "Of course she is. How the hell are we—"

"Maybe our perp has—"

Isaac said, "I have one."

They stared, but he was already trotting off to his Bronco. A horrible moment passed as David held his breath, Riley lit a cigarette without being aware of it, and the diver, Jerry, fought to keep the current from pushing him downriver, while all three waited for the young park ranger to rummage in his trunk. He returned promptly with a three-foot-long bolt cutter with red rubber handles and a rope and called to the diver. "Just let me tie this rope on—"

David shrugged out of his overcoat, pulled the cutters from Isaac's hand, and vaulted over the wooden timbers into empty air before Riley could form the *n* in *"No!"*

The two men on the bridge gazed down.

"I hope he knows what he's doing," the park ranger sighed. Riley said nothing.

As David met the water, he expected hideous cold. He expected icy knives. He expected paralyzing, arctic waves.

He hadn't expected unbearable.

The water forced the air from his lungs, the strength from his muscles. If it weren't for the cold he'd have been sweating from terror.

Evelyn can't survive this. I can't survive this.

A splash that wasn't a wave sounded at his right, and he held out the bolt cutters to the scuba-suited Jerry. The diver, equipped with a strong flashlight on his hood, ripped them from David's rictus grip and fought the current upstream. David followed, though his fingers could no longer cup the water. The current was strong but not over-powering. Cold remained the real enemy.

After an agonizing few moments, Jerry turned tail up and disap-peared under the water. His trail of murky light shone a path to Eve-lyn. David took as deep a breath as his frozen chest would allow and plunged below the surface.

Algae and fleeing minnows stood out in sharp relief against the re-fracted light from Jerry's lamp. Was Christine Sabian down here somewhere? David swam, aware of the killing weight of his sodden clothes, his shoes. He tried not to think, just act.

Then suddenly he saw Evelyn.

In the shifting light, his lungs already threatening to burst, he saw her dark figure swaying with the current as Jerry approached with the bolt cutters. The regulator stayed in her mouth with no indication that she used it. David saw no bubbles. Her hair obscured, then revealed her face. Unreasoning, he gripped her shoulders and pulled.

The chains held, but her eyes snapped open and for one instant they faced each other in their underwater graveyard. Her arms reached for him slowly, as if resigned to this inevitable resolution, to be bound together forever in an icy kiss.

Then the current pushed him and she moved as well. The chains were cut.

David kicked with every last molecule of energy he had, holding on to her with both hands. She came along but felt limp, yielding. The regulator slipped from her mouth and the heavy tank fell behind. He kicked.

In his whole frozen body, only his lungs felt warm, ready to ex-plode in a fireball of pain. He had released breath to ease the pressure but that no longer sufficed. He had to take air in *now*. He had to, or his body would stop and die.

He kicked. Was she still alive? Even with his numb fingers he could detect no movement, not the slightest tensing of her muscles. She could be dead. Or she would be very soon.

He broke the surface and drew in a rasping, frigid breath. He pulled Evelyn's head above the water. Even in the dark night, in moving water, he could tell she was not breathing.

"Here!" he heard over the current.

A series of lights flickered about thirty feet away, and he recognized Riley's voice. They waited on the bank. "Here!"

He swam with one arm, holding Evelyn with the other, through a moving, wavy, frozen purgatory that took all his strength and promised him nothing for it.

Jerry found them and helped support Evelyn's body, propelling them along with flippered feet.

Then David felt mud and the lights were in his face. Silhouettes reached for Evelyn and pulled her in, carrying her limp body off in some surreal pantomime. He began to protest.

Over the din of his rushing blood he heard Riley say, "Better grab him before he drowns, too."

EVELYN RESTED UNDER A heated blanket, which spewed tubes and wires monitoring her heart rate, temperature, and other vital signs. Occasionally her limbs would give a convulsive shake, like a dog throwing off water, but otherwise she slept as one dead. David wanted to wake her but didn't, afraid to throw off her efforts as she fought her way back from the depths. He just waited, perched on the neighboring bed, watching her every breath.

The lights were too bright. He loathed that about hospitals, that the lights were too bright and the rooms were too damn cold. They had given him a dry gown to put on, but the tissue-thin cotton felt only a few degrees warmer than walking around naked, and he stole the blanket and spread off the vacant bed. The nurse berated him for it, but he gave her a blank look and she went away.

Evelyn suffered from hypothermia, and they hoped nothing else. The doctors found no sign of oxygen deprivation, but it was too soon to be sure. They seemed cheerful; the house physician told David that with luck, the mother of all colds would be the worst she got out of this ordeal. David recognized the attempt at humor but could not respond, could not cough up a smile. He had been scared out of his mind. He had seen his life come to one point in time where he *had* to succeed and he had not. He might have lost the one person who could have made his future worth hanging around for. Pretending to be all right was impossible.

He heard a scuffle at the door and looked up as a teenage girl threw herself at Evelyn's bed. Behind her was an elderly woman who, he guessed, had done most of her aging in the past hour leaned in the doorway.

"Mom!" the girl said.

This must be Angel, David thought. *And I'm wrapped in a nightgown and a blanket, hairy legs hanging over the bed. And I thought I'd lost my talent for making good first impressions.*

Angel's crying, Evelyn thought groggily. *I'd better do something.*

It was so hard to open her eyes. She felt as if the cement now encased her whole body, soft but too heavy to move. Each breath made her lungs ache, and what little air she could handle came out in an *oof* as her daughter leaned on her chest, quaking with sobs.

She tried to lift her arms to comfort her daughter. Her efforts produced only a twitch in her right hand, and she was still so damn cold. But she figured one thing out.

It's me. Angel is crying over me.

She smiled.

CHAPTER

EVELYN STOOD WITHIN A loose group of trees in her backyard, wrapped in a bulky sweater and savoring every breath. That the air was tinged with smoke and roasted fowl only made it sweeter. She looked up at the treetops and the bright gray sky and savored those, too.

David left the overwarm house, beer in hand, and joined her in the ring of melted snow around the smoker. He looked around at the white-topped evergreens. "This is beautiful."

"Yeah."

"But my feet are cold. Tell me again why you're smoking a turkey."

"Tradition." Evelyn snuggled into her sweater, though the twenty-five degrees felt downright balmy to her.

"Whose tradition?"

"Mine. Just wait until you taste it."

"It'll taste like ham. Anything smoked tastes like ham. You could smoke an old shoe and it would taste like ham. Three of your cousins are arguing about who gets to sit next to that serology girl, Marissa."

"How do you think I got her to come?"

"What happened to Jason, by the way?"

Her eyes gleamed with a nasty edge. "Oh, Jason. He was told his services were no longer adequate. I think Tony secretly misses his kaffeeklatsch partner, but he got to fire someone, so it wasn't a total loss. It's a little unfair, really. Jason couldn't have known that Kopecki's had anything to do with anything."

"Then there was no reason for him to keep it to himself when I asked a direct question." David's fingers tightened on hers. "I notice Angel is among your guests."

"She wanted to be here." Evelyn happily rubbed steam off the temperature dial. "I told her it was okay if she went to her dad's, that I was going to have plenty of guests and I'd be just fine, but she insisted."

"She refuses to sit next to Ed, that guy from Toxicology," David said. "So do I."

"Be nice to Ed. His testimony about chloroform will be important at Max's trial." She shuddered. "What a circus that will be. Three counts of murder and one attempted. I wish we could prosecute him for Thalia Johnson and Christine Sabian as well."

"Not without their bodies. In spring we'll send the divers out again. I'm sure we'll have plenty of time before the trial comes around."

She watched the flakes of snow drift from the sky. "Defense attorneys are already fighting to represent him."

"I can see it now. He killed because Mommy didn't love him enough. Is that why he picked them? They reminded him of his mother?"

"Yes and no. They resembled his mother, but more than that, they made the mistake of being kind to him. For one brief moment, they each paid attention to him. And then they turned away."

"Like throwing a starving dog a crumb. He wanted more—more attention?"

"What we all want." She reached out her hand. "Love."

He took her fingers in his, pressing gently. They stood like that for some time, listening to the trees whisper over their heads.

"Angel might want to sit next to you, by the way. She thinks you're a hero."

"The jury may still be out as far as your mother is concerned. She keeps asking me a lot of questions, where I am from, that sort of thing."

"She wants to know if you're a nice boy."

"And am I? A nice boy?"

She looked him up and down. Her last wispy memory from her time under the water had been that of his arms around her, propelling her through the icy water to the surface, to life, his hands the only warmth in a frigid world. "I'd say you're a very nice boy."

He smiled.

She leaned over to lift the smoker lid and peer at the browning turkey. "Anything else you have to report?"

He took a deep breath. "That I think I love you, but I'm not going to say it."

The lid settled back with a clang.

He breathed out again. "Impulsive acts always get me in trouble. This time I'm going to go slow and careful."

"Good idea."

He drew closer, trailing a finger along her jaw, one arm sliding around her back. She had a momentary sensation of drowning again, but this time it felt deliciously warm and she relaxed into the waves without hesitation.

"I love you."

She shook her head. "Some people never learn."

ACKNOWLEDGMENTS

I'd like to thank the fantastic staff at the Cuyahoga County Coroner's Office, especially Linda Luke, Sharon Rosenberg, Kay, Dihann, and Bernie and Jim, and of course Dr. Elizabeth Balraj.

I'd also like to thank: those whose brains I have picked for this particular novel—Larry Stringham of the Cape Coral Police Department, Brett Harding, Dr. Valerie Beck-Blum, Dr. Andrew Wolff, the Cleveland Police Homicide Division, and my husband, Russ; Sylvia, my first reader, and Sharon, my most recent; my support system—siblings Mary, Susan, John, and Michael; my editor, Peternelle van Arsdale; and my miracle worker, agent Elaine Koster.